SWEET VENGEANCE

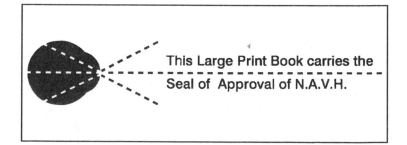

This Large Print Book carries the Seal of Approval of N.A.V.H.

SWEET VENGEANCE

FERN MICHAELS

WHEELER PUBLISHING
A part of Gale, a Cengage Company

Farmington Hills, Mich • San Francisco • New York • Waterville, Maine
Meriden, Conn • Mason, Ohio • Chicago

LIBRARY OF CONGRESS CIP DATA ON FILE.
CATALOGUING IN PUBLICATION FOR THIS BOOK
IS AVAILABLE FROM THE LIBRARY OF CONGRESS.

ISBN-13: 978-1-4328-4803-3 (hardcover)

Published in 2018 by arrangement with Kensington Books, an imprint of Kensington Publishing Corp.

Printed in the United States of America
1 2 3 4 5 6 7 22 21 20 19 18

No More Tears Now;
I will think about revenge

— Mary, Queen of Scots

PROLOGUE

Tessa Jamison counted the time so that she might arrive at a restful place when Death's hand reached out for her own. Each second, minute, and hour, excluding those during which she slept, admittedly few, brought her closer to her inevitable meeting with Death. Surely, she would find peace, or possibly sheer nothingness, in death. If not peace, or a white noise of sorts, if the tenets of her Christian faith were as pure and true as she'd been brought up to believe, she would be reunited with the family she had slaughtered so callously.

Since her conviction ten years ago, the quote from the *San Maribel News Press* had haunted every single minute of her essentially lifeless existence in Florida's Correctional Center for Women.

Slaughtered so callously. A mantra of sorts. *Slaughtered so callously.* The words drummed in her head like a rapid heartbeat.

7

Images of Joel's mangled body, the carnage, the horror of seeing her family.

Dead.

Joel's body was unidentifiable by visual means, the coroner had stated.

Gone in the blink of an eye.

It wasn't until three years after her imprisonment for the murders that the memory of the aftermath of their savage deaths emerged from her safe place — the dark confines hidden deep inside the protective corner of her subconscious. For years, Tessa's mind refused to retrieve the image of their slain bodies. Lily pads. She recalled thinking of lily pads floating in the aqua-blue pool on the fateful day when she'd discovered their bodies. Like a fine French claret, sinewy ribbons spread throughout the aquamarine water, the tomb that held the last whisper of their lives. Their last thoughts. Their last heartbeats. Their last cries. Their understanding that this was indeed the end, that the finality of life was now death.

Tessa hated this part the most. She could not bear to think of their last moments as the dark shroud of Death engulfed them. Had they struggled? Had they cried? Or had they simply taken their final breaths, accepting what was to come as their fate?

These thoughts tormented her. Day and

night, images of their bodies taunted her. Broken marionettes. Their limbs and arms askew, bloated, as decomposition began to set in. Later, she would recall the coroner testifying at her trial. Joel had died defending his daughters. His fingers and arms were covered in defensive wounds, and again, the fact that Joel was visually *unidentifiable.*

"It's as if the victim didn't even have a face," the coroner had testified.

The testimony still had the power to cause her heart to race.

Tessa struggled to keep the bitter prison coffee down as the images assaulted her. Catching her reflection in the small, steel-like mirror hanging above the built-in desk, Tessa no longer recognized the woman she'd become. Her blond hair was now streaked with thick stripes of silver, her once-bright blue eyes were now as dull as the mop-water-colored prison walls that stared back at her. Ten years living, if you could even call it that, in a seven-foot-by-ten-foot cell could do that to a person. She stared at the steel hinges that held her single bunk to the wall. Her bed was a thin, blue-and-white-striped dingy mattress atop rusted springs that creaked with every twist and turn. And the worn gray wool blanket on the bed, which she'd learned to make

9

with military precision, was nothing more than a nighttime battleground. Underneath that blanket she fought the demons that haunted her dreams at night and tormented her days. She'd adjusted to life in prison as well as anyone could under the circumstances, but the anger that grew deep inside her with each day spent behind bars was now barely containable. Ten years of incarceration for a crime she had not committed, of complete and utter hell, had infested and darkened her soul.

The clank of metal against metal, a shrill cry, a moan from someone in the depths of prison passion, were so common now that she hardly noticed them. Each day was the same as the thousand next and the one before it.

In the beginning, she'd simply curled up at the corner of her bunk at night, fearful of what might happen if she fell asleep. Given the nature of her supposed crime, she was immediately ostracized by the other inmates. Other than former cops, baby killers received the worst treatment inside prison.

Dinnertime was the worst. The other inmates' chanting the words *baby killer, baby killer* greeted her as soon as she entered the utilitarian cafeteria each day. It wasn't unusual for a spoonful of food to fly across the cafeteria, smacking her in the face, or to have a glob of instant mashed potatoes smashed in her hair as though she were nothing but a thing to torment. As hard as it was, Tessa refused to fight back. After a few years, she blended in, just like the others. She was a number, an inmate, a convicted murderer. She would die here in Florida's Correctional Center for Women. No one would care; there would be no memorial service to honor the person she'd been. Nothing. She would be carted out in a pine box, and from there, she would most likely be buried in the state's cemetery, where all the other inmates who had died were laid to rest.

Stop, she told herself. *Stop!* It was these thoughts that would kill her. Not the other murderers and drug addicts. Not the child molesters and rapists housed in the men's prison across the road. No, she would not die at their hand, but her own, if she continued to allow her thoughts to return to that day, now almost eleven years ago.

She had died that day because since the moment she discovered the dead bodies of her husband and twin daughters floating in their pool, bobbing, up and down, like the red-and-white bobbers used by fishermen, she'd had no life.

Nothing would change the devastation of what her family had suffered. There was no going back. To this very second, she was as traumatized as she'd been the day the words *guilty of murder in the first degree* filled the courtroom. Nothing would ever bring her a moment of happiness.

Nor did she deserve it. If only she'd stayed home that weekend instead of racing to the mainland to prepare for an indefinite stay with the girls.

The memory of that last day was all too clear to her now, very clear, having emerged in bits and pieces during her ten years in prison. If only she could turn back the hands of time.

CHAPTER 1

October 2021

Tessa rolled over, facing the same wall she'd viewed for more than ten years. Thirty-seven cracks, 192 tiny holes punched in the shape of a small handgun, courtesy of the prison cell's previous "guest." She had often wondered what instrument had been used to make such tiny holes, as any objects that could remotely cause injuries were forbidden. Some days she spent hours thinking about it. It was usually at this point that her circumstances served up a harsh dose of reality. Tears pooled, and she wiped them away with the edge of the wool blanket that covered the thin, worn mattress.

When her thoughts took her back to her previous life, which they did on a daily basis, Tessa did the one thing that helped her to cope with her anxiety.

She exercised.

She lay down on the cold cement floor, hands folded behind her head, and began doing sit-ups. When she reached five hundred, she stopped, a thin sheet of sweat covering her, the hair at the nape of her neck slick with dampness. She stood and began doing jumping jacks, something she'd learned in her seventh-grade gym class. She remembered thinking how stupid some of the girls in her class had looked. A few had developed breasts, some quite large. Jumping up and down with their breasts practically smacking them in the face, she'd been glad to be a bit behind in the physical-development department. The memory brought a mimic of a smile, a rarity. The last time she'd smiled and felt true happiness was nothing more than a distant memory, as though it belonged to someone else.

A lifetime ago.

With the force of an indescribable power, her mind suddenly registered the blatant fact that she'd now been incarcerated longer than her girls had lived. Tears blurred her vision again, and she wiped away the mixture of sweat and tears with the back of her hand. For once, she felt blessed to have the small sink in her cell. She turned on the tap, cold water only — all they were allowed — and she was glad of this missing amenity.

The sharp sting of the cold water brought back the harsh reality of what had become of her life.

One day the same as the next, rarely a variation unless an inmate caused a disturbance. It could be over a stolen cigarette, one's helping of dessert being more, or less, plentiful, or the startling whistle from a guard as they observed the crimes committed by the convicts. Tessa learned that nothing was off-limits where the inmates were concerned. Every item was made even more valuable, as the supply of what counted as contraband was limited and the demand so much greater. Contraband was mostly Marlboro cigarettes, which she never touched as the smell made her sick. Stamps were also a hot commodity, as was bottled water and the digital radios they were allowed. She kept her supply meager so as not to seem covetous. She knew this would set her apart from the other inmates even more. Flashing her wealth was totally out of bounds. And she wouldn't do that under any circumstances. She'd experienced being poor as well as being wealthy. Little good either status did her.

On each Saturday and Sunday, they were allowed visitors. For days afterward, the cellblocks were almost cheery; at least cellblock

C-15 was. She'd been in the same cellblock since being sentenced to prison, despite the crime she'd been convicted of. This was the least violent of the murderers' blocks, as the guards constantly reminded them when there was even the slightest threat to their safety. She did nothing to rattle their chains or that of the others. She spoke only when spoken to and did not participate in cellblock chatter. She had not made friends and did not want to. To what end? To plan a coffee date upon their release, then spend the day shopping at Saks Fifth Avenue? Not going to happen. No way.

Other than her attorney, she rarely had visitors since she had no close family except for her sister, Lara, who was two years younger. Lara had visited all of six times in ten years. Each visit she had asked for money, and Tessa always gave in and would see to it that Jamison Pharmaceuticals released the money her sister had requested. Lara used drugs, and Tessa suspected she worked as a prostitute when her supply of money and drugs was low. They had never been close when they were young since they were raised in separate foster homes after their alcoholic and drug-addicted mother died when they were just eight and ten years old. They'd never known their father, or

16

even if whoever Tessa's father was had also fathered her sister. They both resembled their mother, and neither had really cared enough to discuss the topic when they were old enough to understand that their mother's lifestyle wasn't considered normal.

Tessa remembered feeling relief when she had learned of her mother's death, and the brief flash of guilt she had felt at her own thoughts. She had been in Mr. Pittenger's fourth-grade class, studying her spelling words for the week. Mr. Cleveland, their principal, had quietly entered the classroom, whispered into her teacher's ear, then the two of them looked at her, and she had turned away, knowing that whatever Mr. Cleveland had told Mr. Pittenger wasn't good because they focused on her.

She had already turned her eyes back to the list of spelling words when she felt a tap on her shoulder. Bracing herself, she stood and followed the two men who'd had such a positive influence on her in the past year. Lara was waiting inside the principal's office when she entered. Tessa stood next to her younger sister, and reached for her hand, gripping it tightly as they were told of their mother's death. Both were stoic as they were given the news of their loss. Neither of them cried, accepting the fact that once

17

again, their lives were about to change. Though they had not been told at the time, Tessa and Lara soon learned that the cause of their mother's death had been a heroin overdose.

The rest of that year was spent in foster care. Hard as their caseworker, Lauren Keller, tried, she was unable to find a family willing to take in both of them, and Tessa and Lara lived apart for the first time in their lives. They'd stayed in contact in the beginning, but after two years, Lara stopped answering the letters Tessa sent her sister through Lauren, and their phone calls were few and far between. Tessa optimistically decided that her younger sister must be happy, and she focused on her own set of problems.

She had been in her third foster home for only three months when Hector and Maria Amaya were arrested and charged with fraud. She never knew exactly what kind of fraud but suspected it had something to do with the "other" business Hector operated in their spare bedroom after he thought she and the three other girls she shared a room with were asleep. People would come and go all night long. Some laughed, some cried, and others were bold and vulgar, their Spanish loud and guttural. Tessa had not slept a full night since she had been placed with them, so when she was told she would be relocating to yet another foster home, she was fine with the decision.

She hated leaving the other girls behind. They were all younger than her and looked up to her. Ashley, a pale, thin girl with long blond hair reaching her waist, appeared to be around nine or ten. Tessa knew something very bad had happened to her family, but when she tried to ask her about it, Ashley would just cry, and Tessa held her hand because she didn't know what else to do. Deanna was seven and didn't speak at all. Tessa thought she might have been a bit deaf because she never seemed to react to the loud, boisterous noises at night. Deanna followed Willow, the youngest of the girls, around like a shadow. Willow was small and dark-skinned, with hair so curly it looked like dozens of tiny corkscrews were attached to her head. She was the sweetest little girl, and Tessa thought she had the kindest eyes, especially for one who was so young. She had not seemed at all unhappy with the Amayas, so Tessa didn't spend too much time worrying about her when she left.

In seventh grade, Tessa was sent to live with the Carter family in Davie, Florida, which was a suburb of Fort Lauderdale.

Glenn and Shirley Carter were in their early forties when Tessa entered their lives. Of the three families she had lived with, this one's situation was, by far, the most promising. No trailers or shabby apartments. The Carter family home was a mansion compared to those other places. Painted a pale shade of peach, with a redbrick tile roof and a perfectly manicured lawn with a screened-in swimming pool, Tessa thought she had hit the jackpot. Briefly, she wondered if Lara had had such luck.

She didn't recall how long she had been with the Carters when the nightmare began. Looking back, it all seemed so surreal, so off the charts. Unable to cope with the luridness that plagued her nights, she had focused her attention elsewhere.

School was her savior.

She had studied hard in school and, in her senior year of high school, earned an academic scholarship to the University of Miami, where she studied and earned her bachelor's degree in molecular and cellular pharmacology. She had been a science nerd ever since first grade. In high school, she was a member of the National Honor Society. When she had been offered the scholarship, she knew that receiving it was her only way out of a world of poverty. It had not been easy, but she had delved into her studies and managed to graduate near the top of her class.

The day she had turned eighteen, she packed what few belongings she had and left Glenn and Shirley Carter and her former life behind. Shirley, who'd always asked the fosters to call her Mama Shirley, had truly been sad when Tessa moved out. Sure that she had not known what horrors Tessa had been subjected to, Tessa had merely said her good-byes and never looked back.

After working at Miami University Hospital for a year, she found herself getting bored and applied for a job at one of the largest pharmaceutical companies in the state of Florida.

Jamison Pharmaceuticals.

It was here that she met Joel Jamison, the owner of the company, and after working in pharmaceutical sales for a year, she and Joel became involved. Ten months later, they were married, and one month after that, she was pregnant. Six weeks after learning she was pregnant, she was ecstatic when her doctor told Tessa and Joel that they were going to be the parents of identical twin girls.

At first, Joel had seemed a bit shaken at

the news that they were expecting twins. She had questioned him on this later, and he'd told her the idea of raising one child was mind-boggling. Two at once, he'd said, scared the pants off him. But a few days later, once he'd gotten used to the idea, Tessa remembered he'd become even more excited as together they planned their daughters' future.

"Twins," she had remarked one night as they'd dined in Coral Gables at the stylish Pascal's On Ponce. She was three months pregnant and had already gained sixteen pounds, something Joel had recently started teasing her about. He told her she looked like a starving Ethiopian. She had been truly offended. Not so much for herself but for those in Ethiopia who barely had enough food to exist. He'd apologized, but from that moment on, she was careful not to completely undress in front of him. When their waiter asked if they wanted dessert, Tessa declined, but Joel had insisted she have the key lime raspberry tart, and she remembered wondering if this was his way of telling her that he didn't mind if she was a bit larger than some women at this stage of pregnancy. Of course, she really had no clue about relative sizes, as no one she knew had ever had twins, which led to a discussion on the topic of twins.

Identical twins.

Tessa asked Joel if there were identical twins on his side of the family. At first, Joel seemed angry at her inquiry, but then he brushed it aside, telling her he personally didn't know of any twins but mentioning that he seemed to remember having once been told that there had been a set a few generations in the past.

CHAPTER 2

Tessa forced herself to think of something else, anything but the past. The cellblock was beyond noisy, and she remembered that today was Saturday, one of the two visiting days each week. She planned to finish reading F. Scott Fitzgerald's *The Great Gatsby* for the third time since she knew there wouldn't be anyone anxiously waiting to visit her, to ask if she was okay, if there was anything she needed. That was not going to happen.

She had loved reading her entire life, and it was her love of books that continued to protect her sanity. Lost in the fictional world of the Brontë sisters, she devoured their stories, anything to escape her own reality. Books had been her escape as a child and would apparently be for whatever remained of her miserable life in this cell she called home.

Randall Harper, her attorney, occasionally

visited when there was something new to report. He'd filed an appeal immediately after the sentencing, as was customary after one's client had received a life sentence — in her case three of them — one for each count of murder in the first degree to run consecutively rather than, as was normal, concurrently. Randall had warned her not to expect a decision in her favor, so she wasn't surprised when her appeal had been denied. In point of fact, she really had not cared one way or another. Her daughters were gone, her husband was gone, her family no longer existed. Her life was over, and all the appeals in the world wouldn't change that fact. She had told her attorney not to waste his time on her. It didn't matter where she lived, she would still be grief-stricken and labeled a murderer, despite the fact that she was totally innocent of anything other than, perhaps, stupidity.

Liam Jamison. Joel's half brother. He was the person responsible for her loss, and he had never even been questioned regarding the murder of her entire family. Repeatedly, she had told her story to the police officers. Over and over that fateful Sunday when she had returned from San Maribel. She had begged, pleaded, and finally, she had screamed with such rage, crazed with unparalleled grief, that they'd actually listened to her. She told her story again, over and over, repeatedly, or at least she thought she had because years later, when she had tried to recall the events that had led up to her arrest, she had no clear memory of exactly what she had said to the police that day or any other day aside from her absolute, unwavering conviction that Liam had killed her entire family. Over and over, she had implored them to locate Liam, telling the police she knew he was responsible because he had been molesting her daughters, and that was the reason she had traveled to San Maribel. To arrange a place to hide her girls from the media, which would exploit the horrid act that had changed their lives forever. It didn't seem to matter what she had said; they would not listen. She recalled being whisked from room to room and questioned until she simply stopped talking.

Literally.

She had told the officers on the scene what she knew to be true. When the detectives had taken her downtown to police headquarters, where she was questioned for hours, so long, that her memory of that day, or it might have been days, was still hazy more than ten years later.

Liam was never investigated; in fact, he

was never even located. Sure that Rachelle, her mother-in-law, had whisked him out of the country, never to be found again, Tessa had simply given up on locating him. Rachelle had done a damn good job because Tessa's attorney said he'd hired the best private detectives in the business, and they had failed to locate him. The one thing that they did know was that he had not been in Japan as she had thought when she flew off to San Maribel. He seemed to have fallen off the face of the earth.

The police investigation, what little of it there had been, centered completely on *her.*

Her trial was short, taking almost no time at all and occurring scant weeks after the deaths of her loved ones, making headlines across the country. While the case went to the jury after only fourteen days of testimony, she listened to the talking heads discuss her life, what her motive had been: a 50-million-dollar life insurance policy and Jamison Pharmaceuticals. Virtually everyone agreed that she should get the death penalty for her greed.

The talk of her weekend "getaway" had been the subject of a great deal of speculation. A secret lover in San Maribel. A sudden hate for her children. Revenge for an unfaithful husband. On and on the murders made headlines across the country, and there wasn't a single ounce of truth to any of them.

She had truly lived through a nightmare.

And that nightmare would never end unless she dictated its ending herself. For years now, she had been contemplating how she would go about committing the act that would put an end to her suffering, yet each day, she somehow found another reason to go on. A new book in the library, a rare kind word from a guard, or just the knowledge that it was morally wrong to have acted on such thoughts.

Tomorrow I will rethink my options. She had this thought at least once each day.

The guards were especially watchful on visiting days, their eyes everywhere, never missing the slightest hint of defiance. It could be as simple as one trying to hold the hand of a loved one, a quick sleight of hand in an attempt to pass a joint, whatever the latest craze happened to be in the world of narcotics, or a small weapon. It amazed her how hawkeyed they could be on visiting day, considering how lackadaisical they usually were.

In a different world, she would understand, but she was now a part of this institution that synchronized every minute of her existence with military precision. When she ate, what she ate, when she showered, when she slept, where she slept, what she wore. On and on it went. The only variation to her days were her precious radio, which allowed her to stay informed on the outside world, her books, and the few snacks she was allowed to purchase from the commissary, something she seldom did, again because she did not want to draw any undue attention to herself.

She dampened a much-treasured washcloth and ran it over her face, neck, and arms. Showers were every other day, and she had learned to make do with the small sink in her cell. While she wasn't going to strip off for a full body wash, which she only did when it was lights out, for now, she settled for a quick once-over, then settled down on her bunk with her book while the other inmates prepared for visitors.

At first, it had bothered her when no one came to visit, other than Randall, of course, whom she never considered a real visitor, but now, she was content for the short span of quiet time these weekend visiting days provided her. While her days working in the prison's library were cherished, it wasn't always as quiet as one might think it would be in a library.

So immersed was she in her novel that the whack of a club against the steel bars startled her, and her book flew out of her hands.

"Get up, Jamison. You got a visitor," said Hicks, her least favorite guard.

Who? she wondered, as she had not had a visitor since Lara, and that had been more than a year ago.

Knowing it was useless to ask who, she simply nodded, picked her book off the floor, and tossed it onto her bed. So much for F. Scott Fitzgerald's characters' adventures, but she knew the ending, so it really didn't matter as it was simply a means by which to pass the time, which, unfortunately, she had more than enough of.

"Hurry up. I ain't got all day," Hicks shouted.

Tessa nodded, held her hands out of the small opening for the wrist cuffs that connected to the shackles that would be placed around her ankles when she was out of her cell.

"You ain't going to the public visiting area. You got some fancy-schmancy legal team here," Hicks explained, her Southern accent heavy with sarcasm. "Must think you're special, huh?"

Marcia Hicks was overweight and just as

ugly as she was mean. More than once she had passed by Tessa's cell with a black eye. Tessa wasn't sure if her occasional injuries were from an inmate, another guard, or possibly from home. Nor did she really care. The woman was evil and a bully, which made her well suited for the job of prison guard.

Tessa hated it when the guards tried to antagonize her, anything to get a negative response just so they could send her to the "hole," but to this very day, she had never allowed her emotions to control her actions. She simply nodded as if this turn of events was expected, and let Hicks lead her out of her cell.

Inside, her heart hammered like a Gatling gun. As Tessa walked down the cellblock, Hicks behind her, she kept her head lowered, focusing on the cement floor as she took one step at a time, her thoughts all over the place.

A legal team? Hicks was probably just trying to get a rise out of her. Still, she couldn't help but wonder who'd gone to such great lengths to visit her. The few times Randall visited, they had met in the attorney-client holding room reserved for attorneys to meet with their clients, where they could have actual human contact. One couldn't sign papers or visit with one's attorney in the area reserved for public visitations. But they were headed in the opposite direction from the attorney-client rooms. When they reached the end of the hallway with which she was familiar, with Hicks on her heels, she stopped, waiting for Hicks to direct her to her destination.

"Left, stupid ass," Hicks said before Tessa could ask.

Tessa took a deep breath and released it slowly. She would *not* allow the crude name-calling to affect her, no matter how hard it was not to do so. She turned to the left and walked down a short hallway, which ended with a utilitarian gray door inset with a small pane of wire-covered glass. She had never been to this area of the prison and had no clue what to expect when Hicks jostled her ring of keys and unlocked the door.

Hicks shoved her into the room, and Tessa stumbled, regaining her balance with the aid of an unknown hand that was offered.

When she saw the face of Sam McQuade, tears filled her eyes. Not knowing or caring why he was here, she walked toward him and wrapped her arms around him, not caring that she was being observed by strangers.

"Sam," she said, her voice a soft whisper.

"Tessa."

It was only seconds, but it felt much longer to Tessa when Hicks pushed her away from him. It had been so long since she had had a comforting hug; the utter completeness of the act brought back memories that she had thought were tucked away in that safe place in her mind that she rarely allowed herself to visit. A tingle down her spine settled itself in places that were off-limits to her now.

"Get your hands off her," an unfamiliar voice said to Hicks. "And leave. You're not needed here."

Tessa wanted to shout *"Yes!"* as loud as she could but refrained, knowing what the consequences would be once this visit was over.

It was unlike Hicks not to respond with some smart-ass comment, but the horrible woman left the room without saying a word, signaling her displeasure only by slamming the door behind her. Perhaps these people had the kind of clout that even a bully like Hicks recognized could spell trouble for her if they decided to make an issue of her crude conduct. One could wish.

"Are they all like her?" the man who had spoken asked, nodding toward the door.

Tessa shook her head. "No." Her head was spinning, wondering what was happening. It couldn't be good; that much she was sure of. No one visited a prison to deliver good news; at least she didn't know of anyone who'd had good news delivered this way.

"I assume you're wondering why we are all here," said the man with the unfamiliar voice. He was tall, broad-shouldered, and had a head of the blackest hair she had ever seen. He wore wire-rimmed glasses, a dark blue suit, and a pink tie, which she assumed to be in recognition of it being October, Breast Cancer Awareness Month. "I'm Lee Whitlow, and these are my associates" — he stepped out of her line of sight — "Steven Kilhefner and Bethany Young."

Tessa extended her hand, shaking hands with these three strangers who had most likely come with devastating news, hence Sam's appearance.

Her first thought was that Lara had either overdosed or had been killed. Just the thought caused her stomach to churn with that familiar tugging sensation that she identified as gut-wrenching fear.

Unsure of what she should do, she simply said, "Hello." It had been a very long time since she had had occasion to display her social graces, and she felt totally out of touch with the real world. Prison life was an entity unto itself, and Tessa was stained forever with the stigma of being a convicted murderer. She felt inhuman, worthless, no longer a part of society or anything that mattered because the life she knew had been taken from her over ten years ago. So, whoever these people were, the reason for their visit didn't really matter because she knew that as soon as they said whatever they came to say, Hicks would take her back to her cell, where she would return to the world of F. Scott Fitzgerald.

"Please, take a seat," Lee Whitlow said, motioning to a group of chairs surrounding a low table. She had not even noticed the room's furnishings until now. There was a brown-metal filing cabinet to her right, with a large desk to her left, and folding metal chairs were placed in the center of the room around a low, round table. No windows. Fluorescent lights. *Maybe this is the bereavement room,* she thought as she sat down. Never having been there, it was hard to say, but whatever the room's purpose, Tessa knew her reason for being here could be life-changing.

As soon as she was seated, Steven Kilhefner, a short, stocky man who appeared to be in his early forties, sat beside her and placed a large briefcase on the low table. He removed what appeared to be legal documents, as the files were legal-sized. *No, she thought, this cannot be good.* Her hands shook, and her mouth was suddenly dry.

Bethany Young must have read her mind. She placed an unopened bottle of water on the table in front of her and four more close to the edge. "We talk a lot, our mouths need fuel," she said, smiling, a way of explaining the extra bottles of water. Bethany couldn't have been a day over twenty-one, Tessa thought as she took the water. Of average size, the woman was dressed in beige slacks with a pale blue blouse and wore a smartly fitted navy blazer. Her sunflower-colored hair was pulled back in a sleek ponytail, held in place with a tortoiseshell barrette. Tessa quickly glanced at Bethany's hands, but she wore no jewelry. Girl next door came to mind.

Whatever the reason for the water, Tessa didn't care. She opened the water and drank half the bottle, then steadied what was left in the bottle between her knees.

Sam sat beside her, placing his hand on her shoulder. Again, his touch sent waves of . . . something she didn't want to put a name to through her. She had not felt a man's touch in such a very long time. She tried not to focus on the physicality of her situation, the closeness of the man beside her.

She searched the faces of the people whom she assumed to be the bearers of bad news, and asked, "Could you please just tell me why you're here, and get it over with? Is it Lara? Has something happened to her?" She turned her gaze to Sam, imploring him to answer her questions.

"No, Lara is fine. At least she was the last time she came to the office to pick up a check. That was a few weeks ago," Sam explained. "I keep tabs on her. I'm confident she's doing just fine."

Tessa felt a wave of relief wash over her. While she and Lara weren't close, she was the only family Tessa had left. If something had happened to her, Tessa would be completely alone in the world. This thought struck her so fast, it took a moment for it to register. She *was* alone. She would always be alone even though she was surrounded by hundreds of women just like herself. No, she wasn't like those other women.

She was not a murderer, she truly was *innocent*!

The thought offered little comfort. This was her home now. She had accepted that and learned to live with the court's decision.

Tired of waiting, Tessa focused her attention on Mr. Whitlow, asking, "Why are you here?"

Again, Sam placed his arm around her shoulders. She jerked so quickly the water bottle she had secured with her knees fell to the floor, the water forming a small circle around her slipper-clad feet. "Sorry," she said.

"Don't be," Whitlow replied. "You're nervous, and we understand. Bethany, grab a tissue and give Ms. Jamison another bottle of water."

The young woman pulled a few tissues from a box on the desk and tossed them onto the small puddle to absorb the liquid, then used a clean tissue to pick up the wet glob and toss it into a garbage can beside the desk.

"Thank you," Tessa said. She felt foolish and wasn't used to having people clean up after her. That was her job. Monday and Wednesday, showers, the nastiest of all jobs. Tuesday and Thursday, the library, a much-coveted job. Fridays were spent doling out prescription medications in the prison's infirmary/pharmacy. Another much-sought-after position. Tessa did not care much for this particular assignment either, but given her education and background, it was common sense that she be placed at the "pill window," which was always monitored by guards inside the small area that constituted the prison's pharmacy and outside the window where inmates lined up for their meds. Prisoners must be observed by a guard while taking medication. Inside, an antibiotic or a pill that couldn't be purchased over the counter at the commissary was extremely valuable.

"I know you must be curious why we're here," Whitlow said, stating the obvious.

Tessa nodded, afraid to say anything for fear of the answer.

"Lee, just tell her. You have kept her in suspense too long," Sam demanded.

"The Florida Supreme Court recently ruled that a suspect's silence can't be used against them in court." He paused for effect. "As you know, during your trial, there were several witnesses who stated you remained silent after your arrest —"

"I told the police," Tessa interrupted.

Lee held up a hand. "Let me finish, Ms. Jamison, please. I'm sure you will want to hear what I have to say."

"I'm sorry," she said. "Please go on."

Whitlow continued. "Thank you. I have

read the transcript of your trial. Michael Chen had it in for you. Of that there is no doubt in my mind."

Tessa remembered Assistant District Attorney Michael Chen. She guessed him to have been in his early thirties at the time of her trial. He was smug, she remembered thinking. During the trial, he had done everything he could to draw attention to what he thought of as his brilliant mind, his superiority. That had been her impression even though what he did had little effect on how she felt. She had not really cared one way or another as her life was over whatever the verdict. The trial and Michael Chen's display of arrogance were merely inconveniences to get through.

She had tried to pay attention to the witnesses, but she had been unable to stop the flow of the images that taunted her, the images of her two daughters and her husband that wracked her brain. She now believed she had been in a state of shock after her arrest, and most likely she had suffered from post-traumatic stress disorder.

What she did recall about the district attorney was an abundance of perspiration and body odor. He reeked of rotten onions and sour sweat. She wondered how his assistants could stand to be in the same room with him, let alone seated next to him at the prosecution's table. And the words he'd spouted during his summation were as foul as his body odor. She also recalled that his teeth were crooked and unclean. He made a point of standing next to the defense table when he spoke. Tessa remembered how she would inwardly gag when he stood beside her chair. Short, fat, and smelly summed up this disgusting example of a human being.

"Michael Chen's tactics during the trial were brought to my attention by Mr. McQuade."

Tessa shot Sam a questioning look.

"I was a lawyer before I was a CEO," he explained.

Somewhat stunned, Tessa replied, "I never knew." All she really knew about Sam was he'd been friends with Joel during college, and for the past twelve years, he'd been CEO of Jamison Pharmaceuticals. She knew he held a couple of degrees but assumed they were in the medical and pharmacy field. Sam had been older, and she recalled Joel telling her this once.

"Emory Law," he explained.

Lee Whitlow took the file from Steven Kilhefner. He opened the manila folder and removed a stack of papers. "This is a copy of the Florida Supreme Court's recent ruling. Sam brought this to my attention five months ago, and I agree with the court's decision."

Tessa's pulse increased, her eyes filled with tears. She knuckled the tears before they had a chance to fall. She had to be strong. Tough. If she were headed to death row, then so be it. Her daily thoughts of how she could end her existence were possibly being answered for her. Taking a deep breath, doing her best to evoke some inner sense of bravery, she said, "I do not understand. What does this mean?" She was sure she was correct in her assumption.

"We have asked for a new trial, and our request has been granted," Lee Whitlow stated. "Your conviction has been overturned on the grounds that your Fifth Amendment rights were violated in your first trial."

Feeling as though she had been punched in the gut, Tessa drew in a sharp breath. The room swirled, the fluorescent lights blurred, and a hand reached for her, steadying her as she almost fell from the chair.

It took a few seconds for her to regain her sense of sight and balance. When she had herself under control, she took one of the unopened bottles of water on the table, opened it, and took a long drink. Her throat was dry and her voice scratchy when she spoke. "I still don't understand." A question more than a statement, and she waited for an explanation. "Does Randall know about this?"

"He does, but he's asked me to take the lead. I have read your trial transcript numerous times, as have my colleagues. During your trial, the prosecution sought and received testimony from numerous state witnesses who testified that you remained silent following the murder of your twin daughters and your husband after you were placed under arrest. As I'm sure you know, the state reminded the jurors of your silence repeatedly during their closing statement. Mr. Chen argued that the jury could weigh your silence after your arrest as evidence of conscious guilt. The case law, *Florida v. Horwitz,* was expanded several months ago prohibiting prosecutors from using a defendant's pre-arrest, pre-Miranda silence as substantive evidence of guilt when a defendant chooses not to testify at trial. Because of the recent change in the law, Mr. Chen's use of your silence violated your Fifth Amendment right against self-incrimination, something all are entitled to under Florida's constitution as well as the United States Constitution. In simple terms, the facts that you didn't speak to officers after your arrest, did not testify on your behalf, and the Fifth Amendment to the U.S. Constitution states you had the right to remain silent if you chose to, it should not have been used against you, but it was." Lee Whitlow dropped the papers on the table.

Tessa felt all eyes on her. Unsure of how they expected her to react, she remained quiet, trying to absorb the information she had just heard. Never even giving a thought to leaving Florida's Correctional Center for women, or as some of the other inmates crudely referred to it, *Fucking Cockless Institute,* she had accepted her sentence as it was ordered: three life sentences to be served consecutively, which was the rest of her natural life. How did one get past this? *Shock,* she thought as she tried to summon words to express what she was feeling. Stunned, unable to wrap her mind around the attorney's words, she remained still, silent.

"Tessa?" Sam asked. "Say something."

Shaking her head from side to side, she took another gulp of water, then returned the bottle to the table. "Why? I don't understand. Why now? Why didn't they believe me then? I told the detectives at the scene the truth. My . . . *truth* somehow matters now?"

"It's not always about the truth, Ms. Jamison. Right now it's about your rights, and the law has changed since your conviction." Steven Kilhefner spoke for the first time. "I'm Mr. Whitlow's investigator, but I'm also an attorney. I just choose the investigatory side of the law. I'm going to assist you in getting out of this place while we wait and prepare for your new trial. The circumstances won't be perfect, but they'll be colossal compared to your current . . . situation."

For the second time, the lights blurred, and the room became dimmer. Darkness sought her out, and this time it found her.

CHAPTER 3

Tessa's eyes opened as soon as she smelled the ammonia beneath her nose. She was still inside what she had called the bereavement room, but she was on the floor, her upper body leaning against Sam's chest.

"I'm sorry," she whispered as she tried to sit up. Embarrassed, she stood, using the seat of the metal folding chair to hold on to for support.

Bethany placed an arm around her, helping her back onto the chair she had just fallen out of. "Here, try this," she said, handing her a chocolate bar. "Sugar helps everything."

Tessa took the candy bar, briefly wondering why Bethany carried candy with her.

"I'm diabetic," Bethany said as though she had read her mind.

"I wondered why," Tessa said softly. "Thank you. This . . . news comes as quite a shock."

Sam sat next to her. "Are you okay?"

Was she? Physically, yes. Emotionally, she didn't know. Not wanting to upset or humiliate herself by not showing her gratitude to these people who'd made it their mission to help her, she said, "Yes. I am. The news is just so unexpected, to say the least. I had no idea. Randall never mentioned anything."

"That was because I asked him not to," Lee Whitlow offered. "We didn't want to get your hopes up until we had your conviction overturned."

Hope? She had never had any hope, so when one doesn't have any, there is no chance of losing it. Expect nothing and never be disappointed, a motto she had lived by when she was a young girl, and it had helped her to live her life in prison one day at a time. When she had been accused and convicted of murder, she had picked her earlier self's motto up again.

"I don't know what to say. I'm still shocked," she explained. "I have never heard of this happening in the ten-plus years I have been here."

Whitlow spoke. "That's because the law has changed. I suspect you won't be the last . . . *person*" — he stumbled over the last word — "to receive a new trial after the

47

Florida Supreme Court's long-overdue decision."

Steven Kilhefner cleared his throat. "Ms. Jamison, there is a process we will be going through —"

"Please call me Tessa," she interrupted him.

He nodded. "Tessa, there is a process we'll go through. I need to know that you understand this."

"If you explain, I'm sure I will," she said.

"We will go before a judge next week, and he will issue the terms of your release. Bail will be set, and I'm sure it will be seven figures if Judge Crider's past orders are indicative of his future orders. Sam has assured us that funds for the bail won't be a problem. From there, once the conditions of your release are met, you will be released into Sam's custody. Of course, if there is someone else you prefer, we will suggest this to the judge. However, I would advise you to stick to the plan as we do not want to give the court any reason to change his mind. And it can happen, despite the fact a new trial has been ordered. It is very rare that someone charged with three counts of first-degree murder gets released. The Supreme Court's ruling is in our favor. However, we must follow the law to the letter, or any chance of keeping you out of this . . . place will be gone. Are you okay with Sam as your guardian?"

"Guardian?" Tessa didn't understand.

"It will be in the terms of your release that you have a guardian. If you're not agreeable to this —"

"It's fine by me, as long as Sam is agreeable," Tessa said.

"I suggested this, Tessa. I hope you don't think I was being too forward," Sam responded.

She wasn't sure what she felt about Sam's offer. Since she was unsure about this entire process, it was going to take time for her to get used to the idea. Tessa had a nagging fear that if she allowed herself to get her hopes up, something horrible would happen.

Taking a deep breath, she said, "I don't know what to feel. This is all such a shock. I don't know if I want to chance another trial, another guilty verdict. I have tried to make peace with this" — she motioned to the room around her — "and resigned myself to spending the rest of my life here. What happens if I'm found guilty again?"

The small room was silent, no one offering an answer to her question.

"It's a risk, but we think it's one you

should consider," Lee Whitlow explained. "You are correct that the mere fact that we have succeeded in having your conviction overturned is no guarantee that you will be found not guilty in another trial. But if I didn't think we had a chance at winning you an exoneration, I wouldn't be here."

Tessa knew what it would take for her to be found not guilty at a new trial. "You have new evidence? You have managed to locate Liam?" she asked, her heart racing at the thought. Not that she didn't want him to suffer, she did. But by her own hand.

It was then that an idea began to take form.

"No, we haven't. I have people working on this. Randall's lead investigator, well, let's just say he valued the bottle a bit too much and is out of a job. Has been for three or four years."

Tessa was surprised at this news. Randall had always assured her his team of investigators were the best in the business. She was sure there had been more than one man. It didn't matter at this point.

"I didn't know," was all she could come up with.

"We do have a possible witness," Whitlow stated.

"Who?" Tessa asked, her voice firm. "And

why now?" She was angry. Ten, almost eleven years of her life, she had been living in hell. If there was someone out there with knowledge of her family's murders, she wanted to know why that person was just now coming forward.

"Calm down, Tessa," Sam said. "This is good news for you."

"So you say. Try spending one damned night in this place, then tell me that's *good news.*"

"If you're not willing to go through another trial, I think our business here is over," Steven said. He took the files off the desk and returned them to his briefcase.

"Wait a minute. I didn't say that. I just don't understand. First, it's the Florida Supreme Court making a ruling that allows my conviction to be overturned, and now you tell me there is a witness?" Tessa informed him. "What kind of idiot do you think I am? Of course I want out of this place!" It was at that moment that she realized why her thoughts of suicide had been nothing more than thoughts, something that she would have never acted upon.

Because deep down Tessa had always had *hope.*

And now hope arrived in the form of a

Florida Supreme Court decision and a new witness.

Yes. I will take my chances.

CHAPTER 4

December 2021

Tessa was really surprised that the clothes Sam brought her fit. She had lost at least twenty pounds during the ten-plus years she had been locked up. He had a good eye for size. A pair of khaki slacks, a delicate white blouse, and a yellow sweater, along with the fanciest bra she had seen since her incarceration, and soft, silky underwear, a true luxury. He'd sent a pair of leather Sperrys with a set of footies. He'd thought of everything, or maybe Bethany had chosen these clothes. As far as Tessa herself was concerned, she could have worn a flour sack and been satisfied. She had been given one chance to start her life over, and her wardrobe was the least of her problems.

Once she was finished dressing, Tessa was told to wait in the small office next to the control room where she had just changed into her new clothes. She took a seat and waited for what was to come next.

On the one hand, the two months since Lee, Steven, and Bethany had come into her life had sped by quickly. Once the guards learned of her new trial, they treated her a bit better. Except for Hicks. She was as mean as ever, perhaps even meaner now that Tessa might not be there for her to torment, and tried her best to get a rise out of her. Tessa knew if she had even the slightest blemish on her record, she could forget about getting out on bail while she waited for her new trial.

On the other hand, time seemed to crawl as all she could think about was getting out of jail, planning for a new trial, and figuring out how to catch Liam and destroy the perverted son of a bitch in the most painful manner possible. Lee had explained the terms of her release once the judge entered his final order into the record. Her new trial date had not yet been set, so she would be on house arrest and wear an ankle bracelet to monitor her whereabouts. She would only be allowed to leave the house to visit her attorney, and she could go to church if she chose to. She decided she would. She had to believe that it was God's plan that had sent Lee and his crew into her life, and for the first time since she had lost everything in her life that mattered to her, she was truly thankful to be alive.

The dark thoughts still lingered in the back of her mind, but the bright light of hope was there now, even if it was only a shimmer. If all went as Lee expected, in a few months she would be a free woman. She would be exonerated of all charges, and her record would be expunged.

She had millions in the bank, a successful company that still belonged to her. Rachelle was given $5 million a year as was dictated in her father-in-law's will, but according to Sam, that amount was a small drop in Jamison Pharmaceuticals' financial bucket.

The only downside of this change was that she had to return to San Maribel and the house where the murders had taken place. Sam had taken care of the house and assured her it wasn't the same as she remembered. She certainly hoped not. Just the thought of entering that house again caused her to panic. She had begged Lee to ask the judge if she could rent a place, buy a condo, anything other than returning to the island, but Judge Crider had been adamant according to Lee, whom she now trusted as much as she trusted herself. He cut straight through the flesh to the bone, but she respected that. Life after more than ten years in prison was too short for beating around the bush.

Tessa waited twenty minutes for the Powers That Be to formally release her. It had been confirmed that she would be released into Sam's custody, and that made her slightly uncomfortable. She had always liked him, even more so since she had been incarcerated, as he'd stayed with the company, expanding their production of a new trial drug that would possibly slow, or even halt the growth of cancer cells in patients diagnosed with brain cancer. This could put Jamison Pharmaceuticals into position as one of the top pharmaceutical companies in the country. Still, memories of the moment that he placed his hand on her shoulder and her physical reaction made her feel ill at ease. Though it had been so very long since she had been offered any sort of comfort by anyone, male or female, she felt sure that her reaction was normal given her years alone. But a nagging thought that she couldn't ignore kept popping up: *Am I actually attracted to Sam? How can I even have these thoughts at this pivotal moment in my life?*

The door opened, and Tessa's thoughts were jolted back to the present when the man she had just been thinking about entered the room.

"Are you ready?" Sam asked. There was no humor, certainly nothing remotely suggestive about his manner, but Tessa couldn't stop the faintest tinge of uneasiness when her eyes met his. He wore dark slacks, a light green shirt, and a black jacket. No tie, she noticed, but this really wasn't an occasion where formal dress was required. His dark hair was too long, and his gray eyes were piercing. It bothered her that she even noticed these physical characteristics of his. What did she really know about Sam McQuade? He'd been Joel's friend since college, loyal to the company, but other than that, she really didn't know Sam all that well. He'd been to their house dozens of times, yet she couldn't recall his ever bringing a date to any of the functions she and Joel hosted. It didn't matter anyway. She stopped thinking about past interactions with Sam and turned her attention to the here and now.

Tessa nodded and felt a wash of relief when she had no physical reaction to him as he stood next to where she sat. Taking a deep breath, she looked up at him, and said, "I'm not sure how one is supposed to act at a time like this, but I'm more than ready to find out." When she stood, the weight of her new clothes suddenly felt heavy and scratchy against her skin. After more than ten years in which her only attire was an orange jumpsuit that had softened with time, she almost wished she were allowed to bring her familiar, comfortable clothing with her. But not only did she know that wasn't allowed, but more important, doing so would be a bad way to get started on what she hoped would be the first stages of her new life as a free woman.

"I must warn you, your release is being reported on by all the major news networks, and there are several local network trucks sitting outside the prison. They'll hurl questions at you, but don't answer. Lee is here, and he will take their questions. Just do your best to ignore them. They all want to be the first one to —" Sam stopped talking for a couple of seconds, then went on. "They'll want to hear in your own words how you feel about having your conviction overturned, about facing a new trial, and about being released on bail although you are still under arrest for three murders. Don't react, because if you do, it will be the lead story on the six o'clock news. Stay close to me, okay?"

It wasn't as though she had any choice in

the matter. "Of course," she said. "Is there another exit we can use?" she asked, even though she knew that there wasn't. The freed-convict walk to freedom was always the same; she knew this from being on the inside for so long. But if there were the slightest chance there was another way out, she wanted to know.

"This is it, I'm afraid. As soon as the warden gives us the word, we'll leave. I have a car and driver waiting."

Tessa felt like a true criminal, being whisked out of prison, all eyes on her, all the TV reporters waiting to catch her first moment of freedom on camera. Even though her new freedom might only be temporary, it was still hot news. It was not every day that the person who had committed the most heinous crime of the century so far in Florida was released from prison. Yes, this was big news all right.

Warden Kathryn Ryce entered the room with her usual air of self-confidence. Only one of three female wardens in the state of Florida, she took pride in her position, and while Tessa had no great liking for the woman, she had always treated the warden with respect, and Warden Ryce had always responded accordingly. She was dressed as usual: a dark blazer with a dark skirt and low-heeled shoes, and her auburn hair was pulled into a tight bun. She wore no makeup, but Tessa always thought her an attractive woman in a very plain way. High cheekbones, a full mouth, brown eyes, she was not the angry female many of the inmates claimed her to be. She did her job, and Tessa respected that.

The warden went to the small desk in the corner of the room and picked through a large stack of papers. When she found what she was looking for, she spoke. "Ms. Jamison, I need your signature here." She pointed to a space on the bottom of a legal-sized sheet of paper. "This is an inmate's release form. You may take the time to read through it if you wish, but Mr. Whitlow assured me that he has already gone over all the instructions with you."

Tessa nodded, took the paper, and signed it. She knew its contents. Rules to live by once she walked out the door. They included notifying the local San Maribel Police Department, the Lee County Sheriff's Office, and the Lee County Probation Department. She was required to make all of them aware of her release as though she were a new danger to the community. The judge had explained that since the island was still U.S. soil, and she would be monitored via an ankle bracelet, she would be allowed to stay there.

"If I may, Ms. Jamison?" Warden Ryce asked when she returned the paper to the stack on the desk.

"If you may what, Warden Ryce?" Sam asked, his tone stern.

"Mr. McQuade, I simply wanted to wish Ms. Jamison well. She has been one of the state's most cooperative prisoners, and I simply want to wish her well." She said this as though Tessa were out of hearing range.

"Thank you, Warden. I can't say it's been a pleasure, but I appreciate your kind words," Tessa said, letting both know that she was quite capable of speaking for herself.

"You may go," Warden Ryce said.

"Yes, uh . . . thank you," she said even though the warden had no part in her early, albeit possibly temporary, release from prison.

"Good luck," she said, surprising Tessa.

Tessa gave the warden an acknowledging nod and wondered briefly if the warden really meant it or just said it to every inmate about to leave the prison. *Does it really matter?* she asked herself.

Without another word, Sam escorted her out of the office, through several long hallways, through two steel doors, and finally, the door that led to the world outside the prison gates, a world she had not seen in over ten years.

The door to freedom. The door to a new chance at life.

The door leading to her search for Liam Jamison.

And when she found him, she would make him pay for killing her family and robbing her of the last ten years of her life.

CHAPTER 5

"How does it feel to be free?"

"Are you going to take over at Jamison Pharmaceuticals?"

"Will you have more children to replace the twins you killed?"

Tessa looked up and appeared ready to commit mayhem when she heard the horribly cruel words a local TV reporter had just uttered.

"Don't say a word," Sam cautioned, guiding her to the shiny black SUV parked close to the area where the members of the press were gathered. "All they want is to get a response from you, preferably a negative one. Remember, you don't want to be the lead story on the six o'clock news. Be assured that I have noted who it was who asked that last question. And once this is over, I will personally see to it that she never again works for any television, radio, or newspaper company again. And you can take that to the bank."

She walked as fast as she could, Sam's arm around her waist holding her close to him, away from the reporters, with their hands outstretched, holding smart phones and recorders in hopes of getting a comment on the record. Trying to absorb as much of the outside as she could, Tessa raised her head, letting the warm December sun of Florida caress her face. A cool breeze carried the scent of the inmates' next meal. She reveled in the fact that she would no longer be subjected to the tasteless slop they tried to pass off as food. Seafood, fresh vegetables, and fruit would be her diet for as long as she was free.

She took a deep breath, inhaled the noxious odors for what she hoped was the last time in her life, then, as soon as she reached the vehicle, a door opened, and she slid across the smooth leather seats. She inhaled the rich scent of leather and remembered her own vehicle. Briefly, she wondered if Sam had taken care of that as well but recalled she had asked her attorney to donate her vehicle and Joel's to a worthwhile charity.

Slamming the door as soon as he was inside, Sam spoke to their driver. "Get us out of here, and make sure we're not followed."

Tessa felt as though she were in another world, sort of like Alice in Wonderland, through the looking glass, this large vehicle her own personal rabbit hole, where everything was the same but somehow her perception of it was warped, almost freakish. She closed her eyes and opened them again, hoping to dispel the distorted image.

"Where are you taking me first?" Tessa asked, realizing she had not bothered to ask exactly where she would go immediately upon her release. The words sounded false to her ears; she couldn't even imagine what they sounded like to their driver and Sam. She had been told the process, but until she had actually walked out the prison door, she had resisted really taking in anything beyond getting out the door to the prison.

"You're going home, Tessa," Sam stated. "It's what you agreed to. They" — he nodded toward the back window of the SUV — "won't follow us all the way to San Maribel. Though I suspect we'll have our share of media to deal with there, too."

She nodded, admitting to herself that she had not thought that far ahead. It was her fear of her twin girls' exposure to the jackals of the media that had sent her running to San Maribel all those years ago. And that fear had cost her everything she valued in life. She wouldn't fear the media this time around. She might even find a way to use them to her advantage, but that was for a later time. When she had had a chance to think, time to plan how she was going to get at Liam Jamison, the son of a bitch.

"As soon as we get your ankle bracelet, you'll have some time to yourself."

Tessa inhaled and slowly exhaled. "At the sheriff's office?" She knew this but wanted it confirmed.

"Yes, that, too, was part of the judge's conditions for release," Sam explained.

"I know, it just seems a bit, I don't know . . . sort of like collaring an animal or something."

Sam turned around in the front seat to face her. "That's pretty much the point. While you aren't going to have prison bars around you, you won't be able to come and go, at least not until after a trial or the charges against you are dismissed."

"Of course, I know that, but it still doesn't keep me from thinking it's barbaric. What happens if you remove it?"

"Tessa, that's not —"

"I know, Sam. But humor me. I am just curious. What would happen if it were removed?"

"First, you'd need a massive pair of cutters to remove it, which would then send a high-frequency signal to a receiver. A phone rings, and whoever is in charge contacts the proper authorities, and they begin a search for you. If you leave it on, you're fine. As long as you don't leave your assigned area without permission, you won't have a problem, but they can track your every movement if you do since it's equipped with a GPS. Just so you know." He was dead serious.

"Of course I wouldn't dare remove it. I realize it's what I have to do until after the trial. I'm fine with it, Sam. Really," she added, and gave him a halfhearted smile.

"I know. I'm sorry it has to be this way."

"Me, too, but it's okay. Really." She had not asked Sam why he'd brought her case to Lee Whitlow, but now she needed to know. "Why did you go to all this trouble? Bringing my case to Lee?"

Sam rubbed the bridge of his nose, then raked a hand through his hair. "Because you're innocent."

Not sure of what to say, she said nothing. No one had ever said these words to her. At least not as directly.

"Does Rosa's story have anything to do

with your belief in my innocence?" Tessa asked. Since learning about Rosa's story, she was sure this had influenced Lee and his team probably even more than the Florida Supreme Court's ruling.

"No. I have never doubted your story," Sam stated. "No one in their right mind could do . . . you would never have harmed your girls, or Joel. I know that, Tessa. I have always known that. But I was never called as a witness."

"I don't think your testimony would have changed anything. There wasn't any evidence that required your testimony. In fact, when you get down to it, there really was no evidence against me at all."

"I could have vouched for your character," Sam said. "Not that it would have mattered. The district attorney had his eye on you from the beginning. Any evidence that could have turned their investigation around, they simply ignored. If Rosa had not decided to speak up, they would have fought like cats and dogs against your being released even now. I seriously doubt that they even care whether or not you are guilty. All they care about is not having their precious theory shown to be the garbage it is and always has been and their utter lack of competence exposed to the world."

Rosa. Tessa remembered her well. She had been in her early forties when she came to work for them. The girls were four. It was during this time that Tessa had considered going back to work part-time, with the knowledge that both Piper and Poppy adored Rosa, and she loved them in return.

Tessa had spent many sleepless nights pondering her decision. In the end, she had decided to stay home with her girls. Rosa was a great sitter and kept their large home in shipshape order. Tessa had suspected there was more to Rosa, but her being an undocumented worker who had entered Florida illegally had not been anything she suspected back then. Joel had hired her as soon as Tessa gave her seal of approval. He'd personally taken care of the financial side, and Rosa took charge of their home. To think what Rosa might have witnessed blew her away.

"Thanks, Sam. Really. I don't know what I did to deserve your devotion, and all of this." She gestured to the car, her clothes. "I don't know if I can ever repay you." Financially, of course, she could and she would. That part was easy, but there was no price for gratitude.

"You have thanked me enough. Wait until your new trial is over or the case against

69

you dismissed, and maybe then you'll have something to really thank me for."

A warning voice sounded in her head. *What did he mean? Did he expect something more?* She needed to clear this up now.

"Sam, I'm not interested in —"

"I didn't mean that the way it sounded. If you're proved innocent, that's what I meant. You can thank me then. For that only. Nothing more, Tessa. Joel was my friend. I . . . you know what I mean."

Not really. It wasn't as though they'd been in constant contact since her imprisonment. Yes, he was in charge of Jamison Pharmaceuticals; after all, he was the CEO, and he gave Lara what she needed, but she really didn't *know* Sam well. Yes, he'd been good friends with her husband, but that had been their friendship, not hers.

Uncomfortable silence, then Tessa said, "My social graces need polishing. It's going to take a while for me to get used to this." She looked out the passenger window. "My last car ride was to prison. This is all so . . . unexpected. You just keep on doing what you have been doing, and I plan to take one day at a time."

"Good plan," Sam agreed.

Thirty minutes later, they were driving up Alligator Alley, which was what the locals called I-75. Because of the many accidents that had been caused by the gators in the nearby swamps coming onto the highway, not to mention the endangered Florida panther, the roadside had been fenced off. Not, everyone understood, to protect the drivers, but rather to protect the wildlife. Tessa had always been afraid to travel this desolate road, and now some of the old panic of her past filled her as she stared out at the nothingness. Dried grass, swamps. It wasn't the sunny Florida of postcards and sandy beaches.

"I have never liked this part of Florida," she said.

"Not much to like," Sam commented.

For the next hour, they rode in silence, both of them thinking their own thoughts. Tessa was glad. It would take time to absorb her new reality. People seemed different, and uncaring, at least the few she had had contact with. She had always been the caring type, wanting to make things right for those around her. In doing so, she had ruined so many lives. It had cost her everything that was dear to her.

Wanting to know but afraid to ask, she wondered what kind of changes had been made to her home on the island. She had always thought the place was much too extravagant, too flashy. After a few years of living there, she had gotten used to seeing yachts moored in the deep canals, Bentleys and Lamborghinis casually parked in driveways, their owners uncaring of the damage from the brutal sun. Fearful, yet curious, she wanted to focus on anything but the day that her life fell apart. She knew that once she arrived home, she would break.

Maybe this was all a bad idea. Maybe she should ask the driver to turn around and take her back to the place she had called home for the past ten years. She had accepted the fact the she would spend her life behind bars, and now, this. She was getting a chance to start over, a chance to prove her innocence, and the thought scared her to death. Tessa knew what she would have to do to make things right.

And she would. In due time.

CHAPTER 6

This was almost worse than prison, *almost,* she thought, as the obnoxious female deputy adjusted the bracelet on Tessa's left ankle. Tessa tried to pull her khaki slacks over the giant black ankle bracelet, but they weren't wide enough. Cuffing her slacks into a pair of makeshift capris, she would have to remember that whatever type of slacks or jeans she was able to get her hands on in the next few days would have to be either flared or boot cut.

"While you're wearing the ankle monitor, you must not drink or use drugs; if you leave your assigned area, your monitor will notify authorities; you must pay any and all court costs connected with the use of the ankle bracelet; you must have a job, and you will meet with an officer weekly." The female deputy recited her spiel with about as much enthusiasm as a dead rat. "Do you understand these terms?"

What if I said no?

"Yes," Tessa said instead. "I understand."

"Sign here." The deputy shoved a clipboard in Tessa's face.

Tessa skimmed through the form, stating she was responsible for the care and maintenance of her bracelet.

"I don't understand this. What if it breaks?" She returned the clipboard to the woman without signing it.

"It's fine, Tessa. It's just a formality," Sam said.

The deputy handed the clipboard back to her. She scanned the paper, then signed and dated it, giving it back to her. "If this thing is faulty through no act of mine, what am I supposed to do?" Tessa directed her question to the deputy.

"Ain't no free pass. It means you violated your terms, and you're going back where you belong." The deputy smirked.

Sam held his hand up, preventing Tessa from speaking. "If there is a malfunction in the unit, they'll issue you another. Isn't that the correct procedure" — Sam glanced at the name on her badge — "Deputy Pierson?"

"It depends," she answered.

"On what?" Sam asked, his tone sharp, demanding.

"Ask her," the deputy said. "She ain't about to keep that on her leg once she gets to that fancy mansion. It's all over the news here. I remember *you.*" She practically spat out the last word.

"Let's get out of here before *I* break the law," Sam said, giving the deputy a withering look that promised he would not forget how she had behaved and that she had better hope he didn't use his position in the community to make sure that her career in law enforcement would soon be over.

Turning his back in disgust on the soon-to-be-unemployed poor excuse of a deputy, Sam took Tessa's hand and led her out the side entrance, where their SUV waited.

He opened her door, and she climbed inside, settling in the backseat again. She fastened her seat belt, leaning back in the leather seat, which seemed frivolous now. Being in prison, she had learned that one only needed the barest necessities to live. Even with a fortune at her disposal, Tessa couldn't see herself as the woman of power and position she had been before. She couldn't be that woman ever again, and she didn't want to be.

"Sorry about her." Sam turned his head and said as soon as he was seated next to the driver. "Power-hungry. With any luck, she won't be a deputy much longer."

"I'm used to it," was all Tessa could say.

"Maybe you can begin to get 'unused' to it?" he asked.

Tessa looked at him, saw he was smiling. "I'm not putting the cart before the horse, Sam. If I have learned anything in the past ten years, it's to expect nothing. That way, I'll never be disappointed. Being locked away changes a person. If I'm convicted again, I'll go quietly. That deputy's words meant nothing to me." She had heard so much worse, but she wouldn't burden Sam with stories of her time in what many called the Big House.

"Then let's keep our fingers crossed. Lee Whitlow is one of the best criminal defense attorneys in the country. He will win this, Tessa. I know him. He wouldn't have taken your case on if he thought there was even the slightest chance of losing. I have been friends with him for years," Sam continued.

She had to know. "Why didn't he step up and take my case in the very beginning?" *If he is that good, then why did he wait?* she wondered.

"Lee's wife, Jen, was undergoing treatment for breast cancer at the time of your trial. He came to me then, knowing Jamison was about to launch a clinical trial of a new breast-cancer drug that has since proved to be promising. Unfortunately, Jen passed before we could get her into the clinical trials. We became even better friends. With my background in law, we had that in common, plus he was interested in Jamison's clinical trials, at least the cancer trials."

That explained all the pink ties he wore. "Poor Lee. I had no idea."

"He's been an avid supporter of cancer research since," Sam explained.

"Whatever the reason, I owe him," Tessa said.

"We can talk about Lee's fees later. Your case is the challenge he needs. He's a powerful man and superb attorney. Wait until you see him in a courtroom. Most jurors hang on his every word."

Tessa was only half listening to Sam. They had arrived at the dock and driven onto the ferry now. As they made their way across the bay, she viewed the giant royal palms planted by Thomas Edison in the late 1800s lining the shore of the approaching island. They looked about the same as before, maybe just a bit taller. Most of the finest homes in San Maribel were along the shore. Some of the buildings looked to have been restored, some former homes had been turned into coffee shops, cafés, and high-end boutiques. Not much change. She was glad for that, but as the ferry docked on the shore, on the island on which she and her family had lived, her stomach knotted, and her hands began to shake. This was a bad idea.

"Sam, can't I stay at a hotel? I'm not comfortable returning to you know . . . the scene," she told him.

He leaned across the front seat and reached for her hand, taking it in his own. "I wish we could, but the judge insisted on your going to your home since you actually own it. I don't know why. Maybe Chen, who's district attorney now, put a bug in his ear. He's a real prize. Still hasn't learned what deodorant is for, but he's made a bit of a name for himself. I suspect he's going to run for governor in the next election."

Tessa grimaced. "I remember how disgusting he was. I guess some things never change. I just don't see how he could influence the judge if that's what happened."

"I don't know that he did for sure, but he's very tight with Judge Crider. Having the conviction in one of his most sensational cases overturned solely on the basis of his own conduct and having to retry the matter are bound to cause the man a great deal of concern. Remember, there was not a shred of forensic evidence to tie you to the murders. Despite the weakness of the case against you, he has used it to promote himself in the local halls of power. I'm guessing he is one major pissed-off DA."

If Chen's distress were for any other reason, she might have laughed, but it wasn't. She had lost her family, and nothing could ever replace them or make it right again, as far as she was concerned. Nothing about what had happened to them or to her as a consequence was at all funny.

"Trust me, Tessa. You'll be walking into a completely different home. I think you'll approve of the changes. Since the crime that took place there brought a lot of reporters and just nosy people in general, I took it upon myself to remove the place that seemed to hold so much mystery."

"Why didn't you ever give me details?" she asked. It wasn't his place. Even though he'd had power of attorney over her finances, he had not had her permission to remodel the entire house. Yes, he'd mentioned changes, but at the time she had not cared to ask what they were. Now, however, she couldn't help but be curious.

"I don't know. It didn't seem important at the time. I realize I was wrong not to get your permission for all the remodeling, but as I said, I think you'll be pleased with the changes made."

She had been trying to work up enough courage to ask about her daughters' bedrooms, but she just couldn't. There would be time for her to see for herself, and she wanted to be alone when she did. Unsure if Sam had remodeled their rooms, she tried not to think about it. She would find out soon enough.

As they approached Tessa's former neighborhood, it was as Sam had expected. Television vans were parked along the road, news crews paced back and forth, cameramen and -women hovered nearby, all hoping to catch the first glimpse of her.

"Why don't you drop down so they can't see you? Since I'm in front with Cal, maybe they'll focus their attention on me."

So the driver actually had a name, she thought as she unfastened her seat belt. She folded herself into a fetal-like position on the floorboard, tucking her head between her knees.

"Just stay down until I tell you," Sam instructed. "We're about to make the turn."

"Okay," she called from her position on the floor in the back.

She could hear the shouts from the reporters, several tapping on the rear window, all trying to get their attention as they slowly drove through the throngs of people. Reporters, gossipmongers, whoever. She was a damned sideshow at the moment.

Is this a mistake? Maybe I shouldn't have agreed to this. I'd already accepted my fate, so why chance it now? Too late, she thought as she heard the shouts.

"Do you think the residents of the island want a child murderer in their neighborhood?"

"Are you afraid for your safety?"

"How much did you pay your new witness?"

Tessa placed her hands over her ears to block out the questions reporters shouted at the vehicle. She had not done this since she was a child.

"Don't pay attention to them," Sam called over his shoulder. Tessa didn't answer. She just wanted out of the SUV and a few minutes alone; though with Sam acting as her guardian, she wondered if she would ever have a few minutes to herself. For a moment, she wished she were back in the confines of her prison cell, where she had had all the time in the world to herself.

"People are standing in the street, Tessa. Stay down. Looks as if the entire neighborhood has stepped out for a view. Cal, drive around the block, get out of here, and let's see if these gawkers are willing to stand outside for a while. If we drive around for half an hour, they'll get tired of waiting."

Tessa heard Sam.

"The only way out of this neighborhood is the way we came in. Go to the house, please. I can't put this off forever," Tessa said. "And I'm getting up. My back isn't used to this." She got off the floor, then scooted onto the middle seat. "Go to the house, Cal. I want to get this over with."

And she did. What had she expected? This had been a major news story; her release, albeit temporary, was a big deal. People liked to gossip, and her return to the exclusive neighborhood was going to bring a lot of nutcases out of the cracks.

"Sam?" Cal inquired.

"Go to the house. Tessa's right. There's no point trying to avoid the neighbors," Sam said. "She'll have to face them sooner or later."

"Sam, stop talking like I'm not here."

"Sorry, I just want to make this as easy as possible." Sam did sound a little bit contrite.

"I know, and I do appreciate it. But I'm not a delicate little flower. I know people are curious. This was a tight-knit community once upon a time, though I'm not sure that it still is. Many of the people who lived here were snowbirds, and I barely knew them. I'll be fine."

"I know you will," Sam responded.

As they were driving through her former neighborhood, she could not help but think that this was the place where her girls had spent their entire lives, where they'd celebrated birthdays, had pool parties, where they'd all lived out their lives as a family. Tears filled her eyes when they made the turn onto Dolphin Drive. Several people stood on their professionally manicured lawns as though a circus had come to town, and they were waiting patiently to see the star performer show up.

What had she expected? A welcome home party? Homemade casseroles? An offer to house-sit when she returned to prison?

She tried to keep her focus on the back of the front seat, but her eyes kept darting to the people who came out to witness her homecoming.

"This was expected," Sam said, and nodded to the small groups gathered around the gates to the private entrance of her former home. "Take a deep breath, Tessa."

She nodded but said nothing. Cal punched in the code and the gates swung open. More shouting could be heard as the gates closed behind them. He drove slowly up the drive, and what she had expected to see wasn't there.

Her memory of her former home had been erased. Gone were the eight full-grown coconut palm trees that had flanked the driveway, the emptiness obvious as there were no plants or shrubs replanted in their place. The outside of the house, formerly a soft antique white, had been painted a pale blue. Black shutters had been added, and it appeared as though the glass in the windows had been replaced with something darker, possibly to prevent anyone brave enough to chance a glimpse inside. The automatic garage door opened, and Cal pulled the SUV into the garage. Before she could slide across the seat, the giant door closed, blocking her view of the other changes made to the exterior of the house.

Tessa opened her door and stood next to the vehicle. Waiting. Cal remained in the SUV, and Sam was at her side before she even gave him a thought. This was all so familiar, yet odd. Four cars could fit in the garage along with a million other things, yet it was empty. Hollow. Like her.

Had she expected to see Poppy's and Piper's bicycles leaning next to the door that led to the kitchen? Hers and Joel's, too? The crates of toys she had stacked neatly against the wall ready to be donated to charity? She saw nothing remotely familiar. As though the life she had shared with her husband and daughters had been totally and completely wiped away. Like a stain. One minute it was visible, then, with the swipe of time, gone.

Only memories remained.

Images flashed before her. She squeezed her eyes tightly shut, trying to block them out, as they were not memories of their life as a happy family.

Blood.

Streams of blood.

Aqua water turned a garish red.

Bloated bodies.

Two small white caskets beside a larger, dark casket.

The overwhelming scent of roses.

"No!" she yelled, then realized what she had done. She took a deep breath. "I'm okay." She directed her words to Sam. She would *never* be okay again, and surely anyone in their right mind would know these were simply words to appease those whose sympathetic offerings were given as though they could actually ease the burden of this horrific tragedy that was her life. Tessa truly appreciated any kind words, but they would not change the past, could not change it.

Nothing could right the wrongs of the past. There was no magical potion to reverse the clock. If it were possible, she would have given her soul to save her daughters. And Joel, too.

"Tessa?" Sam asked.

Shaking her head to clear the path down which her thoughts were going, she gave up what she hoped would pass for a half-ass smile.

In a no-nonsense voice, she said, "Let's go inside." And not bothering to explain her outburst, she went on. "I want to get this over with."

Coming from humble beginnings, Tessa had always thought her house a bit on the lavish side — no, over the top — but she'd tried to make it as homey as possible given its size. Italian marble floors, two kitchens, one inside, another outside on the lanai, with a bamboo ceiling, and a large gazebo built around several sections of the swimming pool that branched off in every direction. It was almost like man-made canals, except for the Olympic-size pool in the center. A large fountain, with a separate bar and fireplace in the corner, completed the outdoor part of the mansion.

It had been so many years, and she knew that Sam had demolished parts of the inside of the house, but no matter how many walls were knocked down, floor tiles removed, and new furnishings installed, this was the place where her nightmare had begun. She would never have closure. Many professionals had told her that, in time, she would feel a sense of closure. Yet to this very day, she continued to grieve for her loss, the only difference between then and now being that she hid those feelings so that it appeared to all as though she had accepted her loss.

Never!

Her inner rage had been simmering much too long to cool down now.

CHAPTER 7

She entered the kitchen and stopped when she was just a few feet inside. Slowly, she directed her gaze around the large, airy, open space. The black-and-white tile had been replaced with cream-colored wood. The cabinets were of the same color. All of the appliances were stainless steel. None of the girls' artwork, which had been attached to the refrigerator with magnets, was there. Gone were the pots of fresh herbs she had always kept on hand. Glass jars of her favorite teas no longer lined the windowsill. As it was, this kitchen held no memories for her. It was stark and sterile. Tessa found that she neither liked nor disliked the changes. It was simply a room. *Cold,* she thought, and shivered.

"I'll turn the thermostat up," Sam said, walking past her to the control panel in the formal living room.

Without hesitating, she followed him. The

formal living room had been expanded. The windows facing the canal were unadorned, allowing one a perfect view from anywhere in the room. She took it all in, realizing that Sam had knocked out the wall separating the formal dining room from the living area. Cream-colored sofas, with matching plush chairs, were located in a semicircle opposite the windows. "It's different," was all she could come up with. Her throat suddenly felt dry, and her hands began to tremble. She closed them into fists to prevent Sam from seeing just how nervous she was. Squeezing her eyes shut, again, she could not block the vile projection that swept through her mind.

And the smell. Sharp, pungent, unidentifiable at the time. All this time later she recognized the smell.

Decomposition.

Feeling light-headed, she sat down on the nearest chair, surprised to find that it was leather. Soft and cool. Closing her eyes so that she could block the view, she was still for a moment. The swimming pool, the deck, everything in her line of sight was exactly as they had been that horrible day.

"Tessa, if this is too much . . ." Sam said. He positioned himself on the arm of the chair, which was big enough for two people.

"I just need a few minutes alone." She felt the sudden urge to walk through each room in her former home. Unsure why, Tessa stood up, a bit dizzy, but she was okay. "Maybe you can fix us a glass of iced tea?" she asked, hoping he would take the hint to leave her alone.

He stood and brushed his hands up and down the length of her arms. "Are you sure?"

Shivering at his touch, Tessa had never been surer of anything in her life. The need to see each room was so overwhelming, it was as though she were being guided by some unseen force. She stepped away so that Sam could not touch her. "I need to be alone now. Please."

"Of course. I'll go fix us something to drink."

As soon as Sam had left the room, Tessa headed upstairs, unclear about why but knowing she had to do this now and not a second later. She did not know why, but for some unexplained reason, she could not wait.

When she reached the landing, she looked at the closed doors to her left. Piper's and Poppy's rooms. Side by side, with their bathroom separating them. The master bedroom to her right. She wasn't sure if she should go there first or to the girls' rooms. Again, as though she were being guided by a force unknown to her, she went to the master bedroom, and before she could stop herself, she pushed the double doors open. Expecting to see her former room as it was, with its rich mahogany furniture, the custom-made chairs by the window that overlooked the Caloosahatchee River, she was stunned when she saw that it was empty of all furniture. She thought Sam might have left this room alone. Dozens of boxes were stacked against the wall opposite the door. The windows were bare, the celery-green carpet of her memory had been replaced with shiny hardwood. "Why?" she asked aloud, and walked over to the walk-in closet and opened the doors. Shelves that had formerly been lined with her sweaters, jeans, and shirts were empty. She traced a finger over the surface of the wood. Not a speck of dust. Sam must have hired a cleaning service. She looked at what was once Joel's side of the closet. It, too, was empty. All of their personal belongings, collected throughout the years of their marriage and before, were most likely stacked in those boxes against the wall.

What had she expected? That Sam would remodel the entire house yet leave their personal possessions alone? Truly, she had not given it serious thought until now. The master bedroom had been stripped of everything. Nothing of her past was visible but for the boxes, which she assumed contained Joel's clothes and hers in addition to personal items: her journals, his favorite crime novels. Memories of her and Joel picking out their bedroom furniture, the fabric for the drapes, the chairs, and all the myriad items that went along with decorating a home, flooded her.

She tried to recall exactly how she had left their bedroom the day she left for the mainland. The bed was unmade; she remembered that much. It'd been Rosa's day to wash the linens, so she had not bothered making up the bed. And she remembered thinking this as she hurriedly packed for her so-called weekend getaway. What had happened to the Louis Vuitton luggage she had packed? And all the necessities she had packed for her daughters? It had been evidence — she hated using that word — she knew this, but wasn't it supposed to be returned to the family? Had Sam packed it away with the rest of their personal belongings? She stepped out of the closet and stood in the middle of the room.

Never had she imagined she would return

to her former home once she had been convicted. If she had ever dwelt on returning, she was sure she would have gone utterly mad. Disciplined after years of confinement, Tessa struggled with this new reality, a reality that allowed her thoughts to return to the past.

Inside prison, for the first few years, it was all she could do to *not* think about her freedom, and now that she had been given a sort of freedom, albeit temporary and with harsh conditions that constrained her in a different way, she didn't like the path her thoughts had ventured on since she had learned that her conviction had been overturned and she had been granted a new trial.

Before, she had accepted the fact that Liam had gotten away with murder and it truly didn't matter where she lived because there was no life without her family. Now she wasn't so sure about her future. At least inside prison, she knew the rules. There had been no reason for her to think about the what-ifs and maybes.

All of a sudden, a dozen thoughts were swirling in her mind. She needed something concrete to focus all her nervous energy on. At least until the trial, a date which still had not been determined. Tessa had never been happy being idle. She should see if Sam could find Lara, and possibly she could come for a visit. Maybe she could stay here with her. They could get to know one another all over again, like when they were little, and their mother was still alive. Before they were forced to live apart.

Maybe she could . . . she didn't know, what, be a big sister to her again? Tell her all about her prison life? No, that wasn't a topic Lara would want to discuss. Money, drugs, and the latest fashions were her little sister's passions. In that order. Without money, there were no drugs or fancy designer dresses.

"Are you okay?"

Whirling around, Tessa almost jumped out of her skin. "Damn, don't sneak up on me like that!" she shouted at Sam, who stood in the doorway holding two glasses of iced tea. "Remember where I came from," she reminded him, but neglected to tell him what could happen in prison when someone sneaked into the showers, behind you in the cafeteria line, when a guard's attention was elsewhere. No, he didn't need to know about that.

"Sorry. You looked like you were a million miles away," he said, and handed her the glass of tea.

She took a drink of the tea, reveling in its icy sweetness. "It's been so long," she observed, and she took another gulp of the tea. "The ice, I mean. We don't get ice in prison."

Sam appeared uneasy. "It's the little things, I guess," he said as he stood in the entryway to the bedroom, eyes downcast.

Tessa picked up on his awkwardness, and it took a few seconds for her to realize why. They were in her and Joel's bedroom; obviously, he would feel uneasy here. Or she assumed that was the cause of what she decided was his uneasiness, but she didn't really know him on that level, so she could be wrong.

Disturbed by his interference, she would have to put off going into the girls' rooms for another time, when she was alone. She didn't want him or anyone else around when she entered their rooms. "Let's go downstairs," she said. Though she dreaded doing so, she had to get used to the idea of living in her former home. The changes could not block out her memories of the life she had shared here with Joel and the girls or the scene she had come home to on that long-ago day.

Downstairs, Tessa was at a loss as to where she could sit and not see the pool area, so she plopped down on the bottom step. She needed to know why Sam had not gutted the pool area. Of all the spaces to leave untouched, it was the worst.

Sam sat beside her, and she scooted as far away from him as the step would allow.

"I don't bite," he said.

"Of course you don't. I'm just making room for you," she explained, then patted the extra few inches her moving gave him. Clearing her throat, then taking a deep breath, before she lost her courage, she asked, "Why didn't you fill in that goddamned pool?" Anger spewed from her mouth, surprising her.

Sam shook his head. "I wanted to, Tessa, but I couldn't."

"Why not?"

His face clouded with an emotion she couldn't name.

"It's a crime scene," he explained. "I just couldn't. It would have meant giving up all hope."

A crime scene? All hope?

"But, it's . . . I don't understand," was all she could say. "All these years, why can't I just . . . excavate the entire area?" Tessa forced herself to look out the wide expanse of windows. "The evidence was collected," she insisted, stating what seemed to her to be an obvious truth. It made her nauseated just to say the word *evidence* because throughout her short trial the only evidence had been the remains of her precious family. Tears filled her eyes, and she knuckled them to staunch the flow.

"I could never bring myself to destroy this part of the property. It's always been in the back of my mind that the day would come when a second look was needed. Something in my gut told me to hold off," Sam said.

Tessa didn't understand. "Is there some new evidence you know about that I don't, besides Rosa?" She knew that with today's forensics, the possibility of new evidence was not at all unreasonable. There had been dozens of cases where evidence from as far back as fifty or more years had exonerated those who were innocent. Or, as with some arson convictions, even established that no crime had been committed in the first place. She didn't believe there was any actual physical evidence that could change the outcome of her case, but she admitted to herself that she was not an expert in that area. She was innocent, but a jury of her peers had convicted her of three counts of murder in the first degree. Understandably, she did not have much faith in the criminal justice system.

Sam turned to face her. "I don't think so, but I can't be one hundred percent certain. I didn't want to take the chance in case there was any."

"You should have destroyed the entire grounds," she said, motioning to the pool area. "It's the one area that I would have wanted demolished." She could hear the frustration in her voice, the sheer inconceivableness of Sam's lack of forethought. Screw evidence. There was nothing to find.

"I'm sorry, Tessa. I . . . I simply do not agree," was all he said.

She took a deep breath, gazed at the unfamiliar shoes she wore, the new leather waiting for her to break in. She removed them and the footies she was wearing. She had not worn a normal shoe in years.

"You hate the shoes?" Sam asked.

"No," she quickly said. "It's just that my feet feel confined. It's been a while. It'll take time for me to get used to . . . this." She pointed at the shoes and the ankle monitor. "Flip-flops and socks in prison. What we were allowed to wear. No sneakers. The shoelaces could be used as a weapon, or" — and she had thought of this more than once — "a means of taking one's own life."

"Damn," he said in a hoarse whisper. "I didn't think. I'm sorry. For all of this." He gestured toward the pool area. "If you're okay with it, I can see that it's . . . filled in."

What if there *was* evidence that the police had missed? Having no clue what could have escaped their eagle eye, and remembering that to her way of thinking there really had been nothing one could call an investigation since they had decided she was guilty from the get-go, she couldn't really disagree with Sam's decision just yet. The memories would be with her no matter what was present beyond the wide expanse of windows. Her memory of what she had found in that pool could never be erased.

"No. Leave it as it is. For now. I'm not saying I believe there is still evidence, and even if there is, how are you going to go about your . . . search?"

"You're the sole owner of a giant pharmaceutical company with connections to forensic specialists across the country. I can get the ball rolling or not. Your call."

Should she? She hated to get her hopes up, but at this point, what did she have to lose? She had already lost everything that mattered to her. "Go ahead, do whatever you have to do."

"Are you sure?" Sam asked. "I know this isn't what you had in mind when you came home, but I just couldn't bring myself to destroy . . . the pool area."

She didn't tell him that it would have been the first area she would have chosen to destroy had she been given the opportunity, but that was the past, and the past was prologue. And in her case, it was all she had to cling to — her entire life of happy memories resided here in this house. "Just do whatever you have to. I don't want to know the results unless they provide some new . . . lead." She could not bring herself to use the word *evidence* again.

"All right, I'll get started first thing tomorrow," Sam promised. "Or I can start right now. You're the boss," he said, then added, "I'll make sure Lee is on board before I call in the big guns."

She rolled her eyes. "I think tomorrow is soon enough. I need some time to get used to all this." She motioned with her hand to the space in front of her. "Freedom. Temporary, I know." Suddenly changing the topic, she said, "I want to see Lara. Does she know about my release?"

"I told her when I spoke to her last week."

For a brief moment, Tessa's heart lightened, but then she realized that her sister was basically nothing more than a complete stranger to her now and had been for many years before now. Why the hurry to reunite, to bring up bad memories and broken promises of the past? she thought, but kept it to herself. "And?" she coaxed.

"She told me she would call when she could," Sam informed her.

Tessa nodded but remained quiet, wondering exactly what Lara was up to that would prevent her from making a simple phone call. Eventually, she would have to see Lara. She felt she had no choice, but she wasn't going to push the issue with Sam.

After a few seconds of uncomfortable silence, she cleared her throat. "You'll let me know then?" And that was all she said.

"Of course."

Itching to go back to the master bedroom to search the boxes, she grabbed her shoes and stood. "I'm not sure how this is supposed to work, but I would like some time alone. To explore the house. Familiarize myself, I don't know, just get used to the outside world." She didn't know any other way to explain herself other than just to say what was on her mind.

"Okay. I can see about stocking the refrigerator, get this place up and running again. Is there anything you'd like from the grocery? Publix delivers, so I won't have to leave you."

Tessa shook her head. "Not really." Then,

"Sam, I know you're acting as my guardian, but does that mean you have to monitor me twenty-four/seven?"

Sam stood up and walked down the few remaining stairs, putting distance between them. "Pretty much. I'm to keep you within my sight."

Surely he wasn't serious? Then again, why would Sam make light of her situation? He wouldn't. Incredulous, she replied in a tight voice, "Okay. I see." She didn't really, but was not going to tell him so. She had planned on his being in the house during the day, but around the clock, no. This was going to be a problem. She had to find some way around it, and she would. She had to think and plan. She had to figure something out. It wasn't as though she had a choice.

"I'm going to tell Cal he can call it a day," Sam said. "He'll be driving us wherever we need to go."

Tessa's heart beat double time hearing this. "Sam, where *exactly* does Cal live?"

He shifted his gaze away from her, cramming his hands in his pockets. "Here."

"In my house?" she asked, knowing his statement needed no clarification but still wanting to hear him confirm this. "Around the clock?" she added for no reason.

"It's part of the terms of your release. The

pool house has been converted to a guest-house."

She took another deep breath and nodded, then could not help but wonder if any *evidence* had been compromised during the conversion. "Sam, tell me everything. Don't bullshit me. What other terms of my release have I not been told? I need to know."

Glancing around as though he were searching for an answer from some unseen source, Tessa watched him. "Sam, is there more? Seriously, I need to know."

"No, not really," he said a bit sheepishly.

"That sounds like there is, so just tell me." She wasn't used to playing cat and mouse. In prison, dialogue was fairly succinct and straightforward, at least most of the time.

"I'm to keep you within sight at all times. That's it. Cal's staying here is merely a convenience," Sam explained.

"Basically, I'm not allowed any privacy. Is that it?"

"Tessa, I am not going to sleep in the same room with you. I'm not going to watch you shower or take a bath, and if you want me out of the way, this is a large house with a number of rooms where I can go. I'm not a prison guard, okay?"

He sounded a bit ticked off, but she didn't care. "All right," she relented, "but if something changes, no matter how insignificant you think it is, you'll tell me, right?"

"Of course I will."

She hoped he was being honest with her but didn't tell him so. Whatever it took, she couldn't raise his suspicions. She needed time to prepare. Nodding in agreement, she spoke softly. "I'd like to see the girls' rooms, maybe go through a few of the boxes in the master bedroom. You'll take care of the groceries while I do that?" Her way of telling him she wanted to be alone and that he could do whatever he needed. Groceries, anything, it didn't matter, as long as he was out of her way.

"I have got it covered," he said.

"I appreciate all that you have done for me, Sam. I really do. I'm very sorry if I sounded mad at you."

"I know," he said, and headed to the kitchen.

Finally, she thought.

Alone.

CHAPTER 8

"About time," Tessa muttered to herself as she returned to the master bedroom. She was grateful for Sam's taking her case to Lee, but having him and Cal underfoot twenty-four/seven was going to be tough, given her plans. She would have to make adjustments.

In the master bedroom, she saw the boxes against the wall and decided there was no time like the present. Before she could stop herself, she ripped the heavy-duty packing tape off easily as the tape was dry and yellowed with age. Tessa assumed these boxes had been sitting there for a very long time. Possibly as long as she had been in prison. Had Sam packed the boxes himself? Did it matter who packed them? Maybe. Maybe not.

Removing several pieces of balled-up newspaper from the box, Tessa dropped them into a small pile on the floor. Not knowing the contents, as they weren't labeled, she took her time when she reached inside. Carefully, she removed a stack of envelopes held together with a rubber band. The return address read, *The Bank of The Cities,* where they'd shared a personal checking account. Tessa sifted through a few of the statements. Seeing nothing important, she crammed the envelopes back in the box, along with the old newspapers. No point in making a mess as she would be the one responsible for cleaning the place.

Tessa thought of Rosa and wondered what she had seen on her last day of work. Knowing she had spent more than ten years with information that might have cleared the way for the investigation to focus solely on Liam, or at least on someone other than herself, Tessa wanted to question her privately. She added this to her mental list of people who could have made a difference but, for reasons yet unknown to her, had chosen not to.

The next box held more of the same. She flipped through several file folders, recognizing the deed to the house, car titles, and old vehicle registrations that were once kept in the glove compartment of their cars. She would ask Sam about the cars. Had they been given to charity as she had requested?

She had asked her attorney to see to that but had never followed up on it once she had been convicted. She had no use for them now, anyway, because she would need another vehicle when the time was right. Tossing the box aside, she opened the third box and was stunned when she saw what it contained.

With trembling hands, Tessa removed the sheet of green construction paper, crossing the room to stand by the window where she could see clearly. A crayon drawing of a cutout red Christmas tree was glued to the page. Yellow, orange, and purple squares of different sizes had been pasted around the tree as presents.

Tears blurred her eyes as she remembered the day Poppy and Piper had brought the artwork home. It'd been their first Christmas project in preschool at Saint Cecelia's. Both had been so proud and excited to show her their work. Piper had reversed her sister's work, using red paper to glue her green cutout Christmas tree on.

Tessa had laughed, telling them they were twins but polar opposites in so many ways. They'd asked her if they were polar bears. Tessa explained what she had meant, and it had confused them even more. She had told them that when they were older, they'd understand.

Knowing that day would never come for her precious daughters sent a jolt of rage through her. She held the construction paper against her chest as she took several deep breaths in order to regain some semblance of calm. In time, she told herself, she would avenge their deaths.

In time.

She placed the paper on top of the boxes she had gone through, then continued her search. There were faded family photos, and they took her breath away. One in particular caught her eye. A weekend spent with the girls. They'd hunted for shells, finding hundreds of the little white clamshells that were so common but each unique in its size, shape, and coloring. The girls broke out in a fit of giggles when she identified one of their finds as a kitten's paw, a fairly simple-looking shell, that did look like a kitten's paw, but the name was funny to the girls. Jingle had been another shell they thought silly, and their little-girl laughter had made her day.

She smiled at the memory and placed the photo next to the artwork she planned to take downstairs and hang on the refrigerator door. Why not? It was her home, her children, her memories. She dabbed the tears from her eyes. It was the first memory of her girls that had actually made her smile.

In the next box, several envelopes of photos with their negatives were stacked in neat rows. She put these aside for later — when she could look at her former life without rage and tears, which Tessa didn't see happening at any time in the near future. In fact, ever since her release, it had been worse, not better. In prison, one adjusted, knowing that her new life in prison was all there was. There was no real life, however long her sentence might be.

Now, it was different. All the emotions she had tucked away in a safe place were running rampant. *Just get through this first day,* she told herself. *One. Minute. At. A. Time.*

She pushed the box aside and decided she had to search through one more before going to see the room in which she had spent so many happy days and nights.

Hefting a larger box on top of another so she could see the contents as she peered inside, she pulled the yellowed tape off, then removed more rolled-up newspapers. A man's watch, one of many probably belonging to Joel, but not the Rolex he usually wore. This was a Bravado, with a royal blue face and tiny diamonds representing the numbers. She didn't remember seeing this particular watch but was sure it had belonged to him. It evoked no memory or any real emotion. She looked closer and saw the date showing on the watch. To her horror, she realized that it was the day *after* she had left for the mainland. It had stopped at 6:47 on Saturday, May 3, 2011. Had her daughters been alive then? Had Joel worn the watch while he fought for his life? Their daughters' lives?

What did this mean? Or did it mean anything at all? Was she being paranoid? Maybe Joel's battery had failed, and he'd switched watches. That was highly probable. Since their first date, she had rarely seen him when he was not wearing a wristwatch. He'd been extremely punctual, a trait she had admired, as she, too, respected others' time and thought it quite rude to be late for any event, unless, of course, circumstances dictated otherwise.

She put the watch aside as she made the decision to tell Lee. Maybe it was *evidence.* Hadn't all the evidence been collected already? Had this been missed? Tessa decided the watch had to be important though she wasn't sure how.

With this in mind, she used the tail of her blouse to pick up the watch and place it on the windowsill. Before she went any further, she hurried downstairs. Not bothering to give the slightest glance to the view outside, she found Sam in the kitchen. Apparently, Publix deliveries were fast, too. She had been upstairs just over an hour.

"Do you have a paper bag, or a storage bag of some kind?" she asked.

He turned away from unpacking the groceries to stare at her. "I think I added Ziploc bags to the list." He rummaged through the three brown bags before finding them.

"Here you go," he said, handing her the entire box.

"Thanks," she said, and raced out of the room before he asked her what she needed the bag for.

Upstairs in the master bedroom, once again, she used her shirttail to pick up the watch from the windowsill and drop it inside the plastic bag. Breathing a sigh of relief, she didn't know if she was being foolish, overdramatic, or just careful.

Maybe a little bit of each.

Tessa went back to the box, this time being more cautious as she removed the contents. A checkbook, with a brown-leather cover. She flipped it open. It was a personal check, but only had Joel's name, not hers. Odd, she couldn't remember his having a personal account, either. She saw that the checks were the kind that held a carbon copy of the original. Tessa tried to make out the faint letters on the carbon copies of the used checks, but they were too faded to read. She supposed it wasn't unusual for a man of Joel's profession to have a private checking account, and maybe he'd mentioned it to her, but so much time had passed, she didn't remember. It wasn't important, but just for the hell of it, she added the checkbook to a fresh Ziploc bag.

The rest of the items in the box were an outdated bottle of Tylenol, the red label faded to a slightly orange-yellow, a box of staples, a comb, and a pair of Ray-Ban sunglasses. Nothing unusual. Tessa carried the box across the room and placed it by the window.

Feeling as though she was stalling, she knew she had to do what she had come upstairs to do.

She needed to see the room where Piper and Poppy had spent the last day of their young lives.

CHAPTER 9

She stood in the hall outside Poppy's room, then walked a few steps and stood next to the door to Piper's room. How could she possibly decide which room to enter first? If she chose one over the other, wouldn't she feel a sense of betrayal? As though she favored one twin over the other?

No, this was not the way she should go about this. Tessa paced back and forth, stopped, and closed her eyes. Whatever room she was closest to she would enter first, then open the doors to the bathroom that separated the two rooms.

Her hand touched the doorknob, and she turned it, pushing the door aside.

Piper's room.

Hot tears instantly filled her eyes. Memories assailed her.

The room was exactly as it had been the day she left.

Before she could stop herself, she

screamed, "Sam, you son of a bitch, how could you?"

Tessa ran out of the room, not bothering to close the door. She was at the top of the stairs, and Sam met her halfway up.

"Tessa," he said, and pulled her into his arms. "I wanted to warn you, but I was waiting for the right time. God, I'm sorry."

She didn't bother stepping out of his embrace as sobs shook her. Of all the brutal images she had tried to erase from her mind, this was the worst. It exemplified their utter innocence, which had been so savagely taken.

Pulling away from him, she wiped her nose on the sleeve of her blouse. "Why, Sam? Is there a reason?"

"Let's go downstairs. I've made a salad and a couple of omelets. We can talk down there." He turned and headed downstairs.

Trailing behind for lack of a better choice, she saw that he'd closed the automatic blinds that covered the wide expanse of windows.

"In here," he called from the kitchen.

She reached the kitchen and stood in the doorway. The island that had been added during the remodeling was set for two, with blue place mats and matching cloth napkins.

"Go on, have a seat," Sam said, without

turning away from the stove.

Tessa watched as he slid two perfectly formed fluffy yellow omelets onto two blue plates. Looked like Fiestaware, she thought as she sat down on the barstool.

"I hope you like spinach and mushrooms. It's kind of my specialty. Oh, and Pepper Jack cheese."

Tessa could not remember the last time she had eaten an omelet. "It smells delicious. I like spinach and mushrooms, just so you know."

He smiled. Her heart raced a bit, but she was not going to focus on that. She would probably smile at any man who cooked for her on her first day out of prison.

He removed two blue bowls from the refrigerator. "Another one of my specialties." He set the fruit salad next to their plates. "I'd offer you a glass of white wine, but it's not allowed." He filled a glass with ice and poured the tea he'd made earlier.

She nodded. "Thanks. I was never much of a drinker anyway. This salad looks awesome, just so you know. I haven't had good fresh fruit in . . . a while." Of course she had had fruit, but it had been out of a can.

"Strawberries, cantaloupe, kiwi, oranges, and coconut. Won't tell you my secret fruit-salad sauce. If I did, I might have to kill you."

As soon as the words came out of his mouth, Tessa saw by his expression that he wished he could take them back. "It's okay. Really," she offered. People used that expression all the time. "You don't have to censure your words, Sam. I won't break."

He sat down on the barstool beside her. "Thanks. I'm sorry. That was insensitive. Let's just eat the omelets before they get cold. You eat, then we'll talk. That okay with you?"

She nodded and dug into her omelet. Tessa's mouth practically watered when she took the first bite. Sam was an excellent omelet maker. She took a bite of the fruit salad. "Sam, this is divine! The secret sauce, right?" she teased, and proceeded to finish the omelet and salad. She used the blue napkin, then took her plate and bowl to the sink.

"I take it you approve?" Sam said, still seated at the bar.

She rinsed her dishes in the sink and placed them in the ultra-fancy dishwasher. "I can honestly say it's the best meal I've had in a decade. Thank you."

"You're welcome, though I have to warn you, my culinary skills are limited to just a few simple dishes."

She gave up a bit of a smile. He was trying to make this easy for her. The least she could do was show him she appreciated it. "That's a good thing, I guess, that you know your limitations. I used to enjoy piddling around in the kitchen myself. I used to bake, as I found it relaxing. Maybe I can bake something for you and return the favor."

"I'd like that," Sam said. "Any favorites?"

Small talk; this was easy for her. "I used to make a pretty mean Red Devil's Food cake. A friend in college made it for me once, and it was the best cake I had ever had at that point in my life. She gave me her recipe, I tweaked it a bit here and there, and made it my own. I suppose I could make you one, that is, if you like chocolate?"

He brought his dishes to the sink and stood next to her. "What kind of human being *doesn't* like chocolate?"

She stepped away from him, the closeness causing a zing and zang in places it shouldn't. "I'll make a list of the ingredients, and the next time you make a grocery order, you can get them. Are there pots and pans here? Rather, cake pans?"

"I had my secretary on Google for days ordering household necessities. I'm sure she didn't leave out anything one would normally require in the kitchen. She's very thorough. Let's have a look," he said, and started opening the cupboards.

Tessa searched, too. "Here they are," she announced when she saw a cupboard stocked with every kind of baking pan one could imagine. "She *is* very thorough."

"Darlene's fantastic. That's why I keep her on," Sam explained.

Out of the blue, Tessa wondered if Sam's secretary was more than just an employee.

"She has three of the cutest grandsons and updates me daily on their antics. Jamison was lucky to hire her. Her husband passed away a few years ago, and he left her almost penniless. She's a true peach."

That answered that question.

"Maybe I'll meet her. You know, someday, if I come back to work."

"Highly probable if you ask me. Lee Whitlow is the best of the best, Tessa. He wouldn't have taken on your case if he didn't believe there was a good chance of seeing you exonerated. How about I make us a cup of coffee, then we can talk about what you should expect when it's time for trial, among other things."

She nodded. "Coffee sounds good. I hope it's not instant." She hated the bitter, watered-down version they tried to pass off as coffee in prison.

"I wouldn't do that to you. I had Darlene order a Keurig, too. While it's not a French press, it's decent."

"What is a 'Keurig'? I *have* been out of the . . . loop."

"Sorry. It's a coffeemaker that brews one cup at a time. You put these little pods in." He removed a box from the cupboard. "Here, and press a button."

Tessa watched as the machine did its magic in a minute. "Impressive."

He made a second cup for himself. "You need cream or sugar?"

"Black is fine."

"My kinda girl."

His kind of girl? Why did he continue to drop hints like that? Was she imagining things? Probably, she thought. It had been a long time since she had been on the receiving end of any male attention.

"Tessa?" Sam asked. "You want to sit outside?" He handed her the cup.

Not really, she thought, but she had to start somewhere. It wasn't going to make things any easier if she continued to hide inside the house. "On the dock?" she asked. Away from the pool.

"We can watch the sun go down," Sam

said. "No media, hopefully."

Tessa thought it best to keep her thoughts to herself where the gentle people of the press were concerned. Had she not feared the repercussions on her daughters of the media attention sure to come when she went to the police, so that she set off running to San Maribel, her life would have been quite different. Screw the media. Maybe they were watching her now, taking her picture with a telephoto lens, and her picture would be plastered on the front page of the *San Maribel News Press* tomorrow. Her release was sure to be front-page news.

Sure that he was simply trying to make her first day of freedom as relaxing as possible, given the circumstances, she forced herself to follow him through the large glass doors and out to the dock. Media or no media, dammit, this was still her home, and she had every right in the world to walk outside. The ankle monitor was cumbersome, but she assured herself she had to get used to it.

The blue water of the ocean beckoned her, the briny scent bringing back memories of good times spent boating with Joel and the girls. Surprisingly, there were no tears at this memory, and that encouraged her. She would need to be rigid as hell if she was to get through the upcoming trial. More so if she was convicted a second time.

Lounge chairs were placed on the large dock area, along with side tables. Sam motioned for her to sit. She put her coffee on the table, then reclined in the plush cushions. *Surreal* came to mind. Yesterday, she had been in a prison cell, and look at her now. Enjoying an almost God-like — no it *was* God-like — view of the magnificent sunset. One of her favorite features of the island had always been the lighthouse perched on the very edge of the rocky shore. She had a perfect view of it from the dock, a tall spire framed against the wide sky. Looking at the familiar sight once more, she gave up a silent prayer, thankful for this moment and the opportunities facing her.

She took a sip of her coffee. "This is good stuff, Sam, very good stuff." Coffee had never tasted this good before.

"There is more where that came from," Sam said. "Tessa, I know the next few weeks aren't going to be easy for you. Lee and his team will be here tomorrow afternoon to start prepping you for a trial. I have contacted Harry Mazza. His team is the best in the state. He's quite familiar with your case. They'll be here first thing in the morning to begin their investigation. Are you good with this?"

She drained the last of her coffee. "Of course I am. I'd be an idiot not to be. But I really don't think they're going to find anything." Tessa paused, remembering the watch she had found. "Sam, there were some items in one of the boxes I went through. I'm not sure if I should even be telling you this since it's probably nothing."

"Let me decide," Sam said, all trace of his former, relaxed self now gone.

"I found a watch, a checkbook, and some office items." She hesitated, sure that she was making too much out of what she had found. Overreacting.

"Those were items I packed away when I emptied out Joel's desk at the office," Sam said. "There were five or six boxes if I remember correctly. What did you find that's bothering you?"

Taking a deep breath, Tessa felt foolish. "A wristwatch. I'm sure it's one that must have belonged to Joel, but I do not remember ever seeing it before."

"I don't understand. Joel always wore a watch. Kind of obsessive about punctuality."

"He was. Come inside. I want you to see for yourself." Tessa slid out of the chair, picked up her cup, and headed toward the house. She tried to avoid looking at the elaborate pool area, but it was nearly impossible. She sneaked a look as she entered through the screened-in area. Images of that day filled her mind, but she hurried inside and ran upstairs, with Sam close behind.

"Damn, Tessa. You're in shape. I can hardly keep up with you," Sam said.

She took the Ziploc bag that held the watch and offered it to Sam. "Look at this, then tell me what you think."

Sam reached in the bag.

"Wait!" She searched the room. "Sam, give me back the bag."

"Okay," he said, quickly handing it back to her.

As she had done before, she used the tail of her shirt to demonstrate to Sam how to remove the watch from the bag. "Don't touch it directly, Sam."

He nodded, and as she had done, he used the tail of his pale green shirt to remove the watch from the Ziploc bag. He walked across the room to the window, just as she had done earlier. The sun had set, leaving the room in pale pink shadows.

"Let's go in another room," Sam suggested.

"Not the twins' rooms!" Tessa shouted.

"No, the guest room," Sam said.

Tessa followed him. Surprised to find the room fully furnished, she assumed this was where Sam would sleep. He turned the bedside lamp on and held the watch where he could see it clearly.

Tessa could actually see the change in him as he fully grasped the watch's significance.

"Show me the box where you found this." Sam was still holding the watch by his shirt-tail.

She rushed back to the master bedroom, grabbed the box, and dragged it to the guest room. "It was in here."

"Return this to the bag," Sam instructed. He took a cell phone from his pocket, punched in a number, then walked across the room.

She assumed he didn't want her to hear his conversation. It didn't matter. It was apparent she had been right about the watch.

"Harry Mazza wants to see the watch, Tessa. He's coming over right now. You okay about that?"

"The watch is important?" Tessa asked.

"Could be. Harry thinks it's worth taking a look at tonight. Frankly, I'm not sure why he can't wait until tomorrow, but I have known him too long to question his practices. You were right to bring this to me."

Sam took a deep breath. "Do you remember if Joel was wearing this watch? The day you left? No, forget that. You've already told me that you did not remember his ever wearing this watch, correct?"

She had wracked her brain and simply couldn't remember. She told that to Sam. "That's right. Anyway, I was still in shock. The girls told me about Liam on a Wednesday. Joel was in England on business and did not get back until Thursday afternoon. I was so focused on getting them away from the media, I didn't pay much attention to him. As I said to the police" — she hesitated — "the day I left, my focus was on my children. Only two days before, they had told me that their uncle was touching them." She stopped, closed her eyes. Inhale, exhale. Deep breaths.

"I was in a stupor. Thinking back, I know I was suffering from post-traumatic stress disorder, but at the time, my main concern was my girls." Tessa stared at Sam. "How well did you know Liam?"

"Casually, at best. He wasn't involved in the day-to-day running of Jamison Pharmaceuticals. In fact, other than taking his share of the profits, he wasn't involved in the company at all. It wasn't my business."

Tessa heard more. "You didn't like Liam,

did you?"

Sam sat on the edge of the bed. "Liam was a trust-fund baby. I have never had respect for anyone, male or female, who doesn't have a work ethic. Liam was a nice enough guy, I suppose, but I never thought there was much depth to him. Does this mean I didn't like him?" Sam shook his head as though answering his own question. "I never knew him well enough to decide one way or the other."

"I never liked him. There was just something about him. I could never put a name to it, it was just a feeling. He always made me uneasy. I always felt as though he looked down on me. That he considered himself superior in some way," Tessa said. "He was aware of my background, and I always believed he thought I married Joel for his wealth the way his mother had married Grant for his money. Joel believed the same thing about Liam's mother." She sat next to Sam but made sure there was enough space between them.

"Superior. A good description," Sam agreed.

"Did he date, or have a girlfriend?" She knew Sam would understand why she asked this.

"I always had the impression he was

126

somewhat of a ladies' man," Sam replied.

Tessa leaned down and adjusted her slacks. The ankle monitor caught on the material. "This is a pain, but in a good way."

"Tessa, what do you want to know? I'll be as honest and up-front with you as I can be, but if you don't ask, I can't help."

So she was transparent, she thought as she turned to face Sam. "This is disgusting, but I'll ask anyway. Did he ever strike you as a pedophile? Would you have suspected him of . . . doing what he did to my girls."

"No."

"How can you say that and sound so sure if you didn't really know him? I don't understand."

"He did not strike me as a creepy pervert. Maybe a male whore, but I never had weird vibes in the sense that you're asking. I wish I could be more concrete in my assessment of the guy, but you asked."

She nodded. She had never picked up on any oddities in Liam, either. She didn't like him. Why? He'd been arrogant. A show-off. Cocky. Too handsome in her opinion. But like Sam, she had not picked up on anything twisted about him. At least where . . . children were concerned. And when she actually thought about him in relation to Piper and Poppy, he genuinely seemed to care about them. In the true sense an uncle would. She had never seen the girls' behavior change when he was around. If anything, they were more playful and outgoing when Liam came to the house. It made no sense. Tessa always reasoned that's how these sick-ass people worked. No one would suspect them — Liam — of being a child molester.

A loud banging from downstairs sent her to her feet.

"That would be Harry. A bull in a china shop," Sam observed, as they headed downstairs with the watch.

"Wait!" Tessa said, and ran back up the stairs. She grabbed the other bag with the checkbook and ran back downstairs in under a minute. "He might want to see this as well," she said, a bit winded. "It's a checkbook. I didn't know Joel had a personal account."

Sam took the bag from her.

Another loud bang from the front door.

"Stay here," Sam said. "I'm sure the media hounds are out there just waiting to get a glimpse of you."

Tessa nodded.

She did not want her face made public yet.

CHAPTER 10

Harry Mazza was the spitting image of what one would describe as a science nerd. Black horn-rimmed glasses, brown hair a bit too long and in need of combing, untucked pale blue dress shirt, and wrinkled slacks. Tessa recognized a kindred spirit at once, as she, too, had been a true science nerd in school.

Sam quickly introduced them.

"Yeah, good to meet you, lady. Now where's that watch?" he asked Sam. "I'll need to send it to the lab tonight."

If circumstances had not been so dire, Tessa would have laughed at Harry Mazza. He had no manners whatsoever. But circumstances *were* dire and no laughing matter.

Sam handed Harry the Ziploc bag with the watch in it, along with the bag containing the checkbook. Harry, in turn, took a blue glove from his pocket, snapped it on his right hand, then removed the watch from the bag. He inspected it for several minutes, then took a small magnifying glass from another pocket. Taking his time, he inspected the watch at some length. "I'm going to make an educated guess here, but unless I am mistaken, this watch received a hard blow that made it stop. I can't be one hundred percent sure until we examine it at the lab, but that's my gut impression."

Tessa looked at Sam, then at Harry. "With all due respect, Mr. Mazza, that can't be right. Sam took that watch from Joel's desk after . . . after his death."

"Could be, but until we examine it in the lab, I'm sticking to what my gut says. That watch stopped when it was hit or dropped."

"Sam?" Tessa looked to him for an explanation.

"I'm not an expert in forensics. As Harry says, let's wait until it's properly examined."

Tessa walked into the kitchen, not caring that it was rude. What Harry Mazza implied could not be possible. Sam found that watch at the office in Joel's desk. *After* his death. And the watch had stopped on Saturday, when she was already in San Maribel, and according to the evidence introduced at the trial, the murder had occurred on Friday, before she had gone to San Maribel. Sam had to be mistaken. He'd said there were

130

five or six boxes from Joel's office. She needed to find them and search for the watch that Sam had actually found *in Joel's desk*. A stopped watch with the date of her family's murder was impossible; it literally could not have been in Joel's desk.

Sure that Sam was mistaken, she returned to the living room, where the two men were deep in conversation. She doubted they'd even registered that she had left the room.

"Excuse me," she said. "Sam, where are the other boxes you took from Joel's office? Nothing has been marked."

"I brought all the boxes here. Right after the trial, a month or so, if memory serves me correctly. I'm sure I labeled them."

"No, you couldn't have. None of the boxes I searched had any type of writing on them. To be frank, I found it odd they weren't labeled."

Sam looked perplexed.

Harry peered out the front window. "I'm leaving. The mob looks like it's calling it a night out there. You need to get some security, Sam."

"I did, Harry. I'm not that dense," Sam added. "Just get this to your lab and let me know the results as soon as you can. I'm guessing we have six to eight weeks before the trial."

"I'll have it long before then. I'll send my crew out first thing in the morning, but I don't want the media crawling around while they work. It distracts them, and as you well know, it only takes one little distraction to throw an entire case down the tubes." Harry held Sam's gaze.

"I understand," Sam stated. "Thank you for coming over so quickly. Tessa's very grateful, too." He turned to look at her, raised his brows, and nodded in Harry's direction.

"Oh, of course. I am very thankful. It's very kind of you to battle your way through that." Tessa directed her gaze to the window.

"I'll see you two later," Harry said, then let himself out.

Sam locked the door as soon as he left.

"What security?" Tessa asked. "You said nothing to me about security. Is Cal your security?"

"Part of it. Tessa, surely you didn't think I wouldn't take precautions for your safety? You're major news, and there are those out there who disagree vehemently with the court's decision to let you out on bond, no matter how high."

"There is more than Cal?" This news could ruin her plans. She had not given security the first thought, which showed just

132

how poor her planning was, though she had yet to actually act on her so-called plans, if you could call what she had been pondering plans at this stage. This news of security shed a whole new light on everything she had hoped to accomplish over the next few weeks.

"Of course there is more than Cal. He is just one man. We have hired some of the best in the business. Lee and I discussed this and agreed it was best for your safety."

"And neither of you thought to inform me?"

"Does it really matter? You want to be safe? Do you want to enjoy your freedom once the trial is over?" Sam was pissed; she knew, but couldn't care less.

"You and Lee are too confident, Sam. I don't like that at all. I know you're full of good intentions, but it would have been decent of you to consult with me first."

"We had your best interest in mind. I never thought extra security would be an issue with you. And I still do not see why it is." He paused. "Unless you have plans I'm not aware of?"

She sat down on the bottom step, needing to compose herself and put her game face on. Maybe she needed to come clean with Lee. After all, he was her attorney, and they were legally bound to silence. No, she couldn't tell him of her plan. She knew from being surrounded with jailhouse "lawyers" that if your attorney knew you were about to commit a crime, he or she was legally bound to report you to the authorities.

"Tessa, why don't you tell me the reason you're objecting to your own safety? I hope you're not planning something foolish."

If he only knew the visions that had gone through her mind the past two months since learning of her new trial. With an unlimited amount of money at her disposal, all she needed to do was put the right people on her payroll, and she would see to it that justice was served. Liam Jamison could not have fallen off the face of the earth. There were ways to locate those who didn't want to be located. This was one of the many lessons she had learned while in prison. It was one hell of a place for rehabilitation, she always thought. She heard of ways to get around the criminal justice system and not get caught, though considering from whom she was hearing about it, they obviously weren't foolproof. If they were, she would not be hearing it from people *in prison.*

Liam Jamison had to know his way around the criminal justice system or he would be serving three life sentences instead of her.

Bastard.

"Tessa?" Sam said, jolting her from her reverie.

She had instantly come up with an explanation. "I've been surrounded by guards for over a decade, Sam. Surely you of all people understand my . . . surprise to learn that that hasn't changed; from my point of view, the only difference is that I'm now a prisoner in my own home."

He scrunched up beside her. "Tessa, you knew the terms of your release. The ankle monitor doesn't keep you safe. I took that responsibility when I agreed to act as your guardian. It's my job to keep you safe, so you can testify at trial if you choose to. Lee and I are both confident we can get an acquittal at your next trial if we cannot find enough evidence beforehand to get the charges dismissed. If you're harmed in any way, it's on me."

"What about Liam? That fucking bastard has been living life as a free man while I . . ." Tessa had no words to finish her sentence.

"I know, I know. But if the bastard has the slightest bit of conscience, he's been looking over his shoulder for the past decade. Here is what I can do; I can keep you safe; Lee and I can do our best to keep you out

135

of that fucked-up place you've called home, and when you're a free woman, *you* can hunt the bastard down. But until then, we have to follow the rules. Both of us.

"This is day one. And I don't know about you, but I am tired. It's been a very long day, and tomorrow will be even longer. Let's call it a night, get some rest, and rethink this tomorrow. Deal?" He held his hand out to her.

As much as she hated to admit it, he was right. She needed to sleep, to clear her head. She reached for his hand, "Deal."

"Darlene fixed a room up for you. Downstairs. I'm staying upstairs in that guest room. I hope that's okay?"

"Would it matter if it wasn't?" she asked, still slightly pissed that he had so much control over her.

"You can sleep in the upstairs guest room if you want. It doesn't matter to me. A bed is a bed. I thought it might make it easier on you. Sleeping downstairs."

Of course. Sam was thoughtful, though she hated admitting that just now. "No, it's fine. Which room? There were six bedrooms in this house. Total waste of space." She and Joel had planned on a family, and maybe there would have been that son had he lived. Or two.

"The room where all the books were."

"Ah, my den. Sam, please tell me you didn't toss my books?"

He stood up and took her hands in his. "Actually, I think you'll be pleased when you see what Darlene arranged. Follow me."

She felt odd being led around in her own home. Sam went down the long hall that led to three other guest rooms. "In here," he said, opening the door and turning on the lights.

Tessa entered the room. "Sam! This is . . . a library!" She saw so many of her familiar titles, some of her college textbooks she had hung on to. Floor-to-ceiling shelves held all the books she had collected throughout the years. "Thank you, Sam. This is perfect."

The furnishings were plush and inviting. A fireplace had been added and two arm-chairs now flanked the window — all the creature comforts a die-hard book lover could want.

"I'll tell Darlene you approve. Now, you might want to sleep in one of the other guest rooms. They have been redecorated with all the latest gadgets and gizmos in mind. I'm going upstairs now. I'm exhausted. Night, Tess." He smiled and left her in her new library.

"Good night, Sam."

He waved.

She decided she would sleep in here, surrounded by her books, which held mostly happy memories. It would be the first time that she had slept in this house since she had been arrested for the murder of her husband and twin daughters.

CHAPTER 11

Tessa realized she had forgotten to ask Sam about pajamas and toiletries. Before he went to sleep, she hurried upstairs to the guest room where they'd looked at the watch earlier. She knocked lightly on the door.

"Come in," Sam called out.

Hesitant in case he wasn't dressed, she called out. "Sam, I hate to be a pest, but I need something to sleep in and a toothbrush —"

The door swung open before she could finish her sentence.

"I totally forgot. In one of the guest rooms, I'm unsure which one, but it should be fully stocked with all the things you'll need in the chest of drawers."

"Darlene's magic?"

Sam raked his hand through his hair. Tessa thought he looked incredibly handsome just then. She took a deep breath.

"Actually, it was me. I thought . . . Never

mind what I thought. You should have everything you need in one of the guest rooms and bathrooms. And Darlene did take care of all those bubbles and lotions." He smiled at her, and for the first time in years, she felt glad to be a woman.

Breathless, she nodded. "I appreciate this. Thanks, Sam. Night." She hurried back to the first floor before she did something stupid, but she did hear him laughing on her way downstairs.

She grinned.

She found everything she needed in the room across the hall from the library. The furnishings were warm wood, and the draperies and comforter were done in soft shades of creams and beige, nothing like the dark green and navy colors she had used all those years ago. Tessa found a pair of pink-silk pajamas in the top drawer along with several pair of pastel-colored bikini underwear. She blushed when she thought of Sam's hands touching something so personal. Joel never purchased anything as intimate for her. Flowers and chocolates, which she had adored, but never a set of pajamas and pretty panties. All very feminine. And then it dawned on her. Sam had purchased these things not because he had hoped for any possible future intimacy between them but because he knew she would appreciate fine clothes after her years of wearing an orange jumpsuit. He was thoughtful and kind. Feeling foolish, she was going to indulge herself tonight by soaking in the Jacuzzi tub she had seen when she sneaked a look into the bathroom.

Before, this guest bath had only boasted a shower, a sink, and a toilet. The old had been replaced with newer, modern, much more luxurious fixtures. All done in the same warm shades of beige as the bedroom.

The vanity was lined with shampoos, body washes, razors, everything she would need. She turned the taps on in the Jacuzzi, setting the water temperature as high as she could stand, then added a gardenia-scented bath bomb to the water. Darlene had thought of everything. Someday, she promised herself, she would thank her.

She peeled off her slacks, careful of the ankle monitor before she realized it probably wasn't waterproof. She had to hang her foot over the side, and tomorrow she had to check to see if she could shower with it on. For now, Tessa wasn't going to let a little thing like an ankle monitor prevent her from soaking in this giant tub. She had fantasized about hot baths for years. Prison meant three-minute showers with lukewarm water. For as long as she could, she would enjoy these luxuries.

While lowering herself into the hot, steamy, gardenia-scented water, tears filled her eyes. It had been so very long since she had actually enjoyed anything so simple as a hot bath. She closed her eyes and let her mind wander.

Her first thoughts were of Sam, and the enormous responsibility he had undertaken when involving himself in her case.

Sam was more than he seemed. Sharp, intelligent. Mysterious. Thoughtful. He'd propelled Jamison Pharmaceuticals into areas of research that could change the course of modern medicine. New cancer drugs that changed and lengthened lives. He wasn't a sit-behind-the-desk kind of CEO. Joel must have known this when he promoted him from CFO to CEO early in 2011. Tessa tried to focus her thoughts elsewhere. She did not want to compare Sam to her deceased husband. It wasn't fair to either of them.

Her daughters. They would be almost twenty-one years old now. Maybe they would have had children of their own. Or they would be in college pursuing their studies and looking forward to interesting and productive careers. There were so many possibilities, or had been. Gone with the slash of a box cutter. She shivered. She did not want to relive the day she had come home to find her family, but her mind couldn't stop the images from appearing. She had blocked them out for years, but now, when she tried to relax, they came back in full force.

Tessa drove her red Porsche out of the ferry and made a mental checklist of all the extra things Piper and Poppy would need for an extended stay off the island. Anything to distract her from thinking about the horror her daughters had been subjected to. Her eyes flooded with tears, and her heart raced a mile a minute.

No. Not now.

Concentrate on driving home.

She needed to focus on the items she had to pack. She had to focus on the children, on their escape.

Poppy and Piper would need their summer clothes, swimsuits, and sandals, not to mention all their beach gear. Pails, sand molds for their sculptures, floats, and this year she'd promised them they could get boogie boards.

Their crisp white blouses and navy skirts worn at Saint Cecelia's, the private girls' school they'd attended since preschool, would be left behind. Tessa would continue their education once this nightmare ended.

Both were avid readers, and she would bring their Kindles and make sure the Harry Potter series and a lengthy list of reading material were loaded on their electronic readers. Of course, she couldn't forget to bring their brand-new iPads. As much as she disliked it, she knew there would be times when the quirky games they could access would save the girls from complete and utter boredom. To be sure, she would bring plenty of board games, the collection of their favorite movies, which they never seemed to tire of, and an endless supply of drawing paper with brightly colored markers and pencils. Both girls were very artistic and attended advanced art classes every Wednesday afternoon.

Tessa smiled when she remembered the family portrait Poppy had drawn just a few weeks ago. She'd proudly hung it on the refrigerator with her favorite Harry Potter magnet. It was actually quite good except Tessa thought she'd looked pregnant. She wanted to ask Poppy why but didn't because she feared cramping her artistic style. Maybe it was time to think about another child? Last year, Poppy had asked for a little brother for Christmas. Tessa had laughed, never giving another child much serious thought as she had her hands full with the twins, but now, maybe it was time to reconsider. Joel often hinted he wanted a son. As soon as this horrid nightmare ended, if ever, Tessa promised to give the idea of another child some serious thought.

On her way home after spending parts of the last three days on the mainland preparing for a stay of indefinite length, she was beyond tired as she headed north on Highway 41. Brief flashes of colorful signs zoomed by as she drove past the familiar sights, including the small strip of stores facing the beach. Tessa and the girls had spent many afternoons roaming the stores, shopping, having lunch at their favorite café, and oftentimes spending hours looking for that perfect pair of shoes. Tessa gave a sad grin. Both girls loved shoes, loved trying them on more than anything. Now, however, she wasn't sure there would ever be another innocent mother-daughter outing since they'd told her what happened. A nightmare both girls had endured for almost a year. The fear in their eyes haunted her, twisted her insides in ways she'd thought had been put to rest.

And now those feelings were back with a vengeance; only now, the degradation had been forced on her daughters.

Anger forced her to press her foot down on

the accelerator. Suddenly overwhelmed with the need to be with her girls, Tessa raced along the road. The street was lined with palm trees, and normally Tessa never grew tired of viewing the gallant trees as they stood tall and proud, flanking the road. Now, they passed in a greenish-brown blur.

Tessa thought it a bit too much, but Joel often reminded her of their position, telling her it was his duty to keep his family safe. Kidnapping the children of wealthy businessmen wasn't unheard of. But all the security they'd provided had not protected any of them from the evil that lurked inside the supposed safety of their home.

Tessa's sky-blue eyes filled with tears. Her precious daughters, spoiled by that low-life sick form of humanity. She would see to it that he went to prison for a very long time. If not worse.

She punched in the code that opened the gates to the long drive leading to the seven-thousand-square-foot mansion looking out over the ocean, the house that she and Joel called home.

When she had departed on Friday afternoon, Tessa had hated leaving the girls at such a critical time, but it had been necessary in order to protect them from the media and God knows what else. She had not been too successful in protecting them from their uncle. Maybe she could focus her energies on keeping them out of the spotlight. Once she contacted the authorities, she was certain that everything that had happened would be made public. The media hounds would have a field day. All hell would break loose. She and the girls would need the privacy of San Maribel now more than ever.

Knowing that the twins would be emotionally and psychologically scarred after revealing the abuse they had suffered at the hands of their uncle Liam, she'd immediately taken action. Once she'd recovered from the initial shock, she contacted Jill Ambers Wednesday afternoon. Jill was a good friend as well as a forensic psychiatrist who specialized in the sexual abuse of children. Tessa never dreamed she would need to see her friend on a professional basis but knew that life didn't always go as one expected. That very evening, Jill came to the house to examine both girls. She'd said the girls would need extensive therapy as they'd exhibited a new and intense fear of discussing what Liam had done to them.

How well she knew that some adults could never be trusted, but that was for another time. Now her focus was on her children. She would protect them no matter the cost.

On Friday afternoon, Tessa had gone to the mainland to prepare for their arrival. It was rare for her to take the girls away from home during the school year, certainly not on a Monday night, when their normal routine would consist of deciding what to have for dinner, doing homework, and discussing any upcoming plans for the week ahead, but after Wednesday's revelation, Tessa couldn't imagine keeping them home a minute longer than necessary. Jill had promised to check on the girls that weekend.

Thursday night, after Joel had finally returned from a business trip to England, as they lay in bed, she'd told him she needed a break, some time to herself, said she was mentally exhausted from the kids and all that caring for them had involved while he had been away the past week. He'd accepted her explanation, telling her he had to work on Saturday, and possibly a half day Sunday, but assured Tessa that Rosa, their housekeeper and occasional sitter, would be there for the girls. With Jill's reassurance and believing that the girls were as safe as they could be since Liam was in Japan, she'd quickly arranged for Jamison's pilot and copilot to meet her at the small local airport. She'd insisted they not file a flight plan though the pilot explained to her they would need to fly at a low altitude and stay below eight thousand feet to stay out of class A airspace. She had not cared one way or the other and had sworn them to secrecy, telling both they'd lose their jobs if they told anyone, that no matter what happened, they must remain silent. She ordered them not to tell Joel. They'd sworn their allegiance to her, knowing this had to be terribly important as Tessa was respected and well-liked by all the employees at Jamison Pharmaceuticals and would never make such a request unless it was a matter of life and death.

Jittery as though she were overcaffeinated, she recalled Poppy's odd behavior as she prepared their breakfast on Wednesday morning. She'd been angry and hateful when Tessa woke her up that morning, which was in itself extremely unusual. Poppy never awakened in a sour mood. Piper, on the other hand, needed her quiet time, and Tessa always woke her first to allow her the few extra minutes she needed to start her day. Looking back, Piper had seemed a bit too eager to jump out of bed. How could she have missed the signs?

Both girls were kind, well behaved, and usually polite, or as polite as one could expect from ten-year-olds. The girls had extraordinary talents, which she and Joel encouraged. In hindsight, she should have known something wasn't right when neither wanted to attend their art class Wednesday afternoon. They'd both begged to stay home from school with her, and she firmly told them no, thinking this could become a habit. Then, out of the blue, they announced that they wanted to share a bedroom again. That alone should have sent alarm bells ringing. They both liked their privacy.

And the lights. A week ago, both girls had suddenly begun to insist that their bedside lights remain on. They'd stopped wanting their night-lights when they were five. They'd both been snippy, too. Now she wished she'd taken them in her arms and simply held them. Maybe if she'd done that, they would have opened up to her sooner. The hell with art classes and school. This would remain a part of them for the rest of their lives and define the women they became.

God, how it sickened her to think of Liam, Joel's younger half brother. She'd never liked him, not since the first time Joel had introduced him to her at a family gathering in Miami a few months before she and Joel were married. Handsome, maybe too handsome, with sandy brown hair and coffee-colored eyes, he'd seemed much too eager to please. Slick and phony, she'd thought. And the stories he told were so far-fetched that Tessa had doubted Liam's truthfulness. She'd wanted to tell Joel she didn't like him, but this was his brother, and she had not wanted to hurt his feelings. Joel was totally the opposite of his brother.

Joel's mother had died in a tragic accident when he was twelve. He didn't like to talk about his mother, and Tessa respected that. She knew that he and his mother had been extremely close, and again, she understood and respected his feelings. A year after his mother's death, his father remarried. Liam was born almost a year to the day after his father's marriage to his second wife, Rachelle, a woman ten years his junior whom he'd met at the Viceroy Club in Miami, where she'd tended bar. Joel didn't dislike her, but later, as he grew older, he came to understand that she'd married his father for his money, not for love. Getting pregnant so soon had been a great big bonus, Joel had explained, one that would pay big dividends to Rachelle for the rest of her life.

Joel's father, Grant, would never divorce or abandon the mother of his son, according to Joel. Grant had died three years before she and Joel married, even before she had come to work at Jamison Pharmaceuticals. Thanks to Sam McQuade, who at the time was not only Grant's personal attorney but also the chief financial officer at the company, Grant had left Rachelle a very wealthy woman. Sam had been Joel's right-hand man, and they'd been friends since college.

Had it been only four days ago that life as they knew it turned into a living nightmare?

Tessa recalled the shock she'd felt when Poppy said that Uncle Liam touched her in places he wasn't supposed to and she really, really hated it. Then Piper, the more timid of the two girls, had said he touched her, too, and she did not like it either. She said Uncle Liam told her that if she told her parents, he would kill her and her family. Still, there seemed to be something strange about their stories, and they had both refused to give her any details when she'd asked.

Stunned at the casual manner in which they had told their stories, floored by the revelation, Tessa was momentarily silenced by her daughters' statements. The girls were seated at the small oak table in the kitchen while Tessa flipped pancakes. At first stunned into temporary silence, then, as though struck by a sudden bolt of lightning, her hands had begun to shake so violently that she had dropped the plate of blueberry pancakes she had just made for their breakfast.

The vivid yellow serving platter that shattered on the black-and-white tile resembled mini shards of sunlight, broken forever. Her precious little girls would be broken forever, too, their psyches damaged. Like a kettle of steaming water, rage boiled inside Tessa, spewing forth minutes after she dropped the plate.

"I swear I will kill that son of a bitch!" Tessa shouted as she gathered both girls in her arms.

Even after Joel got home from his business trip on Thursday afternoon, she had avoided telling him what had happened to their girls, what his half brother had done. She didn't know why, but something told her she should wait until her return from the mainland. Jill had assured her they would be fine at home with their father and Rosa for the weekend. Tessa took her friend's words to heart even though Piper and Poppy had begged her not to leave. She told them she had to, that it was very important, and when she returned, she would have a surprise for them. Two days. They would be fine.

As she drove, she tried to pinpoint a time when the girls had resorted to their five-year-old behavior. Why she hadn't paid more attention baffled her. She was a hands-on mother, or so she thought, but she had simply decided the girls wanted to be little girls again, as they'd started to develop early, and she hated this for them, but it was beyond her to control their physical development. She would explain what was happening to their bodies once they were settled. Had this early development been the start of Liam's molesting them? As much as she wanted to ask them what had actually happened, she chose to wait until Jill advised her to do so. They had been so averse to answering any questions about details. It was almost as if they somehow wanted to protect their uncle. No, that could not be true. Could it? Had they actually been . . . raped? Dear God! Surely there would have been a sign.

They'd said they were touched in their private areas. Touched. As bad as that was, she prayed that's all that worthless piece of humanity had done. While that would ruin them, for a while at least, being raped, no, she would not even go there.

One thing at a time. First, she had to get Jill to take the girls. Then she would tell Joel, then they would go to the police station and report the crime.

She felt a fear unlike any she had ever known. Why? Her worst fears had been realized on Wednesday, when her daughters told her about what had happened. She was returning home to whisk them away before the media got wind of what they'd had to go through. Theirs was one of the most prominent families in Lee County, not to mention the pharmaceutical community. Their daughters' molestation would make the local news and possibly the national news.

She drove up the driveway, saw that Joel's car was gone, and felt a wave of relief. She knew she was stalling, putting off the inevitable, but right now all she wanted to do was wrap her girls in her arms and never let them go.

She pulled into the garage, where Joel's own Porsche was always kept. He only drove it when he wanted to impress a client. She shook her head, thinking what a waste. Growing up poor had made her wise with her finances, and this was not a wise purchase, but Joel was a multimillionaire, courtesy of his father's brilliance. He could spend his money however he liked.

The girls' bikes were leaning against the wall. They loved to ride their bikes. Tessa couldn't remember the last time the three of them had ridden together. Several months ago. Maybe that was when Liam began to abuse them. The tote box of toys she had planned to take to ACT, the Abuse Counseling and Treatment center, was still in the garage. She volunteered there occasionally, and many of the battered women had children who came to the center with no toys or games. Piper and Poppy had both cleaned out their closets and asked her to give their toys to kids who needed them.

She smiled. They had good souls. Would they ever be the same again? She didn't know, but she did know she would do everything in her power to see to it that they got the treatment needed to help them deal with the sexual abuse. God, how she hated those words. Especially in connection with her daughters.

Inside, the house was quiet.

"Rosa," she called out. Rosa was probably upstairs cleaning, though maybe not since it was obvious that the downstairs had not been cleaned yet as there were coffee mugs still in the sink, along with three cereal bowls. Maybe she had started upstairs first. Shaken things up a bit. Cleaning a seven-thousand-square-foot home had to be a nightmare at times.

"Piper? Poppy?" She headed upstairs. She peeked into the master bedroom, a bit surprised to find the bed still unmade. She looked around the room, and it appeared just as it had on Friday. Joel had probably told Rosa to leave it until Tessa returned. Shaking her head, she went to the girls' rooms. Both doors were open. "Where are you two?" she asked, her voice slightly raised. After what they'd told her, she doubted they were hiding. They hadn't wanted her to leave.

She searched the bathroom that the girls shared. There were no signs they'd been there recently. She felt their toothbrushes. They were dry as a bone. A chill ran down her spine. Something wasn't right.

Alarmed, she started calling their names as loud as she could, but there was no answer. The pool; they were most likely swimming. Rosa always watched them even though they both were excellent swimmers.

Relieved, she went outside to the giant screened-in pool area. She smelled something odd, like a . . . She wasn't sure, but it was horrible. She walked around the smaller areas of the pool — the girls referred to them as the lazy river — but there was no sign of them. In the center of the screened-in area was the giant, Olympic-size pool.

The water looked strange, the color, off. Like rust, or something. She walked closer to the pool and saw three bodies floating in the pool.

Joel. Piper. Poppy.

She screamed their names as she jumped into the pool. She swam to the deep end of the pool. The smell. It was indescribable.

Horrified when she realized what she was seeing, she screamed.

And screamed.

And screamed.

CHAPTER 12

Tessa sat up in the tub so fast she splashed water everywhere. Her heart was beating so fast it frightened her. She took a deep breath, forcing the images from her mind. Reaching for a towel, she got out of the Jacuzzi, her hands trembling.

She *had* tried to save her girls when she jumped in the pool. But their heads were . . . Dear God, they were inches from decapitation. And Joel. His bloated body was banging against the pool's skimmer.

That was the day her nightmare had begun, and God help her, more than ten years later it had yet to end.

Tessa no longer cared about the luxuries Darlene and Sam had provided. Quickly, she toweled off and put on her new pajamas. Would she ever be able to get the image of that day out of her mind?

Maybe when Liam was six feet under, she

could begin to heal.

At 7:20, a forensic van pulled into the drive, causing a total frenzy among the men and women of the press stationed outside. Tessa watched what was happening outside her house on television.

"Has someone else been murdered?" a reporter from WBBK asked the team as they unloaded equipment.

"Did Tessa Jamison commit suicide?" an anchor from WRAL in Orlando shouted at the men and women there to do their jobs.

Tessa turned off the TV, trying to decide whether to be amused or disgusted.

"You shouldn't watch that stuff," Sam said.

Tessa made herself another cup of coffee and one for Sam. She liked the Keurig. She didn't speak as she waited for the coffee to brew. When both cups were ready, she took them to the living room and put them on a side table. Sam followed her.

"I had complete recall of the murders last night." Tessa had never said this aloud. She was doing her best to keep her emotions under control.

"I heard you," Sam told her as he reached for his mug of coffee.

"I thought I could save them."

He nodded.

"I couldn't."

"Tess, I think I see where you're going with this. It wasn't your fault. You did what any decent parent would do. You wanted to shield your children from those creeps." He gestured, indicating the men and women of the media outside. "I would have done the same thing had I been in your shoes. Stop beating yourself up. You have suffered a loss that I'll never begin to understand, but you have given up ten years of your life when I know and you know that you had nothing to do with their deaths. I have always believed in your innocence one hundred percent. Never for a moment did I think you were capable of doing what was done.

"Let's just allow Harry and his team to do their thing. Lee said that he will be here after lunch. We'll get down and dirty then."

She raised her brows.

"He will prep you, Tess. Run you through the mill. It will be physically and emotionally exhausting for you. But this is his method. And he gets results. Good results. He has *never* lost a case."

He'd taken to calling her Tess. And, she had to admit, she liked it.

"Are you listening to me?"

She nodded.

"Dammit, Tess, don't just sit there and stare at me. Say something."

"Last night, when I was remembering, something occurred to me."

"Go on," Sam coaxed.

"I didn't want to look at Joel's face even though he was on his back, close to me. But I did. I couldn't recognize him. His face was . . . gone. I cradled the girls. Their smell was unlike anything. I have smelled a lot of chemicals in my profession, mixed many, and nothing I have ever smelled could compare to that odor. I can still smell it. I knew the technical reasons for the smell but pushed them aside." Tessa paused. "It was simply death. The smell of their deaths haunted me. Sometimes I gag when I remember them. Sad, huh?" Tears began to roll down her face, and she didn't try to staunch them. Somehow, they felt cleansing.

"God, Tess, I didn't know. I'm sorry."

"We're in the pharmaceutical business. We know what death is, or rather what decomposition is. It's different when it's your family. It never goes away. The girls always smelled like the strawberry shampoo I used on their hair. I can't call up that smell at all, but their death scent, that I can. It haunts me.

"I've tried for years to push these thoughts aside, but I can't anymore. And now, here they are. Digging, poking into the earth, searching for some piece of evidence to exonerate me. Change my life. For the better, and all I can think of is that fucking smell."

"Tess, it's okay to have these feelings. You need to talk about them. Stop persecuting yourself. This was *not* your fault."

Sam got up and went to the kitchen, coming back with a wad of paper towels. "Here," he said, handing them to her. When she didn't take them, he used them to wipe her tears. His touch was gentle, caring.

"Sam, don't," she said.

"Stop it, already! You're punishing yourself for feeling. It's all right, Tess."

She shook her head. "Nothing will ever be all right again. No matter what happens."

A tap on the glass doors interrupted their conversation.

It was Harry.

Sam motioned for him to come inside.

Harry was dripping with sweat even though the December morning wasn't as humid as it normally was. He removed a handkerchief from his pocket and dabbed at his forehead.

"Harry, let's go into the kitchen. I'll get

you a cold drink. Tess?"

They both followed Sam into the kitchen. Tessa stood next to the door that led to the garage, while Harry sat at the bar and gulped down the last of the iced tea. "Thanks."

"What are you even searching for?" Tessa asked Harry. "Didn't they examine every inch of this place already?"

"That's what I plan to find out." He stood up. "I'm going back to the lab for now, but my crew will continue searching. If they find anything to report, I'll let you know." Harry gave a halfhearted salute, then left through the glass doors in the living room.

Tessa and Sam went into the living room and sat down in the chairs near the window. Neither Tessa nor Sam spoke for a minute.

Sam spoke first.

"They may not find anything, Tessa. Everything was searched before, and nothing turned up. And as of now, there are no other suspects —"

"There's Liam, for heaven's sake. How in the hell can you forget him? He's been off the map since . . . since the murders! I know he's responsible for this. My daughters told me. He told them he would kill them and their family if they told. Liam must have known . . ."

How would he have known that the girls told her what he'd done to them? She had told no one, no one except Jill.

"I need to make a phone call, Sam. I'll just be a minute," Tessa said, then raced into the kitchen, where she could speak in private. Her heart raced at this new revelation. Why hadn't she thought of this before?

She sat on one of the barstools with the phone in her hand and dialed Jill's number from memory. It was a weekday. She would be in her office.

"Dr. Ambers' office. This is Amanda," replied a friendly voice.

"I need to speak with Dr. Ambers."

"Are you a patient? If so, I'll be happy to take your number and have her return your call as soon as possible."

"No, I'm not a patient. I used to be her best friend. Tell her it's Tessa, and it's an emergency." She wasn't her best friend anymore, but she didn't care about that now. She needed to speak with Jill ASAP.

"Please hold," the pleasant voice instructed.

She waited.

"Tessa?" Jill Ambers sounded as if she didn't believe it was her.

"The one and only," she confirmed. "I need to see you, Jill. It's urgent. I'm sure

164

you have heard the news. Can you come here to the house? You'll have to go around to the back. The media."

"Tessa, it's so good to hear your voice, and hell, yes, I heard the news. It's on every station. Of course I'll come to see you; just name the time and place. You know, I tried to visit you . . . in prison. They told me you didn't want to see me. Not that it matters now," Jill said. "I'll cancel my appointments for the rest of the day. I can be at your place within a half hour."

Tessa breathed a sigh of relief. She had refused Jill's visits because they were a reminder of all the evil Poppy and Piper suffered. It wasn't Jill's fault, it was the memories. "Thank you, Jill. I'm sorry about the visits. I just couldn't. It . . . hurt. Still does. But that's in the past, and I hope you'll forgive me."

"Of course. I have already. I had an idea that you were suffering. I am a forensic psychiatrist, remember?"

"I know. I need to talk to you about that weekend," Tessa stated, tucking her emotions away in that safe place in the back of her mind. "It's urgent."

"Give me half an hour," Jill said. "I know this probably isn't the right time, but I need you to know how much your reaching out to me means. I have watched the news reports. Hell, I have wanted to smack a few of those plumped-up blond reporters who try to pass themselves off as intelligent. Every time they said your name, it pissed me off."

Tessa smiled. This was the Jill she knew. She had not changed one bit.

"Thanks, Jill. That's what I needed to hear. I'll see you shortly," Tessa said, then hung up the phone.

She returned to the living room and saw that Sam had disappeared. Finally, a few minutes alone. She returned to the kitchen and started brewing her fourth cup of coffee. Sneaking a glimpse out the kitchen window, she saw that the number of media vans seemed to have doubled. Now, in addition to reporters from all the local news outlets, the lead anchors of three of the major networks, CNN, NBC, and CBS, stood outside the entrance, hoping to get the first scoop. It made her sick.

She held the media partially responsible for her daughters' deaths. Had she not feared them, feared how they would report what happened to Piper and Poppy, her daughters might be alive today. She knew their identities would have been protected because of their age, but she had also known

166

that that wouldn't have stopped some nosy reporter from digging deep.

Without Sam under her feet, she decided that now was a good time to go to the girls' rooms. Before Jill came over, she needed to do this. She drained the last of her coffee, rinsed the cup, and set it beside the Keurig. If she were convicted again, she would hate going back to prison coffee.

She rolled her eyes at her own idiocy. Coffee was not important. This was simply her way of coping with stress. Thinking of things that are meaningless. Coffee. The too-large jeans she wore. Ankle monitors, which she did not like the weight of, but it was a small distraction compared to what she was about to do.

At the top of the stairs, she stopped once she was standing outside their rooms. She had to do this, get it over with, as postponing it again would most likely make it worse. A dozen images flashed before her. Before she allowed them to completely take over, she pushed the door to Piper's room aside.

Her body stiffened in shock, the blood drained from her face. She began to shake as she stood in the center of the room.

It was exactly as it had been the day she had left for San Maribel. Her memory of this room was exactly as she remembered it from that last day. Nothing had changed. It was as though she had stepped back in time.

Shaking, she went over to Piper's bed and saw that the lavender sheets were the same. As she had packed their clothes that fateful day, she had been surprised when Piper left the sheets all twisted at the foot of the bed. Carefully, she eased herself down onto the twin-size bed, running her hand across the silky purple comforter. Purple had been Piper's favorite color.

Tessa smoothed the wrinkles from the comforter, then looked at the pillow, and swore it still bore indentations from Piper's head. Tears filled her eyes, and she picked up the pillow, brought it close to her face, and inhaled. She inhaled again and swore she could smell the strawberry shampoo the girls loved.

It was impossible, she knew, given the passage of time. She must be imagining this because it's what her mind wanted her to smell, and scent was a true memory provoker. A trick, she knew, but it didn't matter; any small connection to her daughters mattered, whether real or imagined.

Tessa returned the pillow to the bed, then crossed the room, where she entered the bathroom that separated the girls' rooms. Again, she was taken aback when she saw that it remained precisely as it had been all those years ago. The same red and purple rugs, the red-and-purple-striped shower curtain. She recalled shopping for the girls when they'd decided they wanted their signature colors in the bathroom. Unbelievable, she thought, as it, too, was the same.

She opened the drawers and was surprised to find they were empty. Opening the medicine cabinet, she expected to see extra tubes of toothpaste, a few stray hair barrettes — all the supplies she had put there herself, but it was also empty.

Saddened, but knowing she had to continue with what she had begun, she entered Poppy's room.

Struck by the normalcy of the bedroom as she stood in the doorway, she had trouble connecting her little girls' bedrooms to the images she had seen in the pool. Poppy's favorite color was red. She had always told Tessa it was because her name was a red flower, and they matched. More tears, but had she not cried, she would have questioned herself.

The room was as she remembered. Poppy's bed was made, her red-and-white-striped comforter was exactly as it had been the day Tessa had left for San Maribel, the last day she had seen her daughters alive.

Tessa had so many memories of her daughters in these two rooms. She had always spent a few minutes alone with each of them before they went to bed at night. Twins, but separate individuals, each with a unique identity, she and Joel did their best to encourage each of them to be true to herself. Just because they were twins did not mean they had to wear matching clothes or like and dislike the same things; but there were many things they had in common, and they said it made them feel connected. She had always heard twins were psychically in tune with one another, and she saw this in the girls.

Tessa walked around the room, touching the pillow, and again, she put the pillow up to her face, inhaling, but she didn't smell strawberry shampoo. All she smelled was fabric softener. Odd, as she had not smelled this in Piper's room. Had Sam or Darlene washed the pillowcase? And if so, why not wash Piper's, too?

She pulled the comforter aside and sat on the bed, running her hands back and forth across the sheets. She leaned down to smell them, but they didn't smell like Downy or Snuggle, the two fabric softeners she had always used. This struck her as odd, but everything about her life was odd, from the time of her arrest until now.

She was about to remake the bed when she saw the corner of a sheet of paper sticking out from beneath the mattress. Carefully, she eased the paper out and saw that it was a sheet of the drawing paper the girls used. One side was blank. Odd. She turned the paper onto the opposite side and saw that something had been drawn on it.

She dropped down onto the bed to look at the picture more carefully. It was Poppy's.

There were four sketches of people. After a closer look, Tessa saw that it was their family, but this particular drawing was in charcoal. She remembered when they'd learned to use charcoal in their weekly art classes. Poppy had been quite the artist. Tessa examined the drawing and was able to make out the faces.

One was clearly a picture of Tessa, and the resemblance was impressive. Poppy had drawn herself and Piper, depicting their long hair, which she knew was strawberry blond, and their bright blue eyes. They were identical, yet each had her own unique features. Poppy's nose was slightly more upturned, Piper was over an inch taller. The drawing reflected these slight differences.

At first glance, the man's features were hard to bring into focus as an X had been slashed across his face. She took the picture over to the window to get a clearer look since the sun's rays were lighting up that half of the room.

She scrunched her eyes, as her farsightedness had gotten worse with age. The details were indisputable. The face in the picture definitely belonged to her husband, Joel.

She felt light-headed, and, fearing she might faint, she had to sit on the bed.

Dear God, what does this mean?

CHAPTER 13

Tessa tried to calm herself. She inhaled, then exhaled. Her hands shook like wind-blown palm fronds during a hurricane.

She stared at the drawing again, thinking that surely she was mistaken. Poppy would never do something like this. Joel was her father. She had loved him. She had looked up to him, as had Piper. While they weren't Daddy's girls, they'd always shared a good father-daughter relationship.

With shaking hands, she took the paper back over to the window, where the sunlight gave her a clearer view. The eyes were Joel's, their unique almond shape apparent. The hair was different, slightly shorter than his. He'd always let it grow a bit longer, mostly because he was just too busy to schedule the time for a haircut. The nose and mouth could have belonged to any man. She used her fingernail to try and scrape the red away, thinking that perhaps it was a crayon, but when she scraped her nail across the page, the red remained solid. Most likely it was made by a Sharpie.

This could mean anything. Poppy liked to do what she had always called "shock drawing," a concept she had made up about a year before. . . . It was still difficult to use the words, and even more so now that she was in her daughters' rooms.

She would have to show this to Jill. It might mean nothing, but it was worth having it checked. Also, it was odd. Why would this be here so many years after the fact? Yes, the rooms were intact, mostly, but hadn't the police searched their rooms? Were they not considered a part of the crime scene? She had been in such a state of shock afterward, she had never had an opportunity to revisit their rooms. She could ask Sam, or Lee, but she needed Jill to see this first.

Careful not to fold the drawing but at the same time not wanting Sam to see her find, she rolled it into a tube shape and tucked it beneath the gray sweatshirt she was wearing.

Downstairs, there was still no sign of Sam. Good. She did not want to see him now. He had an uncanny way of seeing right through her. Sure that Joel was never this much in tune with her, she didn't know if she should be suspicious or flattered.

A knock on the door startled her.

Jill. She had entered around the back of the house to the pool area so that she could avoid entering in full view of the mass of reporters gathered at the entrance to the so-called private gated community.

Tessa hurried to open the sliding glass doors. Her face brightened just seeing her old friend there. "You haven't changed one bit in the last ten years," she said, embracing her friend. Jill's dark brown hair sparkled, and her brown eyes were as kind as Tessa remembered. Wearing a pair of black slacks and a teal-colored blouse, with matching teal flats, Jill looked professional but not so much that it would intimidate. *Casual professional,* Tessa thought.

"And don't say I haven't because I know better," Tessa instructed, her eyes filling with new tears.

"Given what you have been through for the past decade, you look better than I'd expected." Jill hugged her back, and Tessa knew that calling her had been the right decision.

They looked at each other for a few seconds before Tessa spoke. "You want to have coffee in the kitchen? Sam got this newfangled coffeemaker — it's a Keurig — pretty neat."

"That sounds perfect. Tessa, everyone has a Keurig now." Catching her mistake, she said, "Shit, I didn't mean that. It's like the Mr. Coffee of the nineties, remember?" She smiled.

"Don't bother walking on eggshells. I'm tough. Prison does that to a person. It's okay, I'm not made of glass."

Tessa brewed two cups of coffee. "Cream, no sugar?"

"You remembered," Jill said, taking the cup from her.

"I had a lot of time on my hands. I probably remember more than most," Tessa explained.

Once they were settled at the bar in the kitchen, she made sure that Sam, as well as Harry's forensic team, were still out of earshot. She took a deep breath and prepared to ask the question that just might blow her away.

"Jill, that day when you examined the girls, you have never repeated what they told you, have you?"

"Heavens no! I'm not allowed to break patient confidentiality. Why are you asking me this now? I didn't even tell Joel. Remember, you swore me to silence? I would never break your trust. And certainly that of the girls. What's happened? I know you wouldn't ask me this if you didn't have a good reason. We have always trusted one another, right?"

"Yes, we have. That's why I called." She removed the rolled-up paper from beneath her shirt. "Tell me your first impression of this." She handed Jill the sketch, doing her best to keep a neutral expression on her face. She didn't want to influence Jill's first reaction.

Tessa watched while Jill examined the drawing very carefully. Though she was sure that she was making too much of this, she still couldn't help herself. She had to know if there was a hidden meaning that her untrained eye had not seen.

"Where did this come from?" Jill asked in the voice reserved for her patients.

"I found it in Poppy's room under the mattress," Tessa told her. "I don't know if it's . . . I'm not sure what to make of it. It certainly appears to be Poppy's style."

"Today? You're telling me you found this just now?" Jill asked, surprise sending her voice up a notch. "This wasn't something packed away?"

Tessa shook her head. "No. I haven't been in the girls' rooms since . . . that awful day.

I would swear they have not been touched. Piper's bed is still unmade; it's exactly as it was the day I left. It's like going back in time."

"Before I say anything, can I look in their rooms?"

"Of course. Let's go," Tessa said.

"No, you wait here. Do you mind if I take the picture with me?" Jill asked.

"Sure. Why can't I come with you?"

"It's a professional thing. I want to see their rooms with no outside influence, and you have already told me more than I need to know. I'll just be a few minutes. Why don't you make us another cup of coffee? I run on caffeine."

"Sounds like you're dismissing me, but I get it. Go on, but don't let Sam or any of those" — Tessa nodded toward the front door — "nosy-ass reporters get a glimpse of you. The window coverings are gone, and those long-range lenses they have now can see the hair in your nose."

Jill nodded, then carefully tucked the piece of paper inside her bag. "No one would dare look inside this," she said, holding up one of the largest tote bags Tessa had ever seen. "It's practically a weapon in itself."

"Hurry," Tessa said. "You know the way."

"Why don't you sit down in the living

178

room? I'll just be a few minutes," Jill said as she headed toward the staircase.

Tessa made another cup of coffee for herself, then went into the living room and sat down on one of the leather chairs. Her thoughts returned to the past. Joel adored their daughters though he didn't spend as much time with them as she had due to his hectic work schedule, but their time spent together was happy and fun. Tessa was the disciplinarian when discipline was needed, which wasn't too often because the girls were well behaved. Not perfect, but they understood what their role in the family was. They weren't spoiled rotten as some of the children attending Saint Cecelia's had been; they had chores and obligations to the family.

Yes, Rosa had taken care of their home, but both girls were required to make their beds daily, keep their bedrooms tidy, and at dinnertime, they helped with the dishes. They were smart and funny, and Tessa had never experienced anything even close to the love that she felt for them. Even Joel. She had loved him, but her feelings toward him were simply not as pure and intense as her love for her girls. Joel rarely, if ever, had reprimanded them. His time with them was mostly without incident.

"Tessa," Jill said, "we need to talk."

Those were the words she had dreaded since calling Jill.

She nodded. "I suppose I can't get out of this?"

"No, you can't," Jill replied, her tone serious.

CHAPTER 14

"So?" Tessa said, when Jill sat down at the bar.

"I didn't find anything unusual. The rooms are the same, but their personal items are gone. Someone had to pack them away. Do you know who, and if so, where they are?"

"I'm not sure," she replied. Had Sam packed their things himself?

"I'd like to find out," Jill said. "Basically, except for the linens, the rooms are empty. I didn't see anything unusual there."

Tessa breathed a sigh of relief. "What about the sketch?"

"It's been ripped from a sketchbook, no doubts there. I'd like to see if we can locate it. One drawing, while it might indicate Poppy was angry at Joel, or a man — and that's a far overreaching educated guess — I wouldn't want to make a judgment without thoroughly searching through Poppy's sketchbooks."

Why didn't I think of that?

"I'm not sure, but I can ask," Tessa said. Jill was right. The rooms were empty other than bedclothes, and that wasn't so unusual. She had remembered the rooms as they'd been when the girls were still alive. Gone were all the knickknacks, posters, all the paraphernalia that made up a ten-year-old's bedroom. *Why didn't I see that?*

"I thought they were exactly as they looked the day I left," she explained.

"A trick of the mind, Tessa. It's what you *wanted* to see. The mind is a miraculous machine."

Did this explain the strawberry scent? The indentation on the pillow? Had her mind been playing tricks on her? Her refusal to accept the obvious, even though it had been a decade ago?

"I'll find Sam and ask him," she said. "I know that he packed up what was in Joel's office, but I'm not sure who packed up the stuff from the house." She had just assumed Sam had. Now, in reality, it seemed rather juvenile for her to have thought so. As CEO of a major pharmaceutical company, when would he have had the time to pack up their possessions?

"I'll wait here," Jill said.

"I'll go find Sam," Tessa said, walking into the kitchen.

Since he was most likely outside with Harry's forensic team, and she did not want to leave the protection of the house, as the media remained at the entrance to the gated community, just waiting like a pack of hungry wolves ready to snatch the first bite of her if she emerged, she dialed his cellphone number, which he had scribbled on a pad next to the telephone, and stood by the glass doors. He answered on the second ring.

"Sam, it's me. I need to see you inside. It's important," she said, then saw Sam as he walked toward the house.

"Two seconds," he said, then hung up.

When he opened the door, he placed an arm around her. "Are you okay?"

"I'll never be okay, Sam; you of all people should know that. However, I have someone here who wants to speak to you." She turned toward the living room.

Jill was sitting where she had left her, with the drawing spread out in front of her. When she saw Sam, she flipped the sketch so that only a blank piece of paper showed.

"It's okay, Jill," Tessa said when she saw her flip the paper over.

Tessa introduced them, surprised that

their paths had not crossed during the investigation.

"Jill wants to see some of Poppy's sketchbooks. Do you know who packed them and where can we find them? It's important," Tessa said. "Show him the drawing," she said to Jill.

Jill turned the paper over and handed it to Sam. Sam held it toward the window, studied it, then returned it to Jill. "What does this mean?"

"I don't know just yet. That's why I need to see her other drawings," Jill explained.

"Sure, that's reasonable. I'm sure the boxes are in the master bedroom. I packed up Joel's office but hired professionals to pack the personal possessions from the house," Sam explained. "Between the three of us, we should be able to find the girls' belongings, the things that were in their rooms."

Tessa heard the hesitation in his voice. Sam had known the girls, too. How could she have forgotten that? It was bound to be stressful for him, or at least she thought so.

"What about Lee?" Tessa asked when she remembered that he was coming over this afternoon.

"We can start now and take a break when he arrives."

She nodded. "Jill, do you mind?"

"No, I cleared my schedule for the rest of the day. I want to help in any way that I can."

Am I ready for this? She had barely been out of prison twenty-four hours, and things seemed to be moving too fast. That was good, maybe. Her life had been so regimented, so routine for so long, it was going to take her a while to get used to the world outside. "Then let's get started," she said, knowing there was no reason to put this off.

The drawing had brought back so many memories of the girls seated at the kitchen table, drawing while she made dinner, talking about colors, why they were named the way they were. Poppy always had an explanation, and this would send them off into other topics of conversation. Tessa always felt so proud of them; they were smart, insightful, open to learning. She had enjoyed these times so much. Tears spilled over, and she didn't bother trying to stop them. *Cleansing,* she thought, as she braced herself for the task ahead of them.

"Tessa, if you don't want to do this, don't," Jill said when she saw her crying.

She shook her head, then took a tissue and wiped her tears. "I need to. It's . . . I just need to do this. I'm fortunate to have this opportunity, I need to take advantage of it." She knew it would hurt, but avoiding the memories wasn't beneficial to her or her future.

"Let's get started," Sam said. "Who knows what we'll find?"

Tessa agreed, but still couldn't keep from feeling frightened at what they might discover. She picked up their coffee cups, went into the kitchen, and rinsed the cups and placed them next to the fancy coffee machine. Returning to the living room, she announced, "I'm ready."

Sam led the way as they headed upstairs. Tessa took another deep breath, hoping to calm her nerves. She had practiced deep breathing over the years and learned to calm herself. In prison, it seemed fairly easy. Now, in the outside world, not so much. She flinched when Sam touched her arm.

"Hey, if you don't want to do this, don't," Sam said. "Jill and I can handle it, right?" He looked to Jill for confirmation.

"Absolutely."

"No, I need to do this. For myself. And my daughters." She motioned for Sam to open the door to the master bedroom.

Inside, stacked against the wall opposite the doorway, were dozens of boxes. Tessa scanned them for some kind of writing but saw nothing. "They're not marked," she said to Sam.

He pulled a few boxes away from the wall, then turned them around so that she could see. "The markings were just facing the wall."

Clearly, the boxes were marked. Why wouldn't they stack them where they could be identified? Though honestly, she realized it had not mattered as she had been locked away for life, and other than Lara, there was no family to claim them. And she doubted that her sister would have taken the time to sort through them even if she thought there might be something worth pawning.

"I see," she said. "Then let's start with Poppy's room. Maybe I can find her sketch-books."

Five minutes later, Sam had both boxes from the girls' rooms moved to the center of the master bedroom. "How do you want to do this?"

"We can each open one box. If we find Poppy's sketchbooks . . ." She turned to Jill.

"I'll have a look at them, and we'll go from there," Jill said.

Sam pushed a large box in front of her, another for Jill, and one for him.

Stalling for a few seconds, Tessa easily

ripped the dried-out packing tape from the box. Inside, she saw stacks of clothes. Tears filled her eyes and trickled down her face like two silvery canals. A deep breath. *I can do this. I owe it to Poppy and Piper.*

A Harry Potter shirt that she remembered buying, knowing there had to be a matching one in Piper's things as both were Potter addicts. She went through the rest of the clothing, deciding she would donate most of it, minus the Harry Potter shirts.

Going on to a second box, she was surprised to find the sketchbooks. She had not thought it would be so easy.

"Here they are," she said. "It appears as though they're all in this box."

"Tessa, why don't you let me go through them first? I know this is hard."

"No, I'm okay," she said, and used the sleeve of her sweatshirt to blot her tears. "It's not all bad," she explained.

"Then let's start looking through them," Jill said.

Grabbing several spiral sketchbooks between them, they flipped through the pages.

"This might be something," Sam said, handing the sketchbook to Jill.

"Okay, let me see what you have found," Jill replied. She took her time as she perused the pages, thumbing back and forth, then closing the book.

Sighing, she spoke. "It's . . . it may be." Jill stopped and seemed to be deliberating. "Tessa, did the girls, Poppy in particular, resent Joel, or men, Liam in this case, in any way?"

She thought about it but could not remember a time when Poppy or Piper had any issue with their dad, or any man, at least nothing out of the ordinary. Joel worked long hours, and Tessa knew the girls were closer to her than they were to Joel, but that's how it worked in their family.

"I don't believe either had any reason to feel anything but love for their father. The only men they were around were Joel, and Liam, and of course, teachers and such at school. I'm sure neither had any issues with men. They were quite open with me. I'm sure if there was a problem, they would have come to me."

"Then why keep Liam's . . . abuse to themselves?" Jill questioned.

"Fear? He told them he would kill them and their family if they told. I'm not a psychiatrist, but I'm sure they took him at his word. Can you imagine how . . . frightened they must have been?" Tessa felt her heart rate increase as it always did when she spoke of this. "Maybe they were simply too scared to tell. It's such a leap of faith to me, as I'm sure it was to them, that their uncle would even consider touching them inappropriately." This still didn't justify her surmise. She had not known her daughters' innermost secrets, and not knowing sooner might have cost them their lives.

Jill draped both arms around Tessa's shoulders. "Don't blame yourself. Actually, it's quite common for victims to protect their abusers. Statistically, eight out of ten children know their abusers, and more often than not, it's a trusted family member or a friend. The girls were afraid; I know this for a fact. They truly believed Liam would harm them, you, and Joel. Those were certainly not their exact words, but I understood what they were telling me."

"Let me see the sketchbook," Tessa stated.

Jill held the book against her chest. "Are you sure you want to see this? They're very disturbing."

"Of course! Good grief, Jill, if there is something in Poppy's art that . . . I don't know, just let me see the damned thing." Tessa held her hand out, palm up.

Jill closed the sketchbook, then handed it to Tessa. Tessa's hands shook as she flipped open the cover on the book. One by one, she viewed Poppy's drawings, her mouth agape.

She tossed the sketchbook back to Jill. "I . . . I don't know what to say. This is horrifying." Tessa wanted to kill Liam, the son of a bitch. How could this have happened without her knowing? And when? Where? She had spent ten years in prison trying to recall when the girls were alone with Liam. There had been a few occasions when they'd had him over to the house for dinner, and of course then he wouldn't have been completely alone with them, but they had dinner parties with Liam and dozens of acquaintances. With her acting as hostess while Joel mingled, there was plenty of opportunity for him to spend alone time with them. In their rooms, possibly the pool house. She couldn't wrap her head around the situation. Both girls, on different occasions; according to Jill, neither one had told the other what was happening until the morning Poppy said something about it to Tessa. Tessa couldn't begin to fathom how this could have gone on in their home without her knowing about it.

Breaking the silence, Sam said, "It's not pretty."

Tessa nodded. "No. I wish I would have . . . well, I hadn't the faintest idea."

The fight had gone out of her, and she plopped down on one of the unopened boxes. She looked up at Jill. "What's your professional take on the drawings?" Drawings of adult male penises with a knife slashed through them. Another of a little girl with a single giant blood-red tear streaming down her face. It was a face Tessa did not recognize.

"Whoever drew these pictures was definitely sexually abused," Jill stated flatly. "Of course, we know it was Poppy. What the drawing indicates to me, the emphasis on the desire to mutilate the genitals, and Poppy's artistic abilities are excellent, is that she wanted to reveal the abuse but was fearful. Possibly, she hoped you would find her sketchbooks and open the door for her to tell. Their behavior, keeping their lights on at night, wanting to go back to sharing a room, crankiness, all are clearly indicative that something was not right. Of course, I knew the girls, but I wasn't aware of this until you told me." Jill sighed. "Of course I asked them questions, gentle questions. I didn't want them to be fearful in any way. They both said the touching hurt. I reviewed the medical examiner's reports, and I remember reading —" She stopped, closed her eyes, then opened them, tears brimming in her brown eyes.

Tessa nodded, remembering the horrifying details from the medical examiner's testimony.

"Son of a bitch," Sam muttered. "I'd like to get my hands on that low-life bastard."

Again, Tessa nodded. Feeling empty and bereft, she wanted to scream, to run through the streets, asking why? *Why my girls? Why? Why? Why?*

They were innocent little children. Thinking of the fear they'd suffered enraged her, but now, with this new revelation, Poppy's drawings, the wall Tessa had built around her emotions came crashing down. *What kind of mother am I? How could I not have known?* Her eyes filled with tears, and she let them flow freely. Jill stood behind her, rubbing her shoulders.

"Let's go downstairs," Sam said.

Tessa stood and followed Sam and Jill downstairs. She wasn't sure what to say. The pictures pretty much said it all, she thought as she trailed behind. "I'll make us some iced tea," Sam told her.

"Thanks," Tessa said, then focused her attention on Jill. "I wish I had found that sketchbook. You realize that I could have saved their lives."

"Stop, Tessa! You're not helping yourself

with those thoughts. I don't want to go all psychiatrist on you, but this wasn't your fault, and as much as I hate it, it was probably inevitable. You didn't know Liam's background any more than I did, or it seems unlikely that Joel knew that his brother was a pedophile, a sick child molester. If he had known, he would never have allowed him to spend any time around Poppy and Piper.

"Whenever someone learns about something like this, it always comes as a terrible shock, especially when it's a family member or a close friend. You just don't think that anyone you know could possibly do anything like this. The people who do these things are totally other people, not your friends, relatives, next-door neighbors. But the fact of the matter is that child molesters do not come with horns on their heads or identification tags that read: CHILD MOLESTER — STAY AWAY. "You are not responsible, Tessa. I want you to remember these words every time you start to think otherwise. You were an excellent mother," Jill insisted. "And don't say a word. We will get through this. Together this time, okay?"

"I will try, but I can't promise," Tessa told her. "Those pictures — I don't understand why they weren't entered into evidence at my trial. Who could have overlooked them?

They had ample evidence that Poppy had been molested. It doesn't add up."

Sam placed two tall glasses of iced tea in front of the women, who were sitting at the bar. "If these sketchbooks were collected as evidence, we would have known about them during the trial. I doubt that even Michael Chen would stoop so low as to not disclose this kind of exculpating evidence. He's an ass, for sure, but he does follow the rule of law as much as any prosecutor ever does.

"More importantly, if these drawings had been available to the investigators, I doubt that you would have even been prosecuted. And if he had allowed these drawings to be presented as evidence at the trial, I'm pretty sure your trial would have ended with a not guilty verdict. These drawings would create reasonable doubt in any jury that saw them, especially given the total lack of forensic evidence against you. Lee will jump on this right away."

"I agree. These drawings should certainly have been considered," Jill said. "Speaking as someone who has given expert testimony many times, I am absolutely certain that no jury seeing them would convict any woman unless there was overwhelming evidence that she murdered the victims. And the one thing that is certain is that there was no such evidence ever presented. Everything was circumstantial at best and pure fantasy at worst.

"But what I want to know is where were they during the investigation? Tessa, did you take the sketchbooks to San Maribel?"

She shook her head. "I took sketchbooks, of course, but I didn't take these. The girls always shared their work with me. It's more than apparent that Poppy hid this particular book away."

"Maybe," Jill said.

"What do you mean?" Tessa took a drink of tea. Her hands were shaky, and her stomach churned. She needed to calm herself, so she took a deep breath and released it slowly, just as she had taught herself to do.

"Just what I said. Maybe it was Poppy who hid the drawings, and we'll never know where, unless we can locate the person who actually packed up her room. Did she have any hiding spots? Most kids do."

"I don't understand," Tessa stated. "What are you trying to say?"

"They weren't discovered during the investigation. It's possible that whoever packed up their rooms found the sketch-books and packed them away without looking at the contents, which would be perfectly normal, and they have been here all this time." Jill turned to Sam. "Is it possible to locate the person who packed the rooms?"

Sam nodded. "I'll get Darlene to check. If anyone can find out, she can."

A loud knock on the front door silenced them.

"Stay here," Sam said. "I didn't tell Lee to use the back entrance."

Tessa and Jill did not speak as they waited for Sam to answer the door.

Praying it wasn't a member of the press banging on the door, she breathed a sigh of relief when she saw Lee Whitlow enter the kitchen.

CHAPTER 15

"I need to take this to the district attorney's office right away," Lee Whitlow said after viewing the drawings. "Sam, find out who packed these sketchbooks. I'll want to speak with whoever that is, and I'm sure the DA will, too. This sheds a whole new light on your case, Tessa. It's possible, if we can locate the person or persons who packed the boxes, and if they can recall exactly where they found the drawings, that there won't even be a need for a trial." He held up a hand. "I can't guarantee that, but it's entirely possible. How is Harry's team coming along?"

"Nothing yet, but they're searching the grounds," Sam said. "So far, there isn't anything new."

Sam introduced Lee to Jill, and the well-trained attorney didn't miss a beat as he acknowledged her with a quick handshake and a very confident smile.

"Tessa, finding the drawings is good for your case. I'm not going to stay now, as I want to get this new information to the DA right away, but I do want to warn you that I have scheduled a meeting with Rosa tonight, eight o'clock, here at your house. I hope I'm not overstepping my boundaries?" Lee explained.

Though Tessa had given him full authority to do whatever he needed, she was surprised at how quickly Lee had arranged the meeting. Using her house as a base for any meeting was for her protection from the media, something that he had told her on his last visit to the prison.

She wasn't sure how she felt about Rosa's returning to her home. If it helped locate Liam, or any new evidence to prove her innocence, she would have to deal with the emotional aspect of her housekeeper's betrayal — her not coming forth before the trial — after she heard what Rosa had to say. According to Lee, Rosa was now a legal resident and no longer feared deportation. She had not asked how that came to be, and truly, she didn't care. All she wanted to know was what Rosa had witnessed on the day her family was slaughtered.

"No, you're not overstepping any boundaries. I'm grateful, Lee," Tessa told him. "If not for you and Sam, I'd still be locked up. I wouldn't have had this . . . second chance. I'll meet with Rosa tonight. Actually, I'm anxious to hear what she has to say."

"Good, then we are all set for this evening. I'll let you know what the district attorney says as soon as I know something concrete," Lee said, then headed toward the front door.

"Go out the back," Sam said. "Those damn newshounds are still hanging around."

"Good idea. I had to push my way through them just to get past the gates to the community. Let's not alienate them just yet since we may need to use them to our advantage. I'll see you all later this evening."

Lee disappeared through the back door as fast as he'd entered through the front. Tessa saw that the forensic team was still sifting through dirt, digging up the perfectly maintained lawn, searching, for something, anything they deemed possible evidence. She didn't care if they excavated the entire grounds. Actually, if she were to believe Lee and Sam, and she was exonerated, she planned to demolish this entire house. She would sell the lot and move on with her life, at least as much as she could. It would never be the same, but at least she would be in control of her life again.

"Do you want me here when Rosa shows up?" Jill asked. "It might make things easier. For both of you."

Unsure, Tessa looked to Sam for direction. "A good idea or not?" she asked.

"Jill knew her, too. It might make it a bit easier, but that's not my decision to make," Sam said.

"Stay." Tessa decided that having Jill present for the interview with Rosa was best for her, and she didn't care what Rosa felt. Sadly, she had really admired the woman at one time. Enough to leave her in charge of her girls. But knowing she might have been witness to what happened to them and had not gone to the authorities, whether she was in the country legally or not, she no longer felt any such admiration.

"I'm going to call Darlene, so she can start searching for the person who packed up the house. She wasn't working for Jamison Pharmaceuticals at the time, but she will know how to find out. Be right back," Sam said, then left her and Jill alone in the kitchen.

Neither woman spoke as they waited to make sure he was out of earshot.

Jill was the first to speak. "Do you trust him?" She nodded toward the living room, where they heard Sam talking in a hushed voice on the phone to someone Tessa presumed was Darlene.

"I do. Very much. He's a good man. I never really gave him much attention when Joel was alive. Once I left Jamison Pharmaceuticals, my entire focus was on the girls, my family. He had been friends with Joel since college." Tessa didn't know why she added that last bit of information, but she needed Jill to know that Sam was legit. Odd that they weren't familiar with one another as Jill had visited all the time and had attended a few of the dinner parties she had hosted. She felt sure that Sam had been in attendance, too, and probably more than once.

"I think I remember him," Jill said. "From a party way back in the day. He's a real hunk, don't you think?" She grinned. "That's not very appropriate, Tessa. I'm sorry."

Tessa thought him quite easy on the eyes, too, as any woman in her right mind would. Was Jill looking for an introduction? A fix-up? She couldn't remember if that was the right terminology, but it didn't matter. She wasn't going to play matchmaker. Sure that Jill was only trying to lighten the somber atmosphere that hung over all of them, still, Tessa wasn't sure she liked the idea of Jill and Sam together. As in a couple. He wasn't Jill's type. Or was he? She had been away for a very, very long time. People change.

"What's troubling you?" Jill asked, going all psychiatrist on her again.

Shouldn't it be obvious? Her life troubled her.

"You of all people should know," Tessa said, her voice sharpened with just the slightest trace of an edge, borderline smart-ass.

Jill drained the last of her tea. "You would think so, but I am not a mind reader. You'll have to tell me."

No way was she going to reveal her thoughts about her and Sam. Realizing that it was juvenile of her to even be having these thoughts about two people she cared for, she pinched the bridge of her nose, looked at the drops of condensation streaming down her glass, and shook her head side to side. "We would be here all night, and then some if I were to tell you all the raging thoughts going through my head right now. I'm pissed, and trust me, that's putting it nicely, that Rosa kept quiet about whatever it is that she knew. She could have gone to anyone. I doubt they would have asked for her green card. It was wrong, Jill, and you know it. She might have information that could have kept me out of prison for the past ten years. Wouldn't you feel . . . anger, something, toward the person who might have held your life in their hands and just let it drop, as if it were a worthless piece of nothing?"

"Of course I would. It's perfectly normal to feel that way. I can't explain the whys of Rosa's behavior, but I do know that fear is a very strong motivating factor for most people. Given the fact that she wasn't in the States legally, in her mind, maybe she thought that what she saw wasn't enough to prove your innocence, so why risk the authorities' discovering she was here illegally? I don't know that any of this is true, but it's a good guess. Tessa, they never had any physical evidence against you. All they had was circumstantial. The odds are in your favor now."

Tessa rolled her eyes. Leave it to Jill to try to make sense of Rosa's actions or lack thereof. "They sure as hell weren't before, and I don't really know that she can offer anything now, at least anything of value."

"With Poppy's drawings, Rosa's coming forth, and the Florida Supreme Court's ruling, I think the advantage is all yours. You're afraid, aren't you?" Jill asked.

Afraid was putting it mildly. Night after night, week after week, year after year, she had spent most of her days and nights reliving what she should have done, what she could have done to save her daughters. Visions of them lying in the pool, in all that blood, tormented her. Joel was not Joel, even in death. It'd taken her almost three full years after their murders to regain her memory of that day. The bits and pieces that hovered on the edge of her consciousness had been enough. Then the full memory of finding them that day exploded in her mind, like a million fireworks going off, and she had lost it for a while, but somehow she had managed to push the memories into a place in her mind that was safe, and any hope of ever proving her innocence was lost. She had learned to get through each day minute by minute, and planned her eventual death, and now she knew it wasn't meant to be.

"Tessa," Jill said. "Are you all right?"

"Sorry, I'm not used to . . . this" — she waved her hand — "freedom. Conversations. Normal people. However, I heard your question, and yes, I am afraid. I have been since May fourth, two thousand and eleven."

Sam chose that moment to return to the kitchen. "Darlene contacted the company that packed up the house. Luck is on our side. Apparently, the owner's nephew was working for the company at the time. Said he remembered the day well because he'd heard about the . . . murders. Darlene has arranged for him to come to the house tonight. I called Lee. He'll be here to question him. He will come before Rosa gets here."

"That's excellent news," Jill said. "Tessa, are you good with this?"

She sighed. "Yes, if it helps find out what happened to my family, do whatever you have to. I would like to talk to him, too. I never came back to the house once I was taken into custody and arrested. It's so damned bizarre. I'm asking strangers to remember what they might have seen in my child's bedroom when I should have known. I hope he can help."

Tessa suddenly felt overwhelmed. The day had been emotionally exhausting, and it was just beginning.

"It was big news here, so if this man says he remembers packing the rooms, I'm guessing he has information of some value. As you said, you never came back to the house after your arrest," Sam said. "You were in shock. You wouldn't have recalled anything standing out."

Tessa thought about this. Sam was right again. "I have tried over the years, nothing other than —" She stopped. "I'd just lost my family. I only recall the blood, their bodies."

Jill placed her hand on top of Tessa's. "I can't even begin to imagine. If you were a patient, and you're not, plus I have never treated anyone who has lost their family in such a horrific manner, but if I had, I would tell them whenever a memory of a tragedy overcomes them, try to consciously replace it with something positive. A special memory, one that brought joy, one that makes one smile."

"Makes perfect sense. I have tried over the years, and I recall dozens of special times with the girls, and Joel, but returning to this house, it's hard not to think of why I had to leave in the first place." Tessa thought at least she could now say this without crying. That was an improvement, but her anger seethed with a mounting rage so strong, it frightened her. She remembered the five stages of grief she had read about in so many books during her prison stay. Denial, anger, bargaining, depression, and acceptance. She would never accept what had happened to her family. Though she could acknowledge the loss for what it was, there was no way in hell she would get past the anger. She could tuck it away in that safe place, as she had taught herself, but never could she obliterate it completely. In her mind, the murders had never been solved, and until that rotten bastard Liam was put to rest, she knew that her anger would continue to play an active role in the person she had become. It was as much a part of her as her eye color, the shape of her hands, the curve of her hips. Her gaze darkened with the pain of the past decade, and Tessa knew happiness would not come easily, if at all. She focused her attention on Jill.

"I wish it were as easy as you say. Then my life would be tolerable. But it isn't, and all the happy thoughts and memories of the past will never change the images burned in my mind. I will try, though, I promise. When Liam is —" She had almost made a slip of the tongue and said "dead" but caught herself. "Brought to justice." Yes, that sounded better. And she really hadn't had time to plan, to plot what she would do when she located him, and there was no doubt in her mind that she would find him, no matter what she had to do. If she went back to prison, so be it. At least she would know her children and husband's murderer would pay for the crime he had committed against them.

At that very moment, Sam's cell phone started to ring. "Yes?" he said.

Tessa and Jill listened to his end of the conversation.

"That's encouraging, Lee. I'll tell this to Tess," Sam said, then disconnected the call. "Lee spoke with Michael Chen. He's agreed to look at Poppy's drawings. If this packing guy has anything to add, he's also said he would listen to what he had to say."

"Listening and doing something about it are two different things," Tessa said. "It doesn't mean he'll do anything yet."

"He won't have any choice if there's new evidence that wasn't presented at trial," Sam said. "Evidence of value," he added.

"Those drawings are vital. I'll stake my professional reputation on it," Jill said. "Make sure and tell Lee to say so to the DA," Jill added. She then said her good-byes, as she had to get back to her office and catch up on paperwork.

Once she'd left, Tessa and Sam sat together quietly for a few moments before Tessa said, "Thank you, Sam. I appreciate all you and Lee are doing. I just hope it's worth all the time and effort you have put into my case. No matter what the outcome."

"You have thanked us more than enough. We need to get down to business, get this case resolved."

Tessa was about to respond when a knock on the sliding glass doors interrupted her.

CHAPTER 16

"What did you find?" Tessa asked, after letting Harry inside. Her tone was doubtful.

"A bone," Harry said. "I believe it's the proximal phalange, the bone closest to the hand. Index finger from the looks of it. The pristine condition surprised me. Florida's heat, though that's not always a consideration with bones. But still, one has to take the elements into account."

"Give me your unofficial report," Sam said.

"In layman's terms, I'd say the finger was sliced off. The bone is sharp, sliced clean where it shouldn't be. There is no sign of a break. It belonged to a fairly young person. Most likely a male."

"What does this mean?" Tessa asked Harry.

"We don't know yet, but we're working on it. We'll extract DNA from that bone and possibly we can find out who it belonged to, decide if it's relevant to your case."

"What is that supposed to mean? You don't think this is an important find?" Tessa asked.

"It's very important," Harry replied. "The only problem is matching the DNA. It could be some random find. A fisherman whacks off his finger cleaning a fish. The finger winds up in the soil, through who knows by what means, and we have found it. A drug dealer in a speedboat tosses out a finger he's removed from a rat, and, hoping to hide all traces, it winds up here."

"It's a good find, Tess," said Sam, "but only if we can match it to someone in your family, which we know isn't going to happen since Lara has all of her fingers, and Harry said it was most likely from a male."

"Why wasn't this discovered before?" Tessa asked. "I don't get it."

"I don't know, Tess," Sam said. "As soon as Harry examines them, we'll know how long they have been here. It's more good news, Tess. A finger is one thing, but several bones, that's a whole different ball game."

"We have to have a match, right? I'd like to know where to start," she said.

Sam seemed to consider her question. "Family first. I'm going to have Lee call Rachelle," Sam told her. "Excuse me."

"I have to head out as well," Harry said, "and head back to the lab."

Tessa waited a moment after both men had departed before she called Jill to fill her in on these latest developments.

"You think she knows more than she testified to during the trial?" Jill asked once Tessa had explained everything.

Tessa nodded. "Darned right I do. There is no way in hell she would sit idly by, waiting all these years, without knowledge of his whereabouts. He's her only son. She's well financed, he's well financed. Enough to take care of him for the rest of his life. That old saying 'money talks and bullshit walks' would apply to the two of them. I never knew her well, but I did know, according to Joel, that she was a good mother and that Liam was the light of her life."

"And all these years he's been off the radar?"

"Yep, all those investigators Randall had searching for him, or at least that's what he told me, and I have my doubts, but nevertheless, I would have thought they could have located him, but nothing. When people don't want to be found, they can make it happen. I learned this in prison from women who sounded like they knew what they were talking about. I feel sure he's living a life of luxury, probably lounging on some exotic beach as we speak, all courtesy of his mother since he has never touched a penny of his trust-fund hoard. He's a low-life son of a bitch," Tessa said, doing nothing to hide the hate in her voice.

"Any man who touches a child is beyond low. Below whale crap, if you ask me. I see a lot of kids in my practice. Their lives were ruined by these sick-ass perverts. Of course, I can't say this to them, or to the family members, but it's rare when a child overcomes this type of tragedy."

"So you think Poppy and Piper would have been . . . ruined, tainted, for the rest of their lives? I thought you told me they would be all right with therapy." Her voice rose a notch.

"I think your girls were strong, Tessa. Like you. They kept their abuse secret for a long time. When I spoke to them, they didn't act like your typical victims. They knew that what had happened to them was a very bad thing. They also knew that telling you was the right thing to do even though they'd been terrified, and justifiably so. Poppy was very angry, as she should have been. Piper was . . . I think she was more damaged. But with your love and support, and intense therapy, I think they would have been okay

214

as adults."

"We'll never know, will we?" Tessa asked, and felt another round of tears fill her eyes. She wiped them with the cloth napkin and blew her nose. "All these years I have beat myself up, over and over, wondering how I could have been so stupid? So blind. It was more than obvious they were suffering. Afraid, as they reverted to their five-year-old patterns of behavior. I will never forgive myself."

Jill cleared her throat. "It wasn't your fault, you know that. Joel wasn't aware of what they were going through, either. I realize I don't have children of my own, but I work with all kinds of abused children, of all ages, and more often than not the parents blame themselves. Unless it's actually a parent doing the abuse, it's not their fault, not your fault. Your case is unlike any I have dealt with. You were whisked away, tried and convicted by a system so convinced they had the right person that they never bothered with a serious criminal investigation. They wanted this case out of the news."

"And why? There was no evidence against me," Tessa said, her anger causing her pulse to race.

"Your trip to San Maribel, the large insurance policy Joel had taken out, plus the company. You planned the trip so quickly, the media thought you had a lover, had something to hide. They found you in the pool with their bodies. You wouldn't speak to the police once they arrested you. In their minds, this was a perfect case of circumstantial evidence. There was no DNA, nothing to connect you to this crime. You had no obvious defensive wounds. Anyone in their right mind should have known you were innocent.

This isn't a large town. Lots of local ass-kissers in the political field. Michael Chen wanted your ass on a platter, and he got what he wanted. When you refused to speak, it sealed your fate. And now, it just might be the key to overturning your conviction. Getting all charges dropped. This is all good, Tessa. Despite the past ten-plus years, you're still young. You can have a full life —"

"Don't you even dare say I can have another family. I cannot and will never have children again! No matter what the court decides."

"I know you feel that way now, but I say, never say never."

"Let's not talk about this, okay? Please?" Tessa begged. Yes, she knew she was just young enough to start over and have a family again, but she would never betray Joel and the girls.

"Fair enough, but it's going to come up in the next few days. Just do what you have to in order to prepare yourself. Michael Chen and the local police are going to do their best to convict you again, regardless of what the Florida Supreme Court says. An exoneration or, perhaps worse for them, having the charges dismissed because the investigation your private detectives are doing turns up evidence of your innocence and someone else's guilt would embarrass them no end. Expose their utter incompetence.

"And let's not forget the media. This is fodder for all the new crime shows on damned near every local and cable channel. Just know you can come to me anytime, okay? I'm with you every step of the way."

"I appreciate your sticking by me, especially after the way I treated you. Denying your visits. Refusing your letters. When I was locked up, I just wanted that to be my life. I'd accepted it, and I still do, but now there's a light at the end of the tunnel. Maybe. And I want to move past this, but it's hard, Jill. Harder than my life before. You know, when I was a kid in and out of foster homes, that was a breeze compared to losing my family."

"Of course it was," Jill said, her voice soothing.

Before Tessa could respond, Sam returned to the kitchen again. Tessa quickly ended her call with Jill so she could listen to Sam's update.

"Harry's expecting the new bones. Apparently, there are quite a few of them, though not large. Pieces."

"What does this mean?" Tessa asked. "The pieces part?"

Sam raked his hand through his mussy hair. "Just that. The bones are small, in tiny pieces. Hard to say if they're human just yet, though the tech is pretty sure they are. They're taking them to Harry now. I spoke with Lee, and he has spoken to Rachelle and arranged for her to meet him in his office first thing tomorrow morning."

Tessa felt a strong surge of irritation. Rachelle's son killed her family. Why would she be so quick to involve herself in the case again? Did she think she could get more money out of Jamison Pharmaceuticals? Or was this her way of playing the role of grieving mother as she had for a decade? Keep the investigation away from Liam.

Tessa didn't know what to say as she had not expected Rachelle to comply so easily. But she was sure the woman had ulterior motives.

"Tess?" Sam coaxed. "Are you good with this?"

"No, I'm not. Her lousy-piece-of-garbage son ruined my life, took my family's lives. Of course I'm not good with it. However, I know it's necessary. I'm just surprised she agreed."

"She's insisted all these years she's had no contact with him. Lee says he wants to go over her testimony, and she's agreed. She also said she would provide a DNA sample. Usually, people who have something to hide aren't so quick to involve themselves in a case that has supposedly been solved. So, think what you will, but again, Tess, this is all good for you. The more people who come forward, the more evidence we discover that wasn't presented at your first trial, the more likely it is that you win this time around, either because the case is dropped or you fight through to an exoneration."

"You believe her?"

"I need to see her. Face-to-face. Lee said she sounded as though she was encouraged by the new evidence. Again, I don't know. Maybe she's just a damn good actress, or maybe Liam really did fall off the face of the earth, and he hasn't contacted her. If he's the ass you say he is, and I'm sure you would know, he just might be the type who wouldn't care if his mother knows whether he's dead or alive."

"He'd need money," she added.

"Liam had a trust fund. Though there hasn't been any activity, at least none that could be traced, and that's virtually impossible in this day and age. We don't know, but we are going to find out. I promise you, Tess. We, I, will find out what happened to your family."

She hoped he wasn't telling her this just to calm her. She knew what had happened to her family. She knew they were killed in such a savage manner that it defied all belief, and she knew that Liam Jamison was responsible for their deaths. Her brother-in-law, the girls' uncle, Joel's brother. She needed him to suffer as she had, to feel such angst, loss, the broken heart that had been her life since she walked into her home all those years ago and discovered their bodies. He had to suffer because Tessa wasn't sure how she could move forward if he didn't.

"Don't make promises you can't keep," Tessa told him. "I don't think I could deal with . . . life, at least a disappointment of this magnitude," she ended flatly. And she knew that she spoke the truth. It was tough enough to get through the days and nights in prison. Now that she was on the outside, in the real world, getting through a minute was ten times harder than she had ever anticipated.

"I'm not making any promises, just so you know. I do have faith in Lee and his team. I don't think you'd be here now if he didn't believe in your innocence. I wouldn't be here, either," he added.

The room was quiet for a moment, then Tessa spoke. "Evil destroyed my family. And it's about time I fought back."

CHAPTER 17

Later, Jill, Tessa and Sam gathered around the glass coffee table in the living room. Tessa sat on the soft leather love seat, with Jill at her side.

Two of the three people who had the power to change her life were expected any moment. She had showered and changed into a pair of navy capris with a matching silk top, again, the clothes courtesy of the fabulous Darlene. The ankle monitor was irritating, but she was already starting to get used to its weight, the bulkiness of it around her ankle its own sort of prison but mild in comparison to the hellhole she had been confined to for more than ten years. Briefly, she wondered if it would ever be removed. And if so, would it be because she was a free woman or because once she was returned to prison, it would no longer be required?

The front doorbell rang, and Sam quickly

stood and excused himself. They'd all agreed he would be in charge of this task as he was quite expert at handling the gentle and not-so-gentle men and women of the media, who continued to linger outside the gates and could be counted on to try to get someone in the house to speak to them.

Lee Whitlow sat opposite her. He'd dressed down, wearing faded jeans and a pale pink polo. Tessa so admired his dedication to his wife and her battle with breast cancer. Had Tessa still been actively employed at Jamison Pharmaceuticals, she, too, would have involved herself in the search for a cure. Maybe if she was released, she could involve herself in the research, but that was a distant thought, one she couldn't pursue until she knew if she even had a chance of returning to her profession. She had been away from the pharmaceutical industry for so many years, she wasn't sure if she could even qualify for employment in her own company, but that was for another time. Now, she had to face the facts, and only then would she be able to make a decision that would affect her future.

Sam cleared his throat, garnering their attention. "This is George Atkins. His uncle owns Atkins Moving and Storage. Have a seat, George." Sam pointed to the plush leather chair beside Lee's.

Tall and pale, with bright red hair, George appeared nervous, his light blue eyes glancing around at his surroundings, and his right leg shook so fast when he sat down that Tessa wondered if he was on drugs.

Thankfully, Lee took over. He made quick introductions, and once that ritual was completed, George seemed to have controlled his spastic leg movements.

Not wasting a minute, Lee began his questions. "Tell me about that day, please. What you observed." Direct, and to the point, Tessa waited for George to explain what he'd seen the day he'd packed her family's life away, or that of her daughters, as she wasn't sure if George had packed away Joel's personal belongings. At this point, she wasn't sure that it mattered.

George appeared to be in his late twenties or early thirties. When he'd worked for his uncle, according to Lee, he'd been young, so given the passage of time, she assumed this was probably a good guess.

He looked at Tessa before he spoke. She nodded, and he began his story.

"I was nervous when Uncle Walt told me I'd be coming with him to pack the place up. I . . . I'd watched the news, so I knew what had happened here. I packed up the kitchen and the dining room." He paused as though he were looking to Tessa for permission to continue.

"It's okay," she said in a reassuring voice, though she felt anything but calm. "Please go on."

"I went upstairs and started emptying the drawers. Clothes and stuff." His face deepened to a bright pink shade. "I was curious, and well, I kinda wanted to . . . brag to my buddies about the job."

Tessa wanted to smack him but controlled herself.

"Tell me where you found the sketchbooks," Lee prompted.

George nodded. "They were in the closet."

Tessa tried to recall if she had seen the sketchbooks the day she had raced through the house packing the essentials she would need for the girls' extended stay in San Maribel. She had grabbed a couple of sketchbooks from Poppy's desk and one from Piper's night table, but she did not remember seeing one in either closet.

"Where in the closet?" Lee asked.

George's face grew red. "The floor, under the board that'd been loosened."

Tessa leaned to the edge of the love seat. Jill placed an arm around her shoulders.

"What do you mean?" she asked him.

"There was no —"

"Would you be able to locate the board now?" Lee interrupted, holding up a hand to silence Tessa. "It's very important," he added.

Tessa thought that was putting it mildly.

"Show me," Lee said, then stood. "Tessa, you might want to see this."

"I certainly do," she replied.

Without saying another word, they all followed Lee upstairs. Once they were inside Poppy's bedroom, Tessa had to force herself not to cry, not to howl in utter pain at the sheer horridness of what they were doing, why they were there.

George hesitated as he approached the closet. "I'm sorry," he said as he looked at Tessa.

She shook her head. "Just show me where you found those sketchbooks. You were doing your job," she added, hoping to reassure him, even though she herself felt as panicky as she had when she had entered this very room yesterday.

He entered the walk-in closet. The floors were the same as they were before. Wide planks of oak that still appeared relatively new. George wedged himself into the far right corner of the closet, then bent over. Tessa held her breath as she watched as he removed a plank of wood at least eighteen inches long. He held the wood out to Lee. "It wasn't this easy before."

Lee examined the wood, then gave it to Sam. "Send this to Harry."

"How were you able to spot this?" Tessa inquired. "I lived here and never saw any sign the floor had been tampered with." Tessa was sure she would have noticed the loose board had it been here before, but again, she reminded herself, she didn't routinely inspect the closet floors. Rosa cleaned in here. Possibly there would be an answer when Lee questioned her later.

"When I entered the closet, this piece of wood just stuck out like a sore thumb. The seams were . . . fresh. Like it'd been recently moved, or replaced. Knowing what'd happened here, well, I just thought I would have a look, and that's when I found those art books."

Lee nodded. "Did you look at the pictures?"

George's face reddened again. "Yes. I did."

"And why didn't you report this to the police?" Sam interjected. "You knew a crime had been committed in this house." His voice was tight, restrained, as though he was holding back a flood of anger.

"I called my uncle. He said to just do my

job and pack the books away. You" — his expression stilled, grew serious — "you'd been arrested, and well, me and Uncle Walt just assumed . . ."

"What? You assumed this was just a little girl's drawings that had been passed over? Dear God, didn't you see what the drawings were? Surely you couldn't have been that naive!" Tessa wanted to shake some sense into this idiot, but it was too late for that; plus, she didn't want to have a charge of assault filed against her, which would certainly land her right back in prison.

George shook his head. "It was wrong. I know that now, and I told my uncle, but he said it was up to the police to locate evidence. If it had been important, he said, they would have found it. I packed the boxes, and when I heard you were being released, I told my uncle that if I was contacted, I would not keep silent this time around. I was a dumb sixteen-year-old kid then. I was afraid."

Knowing his age at the time didn't change the fact that he'd kept crucial evidence out of the hands of the authorities, but Tessa could see his point. He was young, scared. The uncle, now that was completely different.

"It's not an excuse," Lee said. "You're

willing to testify to this? Under oath?"

George nodded. "Yes. I should have spoken up all those years ago, but . . ."

"It's too late for an apology, whatever excuse you have. This might have changed the outcome of my trial. Do you realize the consequences of what you did?" Tessa asked, her voice several octaves higher than normal. "I . . . swear." With that, she walked out of Poppy's room. She was not going to resort to violent behavior and wind up back in prison because this stupid young man had not had the guts to tell the truth. Such cowardice had contributed to her being in prison in the first place.

CHAPTER 18

Tessa wanted to run out the front door, and would have if not for the large number of media people gathered at the gates outside her house. She forced herself to stop at the bottom of the staircase before she acted on the impulse and continued to run outside, only to find herself surrounded by unfriendly reporters of various kinds. Trapped inside her house was turning out to be almost as bad as being in prison, although, to be sure, she didn't have a guard like Hicks teasing and taunting her. The media had taken her place.

"Hey, are you okay?" Jill asked as she came up behind Tessa. "You ran out so fast."

Tessa took a deep breath, hoping to calm herself, but it didn't help. "How can that little . . . punk live with himself? I am so . . . angry! His testimony could have helped my case. I am, I don't know —" She twisted her long hair in her hand. "I feel as if I need to act, to do something other than just sit here and wait on Rosa and Rachelle, and that" — she pointed upstairs — "total jerk. It's hard, Jill. Very hard." Tears surged again, something she was becoming quite used to, and, as was becoming more common now that she was out of prison and did not have to hide her emotions, she let the tears stream down her face.

"I know, sweetie, I know. We are going to make this right no matter what we have to do. I promise. I think Lee Whitlow is top-notch, and I swear I haven't Googled the man. He's smart and seems to know what he has to do for you; and Sam does as well. You're the toughest gal I know, Tessa. I couldn't have endured all this and kept my sanity."

Tessa gave up a halfhearted smile. "Bull. I don't believe that for a minute."

Voices coming from the top of the staircase were heard before Jill could respond.

Lee, Sam, and George came down the stairs.

George held out his hand to her. "Mrs. Jamison, I can't even begin to know what you have been through, but I . . . ." He stammered, and this almost made her feel sorry for him. Almost. "I will do anything I can to help with your new trial. It was totally wrong of me and my uncle not to go to the police and the DA to let them know what we had found."

Hesitantly, Tessa took his offered hand. "Yes, it was wrong, George. Very wrong, but I do not suppose there is any point in my rehashing your reasoning. As long as you're willing to tell what you saw now, I'm okay." To be sure, Tessa was fudging a bit on this, but anger, recrimination, and holding on to the past could not change her future.

George nodded, looking relieved, and Sam led him out the back entrance. Once the people of the press saw him, they were likely to put two and two together, if they hadn't already. And neither Tessa nor any of the others wanted them to get too much of a head start on learning about the new witnesses and what they might testify to.

Lee looked at his watch. "It's almost eight o'clock, so Rosa should be here pretty soon. Are you sure you want to sit in on this one?" he asked Tessa, as they all returned to the living room. "You can tell me what you want to ask her, and I will."

"No, I want to confront her myself," she said adamantly. "I know her, and I need to know why she . . . No, that's not it. I do know *why*. What I want to hear from her own mouth is exactly what she saw that day."

"Fair enough," Lee said. "Though I'll want to question her, inform her what to expect when we go to trial. I don't want her running off."

"Isn't there something you can do legally to make sure she stays here to testify?" Jill asked. "I would hate to see her take off because she was afraid."

"There are a few tactics I can use," Lee said. "I doubt I'll have to. When I spoke to her, she was extremely remorseful, and without having the threat of being deported as an excuse this time around, I don't think I'll have to resort to any legal razzmatazz."

Sam came back into the living room. "I have taken the liberty of ordering take-out from Papa Luigi's. I know the owner, and asked them to call me when they were close, so I can meet them around back," he announced. "I don't know about the rest of you, but I am famished."

Tessa realized that she was hungry and was thankful that Sam had taken the initiative to feed them. Half an hour later, Sam's cell phone rang, telling him their dinner was right around the corner.

There was still no sign of Rosa, and it was way past eight o'clock.

Sam met the delivery driver before he had a chance to enter the screened-in pool area. Sam returned carrying three large bags with heavenly smells emanating from them.

"Hope Italian works for everyone," he said as he took plates from the cabinets and placed them around the bar in the kitchen.

Tessa took knives and forks out of the drawer and put them next to the plates. "It works for me. I can't remember the last time I had real Italian food." She was reminded of the cans of SpaghettiOs she used to order from the prison commissary. Was that considered Italian?

"Lee, Jill, help yourselves," Sam said as he removed paper lids from large foil pans. The delicious scents of garlic and tomato sauce emanating from lasagna, cheese ravioli, and baked ziti filled the kitchen. The tantalizing odor of garlic knots made Tessa's mouth water. A large container of antipasto, with salami, cheese, hot peppers, pepperoni, anchovies, and green and black olives supplemented the carbohydrate-laden dishes. It was a feast right out of *The Godfather.*

As they filled their plates with the food, Tessa half listened for a knock on the glass doors. She forked a bite of lasagna into her mouth, closing her eyes and reveling in the heavenly taste. If she were forced to return to that hellhole of a prison, she knew she would spend many nights reliving this meal. For the next few minutes, the four ate heartily. When they finished, Lee excused himself to make a phone call.

"She's not coming," Tessa said.

Lee came back into the kitchen. "No, she's on her way here. Apparently, she had to call a cab. Said they were running late. Not sure why she didn't call to tell us, but she assured me she would be here within fifteen minutes."

Breathing a sigh of relief, Tessa nodded. "I don't think she ever learned to drive. At least not when she worked for us. She had a relative bring her most days, or Joel would send a car for her. I can't imagine living in San Maribel and not driving."

Actually, she could. It had been years since she had had a driver's license or driven a car. The last time she had driven, she had been racing to get home to the girls. She didn't know if she would even remember how to drive if for some reason she had to.

"If you don't have to learn, you won't," Sam said. "At least she knows how to use a cell phone." His last words were laced with sarcasm.

Tessa discovered that she did not really

appreciate the disparaging comment from Sam, as she knew Rosa, or at least she thought she did. Then again, maybe Rosa wasn't the kind, sweet woman she had led her and Joel to believe. Rosa had not come forward when she could have, and that alone spoke volumes.

What were her priorities at the time of the murders? What did the woman care about? How little she must have thought of Tessa, Joel, and the girls.

This line of thinking made Tessa's blood boil, so she could understand where Sam's sarcasm was coming from. He'd met Rosa on occasion, too, but had never, at least to her knowledge, known her very well.

"She was good with the girls," Tessa said. "They always enjoyed spending time with her, and I thought the feelings were reciprocated, but apparently, I was wrong." She wanted to add more but didn't. Lee was probably aware that Joel had taken care of hiring Rosa and, quite possibly, had overlooked her lack of legal status.

"We don't care how good a housekeeper or babysitter she was. Don't allow yourself to feel pity, Tessa. She might have information that could have turned the entire investigation another way," Lee explained. "If she sees you as sympathizing with what her situation was then, she might think you're letting her off the hook and be more willing to help out in your defense."

"I don't care what her opinion of me is. I want her to tell us what she knows. That's it," Tessa said as she went to the sink and began rinsing the dinner plates and placing them in the dishwasher. Jill handed her the knives and forks. She ran them under the hot water and dropped the knives and forks in the basket in the dishwasher. "I assume you told her to use the back entrance?"

"Of course," Lee said. "The members of the media are still at their posts out front, and I doubt they're going to leave us alone anytime soon. They came to get a story. And, what with Chen thinking about running for governor, this is the biggest story around."

Sam had remained silent during the cleanup, but he spoke now. "Why don't we give them something? Tell them about the bones we found. Get them off our backs."

Lee raised his brows, obviously considering Sam's suggestion. "That might not be a bad idea. But let's wait until Rosa shows up. I want to hear her story first, then we'll decide. Are you all right with this, Tessa?"

Do I really have a choice?

"I'll do whatever it takes, Lee. I have let

you know my position time and time again. I do not want to speak to the media, now or ever, not in a million years, but you or Sam do what you feel is best." She despised the media. They were to blame, at least in her mind, for her racing off to San Maribel in the first place. She had known that her girls' nightmare would become public, and she had had to prevent that. In doing so, she had killed them. By not telling Joel about his brother's abuse, she might as well have put a gun to their heads and pulled the trigger. It was her fault, no matter what Jill or Sam or Lee said. She had put the cart before the horse, and doing so had cost her everything that was dear to her. Everything.

"I want to see what Rosa says, then we can decide," Lee said again.

Tessa didn't have anything to say to that, so she continued to clean the kitchen. Her thoughts were all over the place. It still seemed surreal, being here in her own home, surrounded by familiar yet unfamiliar things. New furnishings, floors, and walls did practically nothing to eliminate the images of what she had found at the pool that horrible day. She doubted that they would ever fade away. Like an old photo that had aged to a blurry finish, the edges of her memory of that day were faded, dried with time, but the actual picture of what she had seen was clear, as sharp as if she had just taken a snapshot of the scene.

It had taken a very long time for this image to return, but now, she could remember every single detail of what she had seen. And there was one detail that had always nagged her about Joel, and she had never repeated it to anyone, for fear they'd think she had totally gone off the deep end, but still, it nagged at her. He appeared so . . . *different*. Yes, she knew he'd been killed, murdered, and she understood the decomposition process, the bloating, all the scientific terms for describing a dead body in water, but she still felt that something wasn't right. Later, after Rosa left, maybe she would tell Jill about it. Jill was a doctor, and she might have an explanation for Tessa's feeling.

They all turned when they heard a light knock on the glass doors. "I'll get it," Sam said, moving to the back of the house.

"Stay calm," Jill coaxed Tessa. "You have nothing to be afraid of."

That was easy for Jill to say. Tessa had everything to fear. Her temporary freedom would most likely be taken away from her, and she would have to return to prison for the rest of her life if things did not go well.

She was simply not going to allow herself to get her hopes up even though Lee and Sam were very encouraging. Going back to prison is what she should focus on. It was so hard to be optimistic when you'd spent a decade of your life behind bars. And it was much worse because she was innocent.

"Tessa?" Jill said. "Are you okay? You seem like you're a million miles away."

Tessa agreed. "Sorry. I was. I do that a lot. I'll be fine."

"Let's get this over with," Jill told her. "Rosa is waiting."

Taking a deep breath, Tessa could not help but feel a bit anxious. It was time to hear from the horse's mouth exactly what her former housekeeper had witnessed.

CHAPTER 19

Rosa had not aged well at all, Tessa thought as soon as she saw the woman. Her dark hair was now a harsh steel-gray color reminding Tessa of a used Brillo pad. Her once round, honey-brown eyes were heavy lidded, making her appear as though she were squinting. She wore a dark skirt and a faded, floral-print blouse that looked as though it came from another century. On her feet were brown sandals that revealed callused heels and toenails with chipped orange polish that were much too long and in need of a trim. To say she had aged and let herself go would be more than kind. In her early sixties now, she looked as if she could already be an octogenarian.

Tessa would not have recognized her had she run into her on the street or at the mall.

"Miss Tessa," Rosa exclaimed as soon as she saw her. Her Mexican accent was virtually nonexistent. "I missed you so much, and the girls, too."

Tessa was not sure how to respond, so she didn't. Tessa was shocked that the older woman seemed so . . . *normal*. As though they were the best of friends, and Tessa was simply returning from a long vacation instead of ten years in prison as a convicted murderer. "Rosa," she said, finally acknowledging the older woman.

Lee and Sam were seated on the sofa, Rosa in the chair opposite. Tessa chose the chair that faced the pool area. Jill sat on the arm of the chair, her left hand casually resting on Tessa's right shoulder.

Lee waited a few seconds, then removed a legal pad and a tape recorder from his briefcase. He went through the legal spiel with Rosa, making sure it was on record that she was here of her own free will and that no one had coerced her into making a statement. He handed her several papers for her signature. As soon as she finished signing them, Lee returned them to the briefcase.

"Can you tell us what you saw on the last morning you were at this house? In as much detail as you can remember. Any detail you think may not be important, probably is, so I want you to tell me" — Lee looked at

Tessa — "us everything that you saw and heard."

Rosa nodded, her steel-gray hair coming loose from the bun coiled at the top of her head. She reached up and tucked the hair back into the bun, then smoothed her skirt, crossed her legs, and sat up straight. She continued to stare at Tessa, then began to speak. "It was Saturday morning, the day after Miss Tessa went away. I went upstairs to do the beds after I had breakfast with the girls. The girls had their cereal and stayed in the kitchen." She paused, removed a tissue from her skirt pocket, blotted her eyes, then went on. "I decided to do the toilets first —" She stopped speaking, took a breath, and looked directly at Tessa. "I usually do the toilets last, but not that day. I don't know why I changed my routine. I cleaned the master bathroom first, then I cleaned the girls' bathroom. All those bright colors. They made me smile."

Lee interrupted her. "So, you changed your routine that day, correct?"

Rosa nodded. "I did."

Lee scribbled something on his legal pad, then asked Rosa, "Did you plan on changing your normal cleaning routine that day or was it spontaneous?"

She looked to Tessa, then Jill as though

they had answers. Tessa was not going to help in making this easier for her, and neither was Jill.

"I don't understand," Rosa stated.

"When you headed upstairs while the girls were eating breakfast, was it your intention to strip the beds first?"

"Yes, yes, it was."

"And all of a sudden, out of the blue, you're in Mr. and Mrs. Jamison's bedroom and decide to do the toilets first? You don't know why? You had a sudden change of mind for no reason at all?"

Rosa seemed confused. "I don't know, I just decided to do the bathrooms. That is all I can tell you."

Lee made another note on his legal pad. Tessa watched Rosa and could see that the woman was nervous, uncomfortable at being questioned so closely.

"Okay, you had a change of mind. I'll accept that. Do you recall how much time you took cleaning the bathrooms?"

"Maybe fifteen minutes. I only did the toilets. Not the showers, tubs, or floors."

"Okay, you finished the bathrooms. Walk me through your next round of duties," Lee instructed. He was relaxed, and Tessa could see that he was in his element questioning Rosa. She could only imagine the effect he'd have on a jury while questioning or cross-examining a witness.

With all eyes focused on her, Rosa adjusted her position, her rigid stance slackening. She tucked stray hairs back into her bun. "I went to Poppy's room first. She is, *was* very particular about her bedroom. She always helped me to clean. That morning, she had made her bed, so I didn't want to undo her work, so I decided I would change her bed the next day. I went to Piper's room and stripped her bed."

Lee held up a hand. "Stop for a minute."

Rosa nodded.

"Did you replace the sheets on Piper's bed then or later?"

"Then. I remember I used the lavender sheets. They were her favorite. She liked all shades of purple."

Tears filled Tessa's eyes as she listened to Rosa talk about her daughters and their likes and dislikes.

"What did you do after that?" Lee asked.

Rosa appeared troubled at the question. Her eyes downcast, she picked at her nails. "I was going to change the linens in the master bedroom, but when I went into the hall, I heard voices downstairs. Very loud voices. Angry-sounding voices."

Tessa's heart rate sped up and skipped a

beat. She leaned in to hear Rosa's next words.

"Go on," Lee encouraged.

"They were yelling, the men, and it frightened me. I had never heard Mr. Jamison scream and carry on like he was. I called Roberto, my brother, from the portable phone he had brought me that day. I asked him to come back right away. I did not want to stay at the house. I wanted to go home so I did not have to listen to the men hollering. I was scared stiff."

Men? Tessa was shocked.

"You say 'men.' How many?" Lee asked.

"Two. At first," Rosa said, "Then Mr. Jamison . . . he just stopped yelling. The other man stopped, too. I heard a loud, very fast banging on the front door. That is when the yelling stopped. I waited because I thought that Mr. Jamison and the other man are arguing about business and have forgotten that they are not at his office. I wanted to check on the girls, so I went downstairs." Rosa hesitated and looked at Tessa. "I stopped when I heard the other man."

"Why? Did you know this other man?" Lee asked her. "What made you stop, and where exactly were you?"

"I was there." She pointed to the bottom of the stairs. "The wall that used to be there

246

blocked the view from the kitchen, where I heard the voices coming from. I didn't see the other man. Just heard him, and I had never heard him before."

"Was this other man in the kitchen?" Lee asked.

"Not at first. I think that Mr. Jamison let him in, then the man followed him back to the kitchen." Rosa shot a pleading look at Tessa again, as if she were begging for her forgiveness.

"Where were the girls during this argument?"

"I think they were still in the kitchen at that point."

"So, the girls are in the kitchen, presumably having their cereal, their father is screaming at one man, then another knocks on the front door, Mr. Jamison answers it, invites this strange man into the house, and this third man then follows him back to the kitchen, where the first two men continue to yell and argue? Would you agree that this statement is accurate?" Lee looked at Tessa and gave a slight nod.

Tessa was trying very hard to keep her emotions under control and not react. Lee had obviously sensed this. It was all she could do to remain seated. She wanted to strangle Rosa, wanted to shake her until she . . . what? Tessa took a deep breath, letting it out slowly. It would not be a good idea to lose her temper at this point.

"Yes, that is a true statement," Rosa agreed.

"Did you recognize the two men, or at least their voices? Had you ever heard them before that day?" Lee continued with his questions while they waited.

Rosa nodded. "I knew the younger man, Mr. Jamison's brother, Liam. He was in the kitchen with Mr. Jamison when the other man knocked on the front door."

"What did I tell you!" Tessa shot off her chair. "That worthless son of a bitch killed my family! I want him found now. I don't give a good rat's ass how much it costs or what you have to do to find him!"

"Tess, calm down." Sam reached her in three giant steps and wrapped his arms around her. "This isn't going to help us right now. Give us a minute, okay?" Sam tossed over his shoulder as he led Tessa to the kitchen. "Sit down," he said, then took a glass from the cupboard and filled it with water from the tap. "We need to hear what Rosa has to say, okay? I can only imagine how hard it is, but it's what needs to be done right now. She has already helped you, you realize this? Whatever else she says, her story confirms that the murders took place on Saturday, not on Friday, as the state said at your trial. You were in San Maribel all day Saturday and could not have committed a murder in San Maribel. Once the DA hears Rosa's account, it will not matter what else we learn. He will have to drop the charges unless he can disprove her story."

Tessa took a drink of water. "Okay. I can see that. But I want to know more. Who in the hell was here that day? Joel never conducted his business at home, let alone in the kitchen, where Poppy and Piper would have been having their breakfast. I don't know if I believe her, Sam. She could be making this up, just to cover her ass."

Tessa blew out a breath, which caused her hair to fly in front of her face. She was more confused now than she had been before. How could a person keep something of this magnitude to herself? And how in the world could those who conducted the investigation, no, the witch hunt, with her being the prey, *not* have known of this? What kind of incompetence could lead to her being charged and convicted of murders that were supposed to have occurred on Friday when all the victims were still alive on Saturday?

"I know it's tough, but we need to listen to her story. Lee will pick it apart, and won't stop until he's satisfied. Remember, he has *never lost a case.*" Sam emphasized the last four words. "Trust me, okay?"

Trust? Not something she had experienced much of in her life, at least until she had met and married Joel. Her mother was a drug addict, she had no clue who her father was, and Lara, her only living relative, at least that she knew of, hadn't even bothered to call her and ask how she was doing. Trust? It had never come easy for her.

"I'll try," she said.

"Let Lee do his job," Sam said as he led her back to the living room.

"Are you all right?" Jill asked. "I can give you something if you need it."

Tessa gave her a halfhearted smile. She pointed to the ankle monitor. "Rules. No alcohol. No drugs. But I appreciate your concern. I'm going to be . . . I'm dealing with this now." She looked at Rosa, who was cowering in her chair. The woman was afraid, there was no doubt about that. But she was no longer in fear of deportation, and according to Lee, her entire family were all now legal citizens. What else could she possibly have to be afraid of?

"Are you sure you want to listen in?" Lee asked her. "I can do this at the office."

"No. I'm fine. Just do what you have to do." Tessa never wavered as she said this, looking at Rosa the entire time. "I want to hear what happened in my house the day my family was *slaughtered.*" She remembered that word, the very one that had been used by the prosecution and the media to describe what *she* had supposedly done before she left for San Maribel on Friday.

Lee nodded and turned to Rosa.

"Rosa, did you hear anything specific from the younger Mr. Jamison? From Liam Jamison?"

Rosa nodded.

"Tell us what you heard him say," Lee instructed. "Word for word."

CHAPTER 20

Almost immediately after Lee said this, his cell phone buzzed, and he excused himself to take the call.

The tension in the room intensified when he left the room. Rosa squirmed in her chair, trying not to focus on Tessa.

Tessa had a dozen questions floating through her mind. So Liam had been here that day, not in Japan as she had been led to believe before going to San Maribel. Just as she had always been sure of, he was the person who killed her family. But who was the third man? Someone from Jamison Pharmaceuticals? And if so, who would come to their home? What was being argued about? The company was stable and thriving, though she had to admit she hadn't been involved in the day-to-day operations since she had left her position to start a family. Joel never complained to her about the inner workings of the company. She had just assumed that there wasn't anything to complain about. They were a healthy, happy family, blessed with loving children. Their lives hadn't been perfect, but close.

Or so she had thought.

Lee returned. "Tessa, I need to speak to you and Sam."

Her pulse increased again, and for a minute, she feared that her heart would burst from her chest.

"Jill?" she asked.

"You mind waiting here?" Lee asked Jill, nodding in Rosa's direction.

"Not at all," Jill said.

Tessa knew this was Lee's way of asking Jill to watch Rosa, make sure she didn't decide to disappear again.

As soon as they were out of eavesdropping range, Lee spoke. "That was Harry. He says the watch stopped on the date it showed, said it was hit, slammed against something hard enough to do the damage. There's DNA on it, too."

"That can't be right! Sam said that he packed up Joel's desk, and the watch was in his desk. It's impossible, right? He couldn't have put it in his desk, not then. He wasn't alive."

"I'm just telling you what Harry said. The impact on the watch, by whatever means, caused it to stop on the day of the murders. That means the murders occurred on Saturday, not Friday. It supports Rosa's story about her last day working being on Saturday, not Friday. As to how the watch got to Joel's office, I'm sure there is an explanation, but I haven't a clue what it could be. But I will find out, I promise," Lee said.

Tessa had taken in so much information in the past forty-eight hours, she couldn't process this last bit. "Have you given this information to the district attorney?"

"Not yet. I wanted to tell you first."

"What's Harry's plan on the DNA?" Sam asked.

"He'll run it against the samples taken at the scene, see if there's a match."

"A match? Who else's DNA would be on that watch, other than Joel's?"

"That's Harry's job to find out. Remember, Rachelle will be at my office tomorrow morning, and she's agreed to give a DNA sample. If Liam's DNA is on that watch, it's just one more fact to take to the DA."

Tessa dropped her head in her hands. Her head was pounding, and she was feeling nauseated. "So you're saying that Joel's watch might have stopped during a fight or something, and if Liam's DNA shows up on the watch . . . What does this mean?"

"Let's wait for Harry. He knows the case, knows what to look for. We will get to the bottom of this. I'm going to call Michael Chen right now. Sam, you okay with questioning Rosa? I don't want her taking off or thinking she's off the hook. The events that took place, at least those she witnessed, need to be documented. I want her scared. And don't be easy on her."

"I can do that," Sam agreed. "You leaving now?"

"I want to get to Chen before any of this makes the evening news. The damned media are still stalking the neighborhood. We need to stay alert until we figure this out. Maybe I can get Chen and Judge Crider, the old son of a bitch, to dismiss the charges since the murders could not have happened on Friday as the state alleged. At the very least, get him to give us a date for a new trial. Something they can focus on while we investigate.

"If the evidence I have to take to the judge holds up, there won't be a need for a new trial. Now, Sam, Tessa, go see what else Rosa knows. I'll see you both tomorrow morning at my office, that is, if you want to see Rachelle?"

"I do," Tessa replied. "I want to look into her eyes and tell her what an evil bastard she gave birth to."

"I understand. Now, Sam, go before she relaxes, gets too comfortable. I'll call if there's anything new to report."

Tessa and Sam returned to the living room. Rosa remained as she was. Jill had moved to the sofa and was sitting near the end closest to Rosa.

"Lee had to leave. A big break in the case. I'm going to continue with the questions, Rosa. I'm an attorney and have been working alongside Lee, so I'm as familiar with the case as he is. However, you may leave at any time; that's your legal right. But we will issue a subpoena when and if this goes to court. You will be forced to testify to what you saw and heard."

Her face paled. "But I thought if I told you what I saw . . . there would be no court, no trial."

"It's a possibility, but there are no guarantees. Those papers you signed, it's all clearly outlined. Up to you, Rosa."

Tessa could see that Sam was not going to be as sympathetic and objective as Lee.

"I will tell you what I saw," Rosa said. "I want to help Miss Tessa."

Sure she does, Tessa thought. That's why it took her ten years to decide to come out with what she had to say. Tessa wanted to slap her silly. The pent-up anger she had kept hidden all these years was not going to remain inside. It was ready to explode. But she would control her violent thoughts, both because it was not in her nature to be this way and because she did not want to end up in jail this time for a crime that she did commit. Unless it was for killing Liam Jamison, that son of a bitch.

Nonetheless, the thought of harming this woman who had changed the course of her life was there, and Tessa thought that given what she had been through, her feelings were probably a natural reaction.

Sam took the legal pad Lee had left him, read through the list of questions, then put it aside. He took his cell phone and set it up to continue recording Rosa's testimony.

"We left off with you about to tell us what you heard the younger Mr. Jamison, Liam Jamison, say."

Rosa pulled herself upright again, her upper body perfectly straight. "How should I say this?"

"Any way you're comfortable. As long as it's the truth," Sam said.

He was not cutting Rosa any slack. Tessa appreciated this more than he knew. She needed someone on her side this time around. Someone who believed in her. Sam

McQuade believed in her.

Jill sat beside her again, but this time she wasn't as relaxed. Maybe she didn't trust Sam. Lee was good, but if he trusted Sam in his place, then Tessa would, too. She whispered to Jill, "It's okay. Sam knows what he's doing."

"You read me well," Jill whispered back.

Sam cleared his throat. "Rosa?"

She nodded. "I was at the bottom of the steps, and they were arguing. I was very frightened —"

"Rosa, you have said that more than once. I want to know what you heard Liam Jamison say."

"He said to Mr. Joel . . ." Rosa's eyes suddenly filled with tears. She took another tissue from her pocket and blotted her tears. "He said that he knew about the girls."

Tessa actually felt the color drain from her face. Her hands started shaking. She took a deep breath. "What do you mean?" She could hardly get the words out of her mouth.

Rosa's head bobbed up and down, her bun finally coming completely undone. She didn't bother trying to fix it again. "He said he knew about the girls."

She looked at Sam, praying he would get her to clarify what she had just said.

"Liam Jamison said *he* knew about the girls?" Sam asked her again. "You heard him say those exact words to Joel? Is that what you're saying?"

Rosa nodded.

"Is that all you heard?" Sam asked.

"No."

The room was as silent as a tomb. Tessa felt as though she had stepped out of her body and was looking down on Jill, Sam, and Rosa from high overhead. The word *surreal* came to mind. An out-of-body experience.

"Tell us what you heard," Sam persisted. "Exactly as you heard it being said."

Tessa watched Rosa. She could see that this wasn't easy for her, but again, she could have made a massive difference all those years ago and had chosen not to. She reminded herself of this each time she started to feel the least bit of sympathy for the woman she had trusted with her daughters' lives.

"I . . . I heard him tell Mr. Jamison that he knew about the girls. That's how he said it. I swear to you," Rosa repeated. "Just like that. He said he knew about the girls."

"Okay," Sam said. "Did you hear him say *what* he knew about the girls?"

She shook her head. "That is all I heard.

He did not say . . ." Rosa appeared to be searching for the right words. "Specifically. Yes, that is it. He did not say specifically what it was that he knew."

Tessa couldn't remain silent. "You're saying that Liam said that to Joel? Not the other way around?"

Again, Rosa nodded.

"I think you're confused," Tessa told her. "You're not telling the truth."

"Tess," Sam chided. "Let me do my job."

How could he expect her to keep quiet?

"Calm down, Tessa," Jill said reassuringly. "Let Sam finish what he needs to do."

Tessa sighed, exerting an iron will of control, then motioned for Sam to continue with his questions. The mood in the room was grim, dark. She had a fleeting thought, wondering if this is how her girls felt when they'd heard the arguing that morning in the kitchen. *If* that's what they heard, and still, she wasn't convinced Rosa was telling the complete truth.

"So, you are at the bottom of the staircase, you hear both Mr. Jamisons, Joel and Liam, arguing," Sam stated in a matter-of-fact tone of voice. "Liam says to Joel, 'I know about the girls' and you just continue to stand at the bottom of the stairs?"

"I was very afraid and wanted to take the

girls to their rooms upstairs, and I was about to when the loud banging started on the front door. They stopped shouting." Rosa looked down, reached for her wadded-up tissue, and blew her nose. "I waited, too. I thought it was Roberto coming to get me, but then I realized that he could not have gotten here so fast. You know? It had only been a few minutes since I had called him. He worked over on Alhambra Drive, not all that far from here, but it still takes at least ten minutes to get from there to here. So I waited to see who was at the door knocking so loudly. I thought maybe Miss Tessa had come back, but it could not be her because she had keys. And she always came in through the garage and entered the house through the kitchen door."

Sam looked at Tessa for confirmation.

"At least that's true," she said.

"Go on," Sam coaxed Rosa.

"Mr. Jamison, Mr. *Joel,* answered the door, and Mr. Liam followed him. I thought that now is my chance, so I ran to the kitchen and told both girls to go out to the pool immediately. They did as I said. No questions because I think they did not want to hear their father and uncle yelling in front of them. They had shorts on, no swimwear, but I said to them, hurry out and go swim."

"Stop!" Tessa shouted, no longer caring what Sam or Jill said. "How in God's name could you *not* come forth with this information? I have spent a decade rotting in a prison cell! I lost my family, Rosa! Everything dear to me was taken that day, all that I loved . . . and you . . . you just *up and left.* You walked out the door just like it was a normal day. How could you?" Her voice was loud and harsh, but she no longer cared.

Sitting here and listening to Rosa talk about *that day* as though it were just any other cleaning day at the Jamison residence made her seethe with rage. She didn't care whether her words hurt Rosa or not. Glaring at the woman, knowing her eyes shone with hot anger, she could not stop herself. "You're nothing but a coward, you know that? You left two innocent little girls alone to . . . die!"

"Miss Tessa —"

"Shut up! You. Ruined. My. Life. You. Watched. My. Family. Die!" She spat the words so contemptuously, she surprised herself.

Sam held up his hand. "Calm down, Tess. We're not getting anything accomplished. I understand your anger. We all do. We will find out the truth. No matter what. I swear."

He said this while staring at Rosa.

"I am very sorry, Miss Tessa. I cannot change what I did that day and afterward. I live with it every day of my life. I am not a happy woman. I . . ." She blotted her eyes again. "I pray for their souls at church. I swear to you." At that admission, Rosa began to sob in earnest, then genuflected. Tessa felt a twinge of compassion for the woman, but only a twinge.

"Jill, why don't you and Tess get us something to drink?" Sam asked. "I think we could use a break."

"Come on, Tessa." Jill took her friend by the hand and led her into the kitchen.

For a minute, neither spoke as Tessa removed glasses from the cupboard while Jill took four cans of Coke from the refrigerator. Tess filled each glass with ice, found a tray, and placed the glasses on it, along with the Cokes. "Why do I feel like strangling the life out of that woman? Can you tell me that? I can barely stand to look at her," Tessa said.

"I don't know of anyone in their right mind who wouldn't feel exactly as you do. Her inaction has changed many lives, Tessa. As long as you're not planning on acting on those thoughts, as a psychiatrist, I would tell you your reaction is perfectly normal."

If she only knew how serious she was, but even through her rage it wasn't Rosa she ultimately wanted to punish.

It was Liam.

CHAPTER 21

Twenty minutes later, after they'd had a chance to calm down, and Tessa was in control of her emotions, Sam asked Rosa if she wanted to go home or continue.

"I will stay as long as I need to," Rosa told him. "I want to help. Honestly."

"Okay, let's go back to your telling the girls to go to the pool. What did you do next?"

"I thought I needed to watch the girls, so I slipped inside the pool house. I could watch them from the window. The girls seemed okay, and they sat by the edge of the big pool. First they put their feet in the water, then, a few minutes later, they got into the pool. It was okay for them to do that; they were very good swimmers, but Miss Tessa always wanted me to watch them at the poolside. I always did." Rosa closed her eyes. "I stayed by the window and watched."

"How long?" Sam questioned.

Tessa's heart was beating so fast, she had to take several deep breaths to calm herself.

"I think it was at least half an hour."

"And during this time that you were in the pool house, watching the girls, did you see anything unusual, hear anything?" Sam asked.

"No, not then. I just watched Poppy and Piper playing in the pool. They were having fun."

Tessa could visualize both girls in their pool. They had all kinds of games they played, some were the usual. Marco Polo. Dive for gold. Mermaids. And they had their own games they'd made up, which consisted of going underwater to see who could hold her breath longer. It was something she did not approve of, and she had told them so, but she knew they still played the game, and as long as they didn't take it too far, she hadn't told them she knew. Another was to close their eyes, float on their backs, and see where they ended up when they decided to open their eyes. Endless games that were, for the most part, harmless, but Tessa insisted an adult be at the pool when they were swimming, or playing, despite the fact that both were excellent swimmers.

"You watched the girls playing for half an hour and saw nothing unusual. What did you see after the half hour you watched the girls swimming?" Sam asked, and Tessa could hear the impatience in his voice. He was walking her through her story like a child, and she knew why, but it was frustrating, to say the least, to sit here and listen to Rosa tell about her memories of that fateful day.

"Mr. Jamison came out to the pool area, the living area. Liam followed him, and that other man."

"Who was the other man you saw?"

Rosa looked down again, then met Tessa's stare. "I had not seen this man ever, but I had seen him. Sort of."

Sam was losing his patience, Tessa could tell. He rolled his shoulders, raked his hand through his hair, took another sip of his soft drink. "Okay, Rosa, you're not being very clear. Explain what you mean by you had seen this other man, 'sort of.' "

"He was . . . like Mr. Jamison. Like Joel."

The proverbial 'you could hear a pin drop' came to mind when Tessa heard what Rosa had said.

"You need to be very clear, Rosa. Beating around the bush isn't helping you, and it's not helping Mrs. Jamison. I want you to tell

267

me the truth. You have mastered English, and I know you're not having trouble coming up with the right words. I'm going to give you one more chance, then we're done." Sam waited for her to speak.

"It was just as I am telling you! I have no other way to explain what I saw, other than the man looked just like Mr. Jamison, Mr. Joel Jamison, not like Liam. I thought . . . I know it sounds very odd, but that man looked like he could be Mr. Jamison's twin brother."

Tessa struggled to hide her confusion. "I don't understand. Are you telling us that this . . . other man, the one banging on the front door, looked just like Joel?"

"Yes, Miss Tessa. He looked just like your husband."

She turned to Sam. "I don't understand." This couldn't be right. While Liam and Joel were half brothers, they really didn't resemble one another all that much. Both were tall, but Joel was fair where Liam was olive-skinned, as was Rachelle, his mother. There were a few similarities in their build but nothing that could make one conclude they looked exactly alike.

"Tell me about this other man," Sam said. "Every detail you remember."

She watched Sam. Expecting him to be as

stunned as she was, she was surprised that he didn't appear the least bit rattled at Rosa's description of the other man.

"I just saw him for a few minutes. He was tall like Mr. Joel. Is it okay if I call him that?"

"Yes," Sam replied. "Go on."

"He got up in Mr. Joel's face. I think he yelled, but I couldn't hear. It just looked like he was very angry, and Mr. Joel, well, he seemed shocked, then he became very angry, too."

"What was Liam doing during this exchange between Joel's visitor and Joel?"

"I think he was hollering, too, but I couldn't hear what any of them were saying. It just looked like they were all very angry. I only wanted to make sure the girls were okay, but I could see them from my spot at the window. They had gone to the end of the pool, and this brought them closer to the three men."

"Did you come out of the pool house? Did it ever occur to you to get the girls out of the pool and take them somewhere safe, away from the men?" Sam asked her.

"Yes. But I knew I had to wait until the men had calmed down. I assumed they were arguing about business, or whatever it was that Mr. Jamison, Liam, I mean, said he knew about the girls. So I just waited. I saw that the girls had swum to the other end of the pool; as you can see, it's a very big pool." She waved toward the glass doors that led out to the pool.

"I was sure they couldn't hear the men, so I went to the kitchen, well it's not really a full-sized kitchen, but it had a small refrigerator. Miss Tessa always had snacks for the girls in the pool house. There was a sink and a coffeemaker. I made a pot of coffee and sat at the bar. I was going to stay there, keep an eye on the girls, and as soon as the men were gone, I was going to bring them back inside and call Miss Tessa."

"But that isn't what happened, is it?"

More tears from Rosa. "No, it was so horrible. I can't describe . . . when I peered out the window to check on the girls, they weren't in the pool. I thought they'd gone back inside the house. This is what I thought because I did not see them go inside from the window of the pool house. I assumed they had all gone inside, and I was very scared. I knew that Roberto was probably waiting outside the gate for me because that's what I told him to do when I'd called him."

"We need to wind this up, Rosa. It's late, and I'm sure you're stalling. I want you to tell me what you saw when you finally decided to come out of the pool house to meet Roberto."

There were more tears and nose-blowing from Rosa, but she knew the enormity of her situation; at least Tessa thought so. Rosa shifted her shoulders back again, then seemed determined to finish the story she should have told more than a decade ago.

"When I left the pool house, I knew that Roberto would be waiting in the front outside the gates, so I went out the side door . . . and that's when I saw him running from the garage. And when I saw who it was, I stopped and waited. I didn't want him to see me. I was so scared, and I knew that, well, I was not here legally. We had all come from Mexico and were just thankful to be safe. It took many, many years, but my entire family are now American citizens. I did not want to return to Mexico, with all the drug lords and killings. It is a very bad place to live. Mr. Jamison knew I was not a citizen when he hired me but assured me that he would do everything in his power to assist me and my family so that we could be here legally."

"Rosa, I don't care about your legal status, and Tess doesn't either. It's of no relevance whatsoever to the current situation. It wasn't then, and it's not now. Get to the point." Sam was being hateful and didn't seem to care.

"As I waited by the corner of the house for my brother, I saw him. He came out through the garage door, and he ran across the lawn, then through the gates. I saw Roberto, and I ran to get in the car with him. I had to leave because I did not want to get involved with the police."

"Why would you think this argument these three men were having would involve the police?"

Rosa, who had appeared weak and frightened before this, all of a sudden seemed courageous when she spoke. "Because Mr. Joel had blood all over him when I saw him running away from the house."

CHAPTER 22

"But that's impossible!" Tessa shouted, rising from her chair and lurching toward Rosa as if she meant to do her harm. "You lying bitch! You have lost your mind! There is absolutely no way you saw my husband running from his own home, and with blood all over him." Enraged, she turned to Sam. "Do you believe her?"

"Rosa, you have to be mistaken," said Jill. "Mr. Jamison was later found in the pool with the girls. Maybe you imagined this? You were so frightened when you saw the . . . bodies in the pool, you were unable to handle the shock. You were traumatized by what you saw in the pool, and this account is the result of post-traumatic stress disorder."

"No! No! Never! I know what I saw that day. I am a lot of things, but I am not a crazy woman. I did not see any bodies in the pool, not then or ever. This I swear to you on all that is holy. I only saw what I saw. When I heard the news, later, I thought that this horrible crime must have happened after I left with Robert."

Is it possible Rosa is telling the truth? Tessa had more questions than answers and could not see how any of this would help her as regards seeing Liam brought to justice or taking her revenge on him for what he did.

"Would you be willing to submit to a polygraph?" Sam asked her.

"What is that? I do not understand the word you just used," Rosa asked, her tone filled with skepticism.

"It's a test that determines if you're telling the truth or lying," Sam told her. "If you're telling the truth, this test will prove it."

"Then I will take the test. I am not a crazy woman, I swear to you, I did not see . . . bodies. And I am not lying. I saw Mr. Jamison, Mr. Joel. He was running, and there was blood all over him. I never went back to look in on the children. That is something I will have to live with for the rest of my life. For that, I will never forgive myself. I may not be a smart and educated woman like Miss Tessa and Miss Jill are, but I do not say things that are untrue. I admit I was very wrong not to come forward to the police. I told you why, and I have never had a peaceful day since."

Is she telling the truth? It was so bizarre, Tessa had a hard time wrapping her mind around the implications if she *was* telling the truth. It made absolutely no sense at all. How could Joel be in two places at once? And this other man, who was he? Was Rosa sure of her description of him? Tessa didn't know. How could she? All she did know was that she was more confused than ever, and almost wished she were back in prison. At least there, her days were predictable.

"I can arrange for the polygraph first thing tomorrow morning. I'll send a car for you," Sam told Rosa. "That is, if you're sure you want to do this. You may want to consult with an attorney, talk this over with your family first."

"No! I will say what I saw. I did not come forward ten years ago. That is *my* crime, and I will go to jail for that. I deserve whatever punishment the court decides. I did not imagine what I saw. The image is very, very clear to me today, the same as it was then. I have agreed to help Miss Tessa now. I will do whatever I have to do for her."

Tessa, who had taken her seat again as Rosa spoke, couldn't remain quiet any longer. "Rosa, how could you see Joel? He

275

died at the same time the girls did. Is it possible it was Liam you saw? Or the other man who you said looked like Joel?" Tessa tried to speak as calmly as she could, but it was very difficult, almost impossible.

"I have told you exactly what I saw, and I will take the test Mr. Sam mentioned. It was not Mr. Liam. He has that dark hair, not like Mr. Joel. And it was not the other man, either. By that time I had known Mr. Joel for ten years. There is no way I could mistake someone else for him."

"Sam?" she asked. "What do we do with this?" She shifted her head toward Rosa.

"Let me call Lee. I'll be right back." Sam went to the kitchen, leaving the three women alone.

An awkwardness permeated the room. Tessa could not wait until Sam returned before resuming her questioning. "Rosa, I know that you're not . . . crazy. But I know from personal experience when you see something that is so violent, the mind does strange things. It took me years before I could completely remember the day I came home and discovered the bodies in the swimming pool. It was the worst day of my life, and there is nothing I can do or say to bring my family back. They're gone forever, but I can see to it that they get justice. I did not murder my family."

Tessa said this without tears. "I loved them with my entire heart and soul. They were my life, my reason for living, you know that. I understand you might have been confused at the time. I certainly was when I found them, and I believe it's part of the reason I went to prison. I was so stunned, Jill's diagnosis of post-traumatic stress disorder is probably accurate. I should have spoken up in my own defense. People can have this and not even be aware of it. I wasn't sure I had this for several years. It was not until I had lots of shitty prison counseling, and did a lot of reading, that I realized I'd suffered from this, and probably still do. It's not a crime to admit you were wrong," Tessa pleaded, hoping to make an impression on Rosa. Tessa was most likely in shock the day she found her family butchered in the pool, too, so at least that part she could identify with. Rosa's not telling the police what she had seen that day, well, that wasn't quite as easy to understand.

Rosa's hair had come completely unraveled now, the long gray strands nearly reaching her waist. "I am so sorry, Miss Tessa. You know I . . . No, you have lost your family. I cannot ask you to forgive me, or understand. But I will do what I can to make this right. I will take the test, then I will go to jail. I deserve to."

"You're not going to go to jail, Rosa. Even if you committed a crime by not coming forward to tell the police what you saw that day, it was more than ten years ago. That is way beyond the statute of limitations for whatever crime you might be guilty of. So you are not going to jail."

"What is this statute of limitations you just referred to, Miss Jill? I do not understand. I am guilty of a crime and should be punished."

"The statute of limitations says that after enough time has passed since a crime was committed, the guilty person cannot be tried for that crime. There are some exceptions, like murder, for which there is no such thing as a statute of limitations.

"All we're trying to do is bring new evidence to trial, though we're hoping this doesn't even go to trial. We just want to find the person or persons who committed these horrible crimes, and see to it that they're finally punished," Jill explained in her most professional manner.

"Really?" Rosa asked, amazement in her voice.

"It's very possible you won't even have to testify," Jill said, turning to look at Tessa.

"She's right, but as Sam and Lee said, there are no guarantees. I'm only here now because of a new ruling by the Florida Supreme Court. If there is no new, *convincing, provable* evidence, I will return to prison and serve out the remainder of my three life sentences."

"I stand behind what I saw. I am not quite sure how the court works. I have always been told to tell the truth. This one time in my life, I ran like a coward. About that, you were absolutely right. I will tell the court the truth about that, too. But I cannot lie about what I saw, Miss Tessa. I know it was Mr. Joel I saw running from the house. I worked for you and him for ten years. There is no way I could mistake anyone else for him. I don't understand, uh . . . the circumstantial way so much, but I understand truth."

Sam came back into the room. "Lee has arranged for a polygraph tomorrow morning, as soon as his meeting with Rachelle is over. He couldn't give me an exact time but wanted me to ask Rosa if she would be willing to wait in his office."

"I will do what I must. I have told Miss Tessa and Miss Jill that I will tell my story. I will tell exactly what I saw that horrible day."

Rosa seemed to have a newfound confidence. Why, no clue, but Tessa wasn't sure if it was a good thing or a bad thing given what she said she had witnessed. There was no way it could be possible, but if it's what she believed, and if the DA thought it worthwhile, then so be it. But even if the DA did not believe what she says she saw, the fact that it was Saturday and her family was still alive meant that she could not have been the killer and the state's case was impossible since it relied upon the deaths having occurred on Friday, not Saturday or later.

She was so very tired, mentally and emotionally. At this point, all she wanted to do was right the wrongs of the past, and if it took an insane story by her former housekeeper to convince the DA and the judge that there was new evidence that meant she could not have killed her family, then it is what it is.

CHAPTER 23

Sam arranged for Cal to take Rosa home and remain near her house for the rest of the night in case she decided to take a sudden trip. He would remain there until it was time for him to take her to Lee's office the following morning. Of course, Sam didn't mention the surveillance part to Rosa.

"I hope she doesn't climb out the window," Jill said. "Though I am convinced she thinks she saw Joel. I don't understand, but if she did see the . . . bodies, then this could be her way of coping. People are unique in finding ways to cope when they have been traumatized. It's my professional opinion this is what Rosa has been doing all these years to cope with her guilt."

"She seems so damned sure of what she saw. We all know it's impossible. I don't know if we, Lee and his team, will be able to convince her that she could not have seen what she says she saw. Sam," Tessa asked, "what do you make of her story?"

He rubbed the dark stubble on his cheeks. "She's convinced she saw what she says she did. She thinks she saw Joel, so it might be something worth checking into."

"You're not serious, I hope," Tessa barked.

"I am very serious, Tess. Tomorrow, we'll have more to work with. Harry's put the rush on the DNA, so we will have physical evidence if we can get a match on the bones. And remember the watch. Harry was able to get DNA from that as well."

"And we all know Joel's DNA will be on his watch. I can't see how that is going to prove anything other than that the watch belonged to him."

"It's not the DNA so much but the time the watch stopped, the date. And where and when the watch was located. I packed that myself, so I can testify to that if it comes down to it, but personally, neither Lee nor I think this will ever hit the courtroom a second time. Michael Chen is an ass, but for an ass, he's actually pretty smart. If his big, history-making case turns out to be a disaster, as it will since the victims were still alive after you had arrived in San Maribel, he'll find a way to use it to his advantage. Lee seems to believe he's going to make a run for governor."

"Sam, do you think Rosa is telling the truth? You said you packed Joel's watch yourself. It was in his desk. This was after his death. How do you explain that?"

Sam took a deep breath and pinched the bridge of his nose. "I can't."

"So what exactly does this mean? I know I'm wiped out, and you are as well, but I don't think any of us actually believes that Joel put that watch in his desk for you or anyone else to find. Given the significance of the date and time, it's impossible."

Tessa was so mentally drained, it was becoming hard for her to apply reason and logic to the facts as they were becoming available to them.

"You're probably right, Tess. But right now, I'm virtually certain that Lee can get your case tossed out; meanwhile, we will continue to dig deeper into what we find. I don't want to be a bummer, but I'm calling it a night. I have got to get up with the chickens, and that's not that much longer."

Sam stood and stretched. His shirt was untucked, and when he stretched, he revealed a muscular waist. Tessa tore her eyes away before he caught her looking.

"I need to get out of here myself. I've got a client early, and I can't reschedule, but I will cancel the rest of the week. I want to be here with you, this time, every step of the way," Jill said.

"You can stay here; there's plenty of room," Tessa said, hating to see her leave. Their friendship had picked up right where it left off, and despite the years, and Tessa's refusal of her letters and visits, it was just like old times. Easy and relaxed, with each knowing what the other thought before the words came out of her mouth.

"I know, and I will another time. Maybe tomorrow. I have a bit of reading to do when I get home, so I'll call it a night. I'll call you tomorrow as soon as I finish with my patient." She leaned in and gave Tessa a hug.

"Watch yourself when you leave. Those media whores are still hanging out by the gates," Tessa reminded her.

Jill laughed. "I'll watch for them, and if they give me any crap, I'll flip them the bird. That should give them something for tomorrow's front page."

Tessa laughed, too, and for the first time in a very, very long time, she felt just a moment's happiness. "I don't know if I'd go that far," she added.

"Of course I would never do that, but I did get a smile out of you," Jill said. "Are you okay? Seriously, do you think you're going to be able to deal with . . . everything?"

"I'm just grateful for the chance," Tessa said. "It was never going to be easy, I have realized that all along, but I want to do whatever I can to find . . . the person responsible." She wanted to say Liam, not the wishy-washy "person responsible," but she didn't for fear she would actually slip up and tell Jill what she was planning to do when she found the bastard. Even though she had no formal plans, they had to find him first. Then she would seriously begin to plan his death.

"I'll be here every step of the way," Jill said. "Now, I'm going to sneak out the back." She grabbed her giant tote bag, and Sam waited by the door.

"I'll walk you to your car," he said to Jill, then to Tessa, "Wait here."

She sat down on the sofa, totally exhausted. It was almost midnight. Another long day tomorrow, but she didn't care. She thought about Rosa and her absolute certainty that she had seen Joel running from the house. Covered in blood. It was so absurd, she couldn't believe Sam was actually considering looking into her claims.

Tessa felt sure the watch found in Joel's desk was . . . was what? Suddenly, she didn't know what she felt so sure of anymore. Granted, none of this made any sense whatsoever, but she remembered that day. *Horrified* hardly described her reaction to what she had seen, but she clearly remembered that when she had seen Joel's body by the pool's skimmer, something about it hadn't seemed right. It was Joel, she knew that, but she had always had a nagging thought that the man that was Joel, the bloated, decomposing Joel, had not been . . . *Joel.* Of course, scientifically, she knew why the body didn't appear to be her husband's body. The face was gone. Slashed so badly with the box cutter that the medical examiner's office had needed DNA to make an accurate identification. And, of course, the DNA was an exact match, so what was it about his body that had bothered her all these years?

Everything, of course — he was her husband, the father of her children. Their twin daughters. As though jarred by a jolt of lightning, Tessa had a flashback from a conversation she and Joel had had years ago. They'd been having dinner at a fancy restaurant. She was pregnant with the girls.

Tessa asked Joel if there were identical twins on his side of the family. Joel had seemed angry at her inquiry, but then he'd brushed it aside, telling her he personally didn't know of any twins, but she remembered he had said something about once having heard that there was a set a few generations before him.

Had she imagined his reaction to her question? Had he actually been angry? She didn't remember the exact tone of the conversation, so it's possible she was reading more into an old memory than she should.

But hadn't he acted strangely when they learned that they were having twins? Yes, she was sure he had, but then he had explained it away by telling her it was scary enough being a parent to one child, even more so to two at once. Those might not have been his exact words, but they were close. And he had been rattled when she asked him about it later. She didn't recall where the conversation had ended, but the discussion of twins had provoked Joel for some odd reason. Of course, once the girls were born, Joel was truly a devoted father. He changed diapers, helped with the 2:00 A.M. feedings, helped her bathe them.

Dear God, had he . . . No! She wouldn't even allow her thoughts to travel down that sick road. Joel had his faults, but he was a good father.

Sam opened the sliding door, and Tessa jumped. She placed her hand on her heart. "I am definitely jumpy tonight," she said, her voice sounding fake to her own ears. There was no way she would even consider sharing her thoughts about Joel with Sam.

"I think you're just tired. Let's call it a night, and tomorrow, we'll get a fresh start." Sam stretched again, and she looked away.

"Yes, I am bushed."

"I'll lock up and see you in the morning," Sam said.

"Thanks, Sam. For everything," Tessa said. "Night."

"Good night," he called out.

Tessa had planned to take a hot soak in the Jacuzzi tub, but she was too tired after the emotionally strenuous evening she had just been put through. She had showered earlier, and that would have to suffice. So she quickly washed her face. She brushed her teeth, reveling in the real toothbrush, not that flimsy excuse for one she had to use in prison, though she had to remind herself not to get too used to these things as there was no guarantee that she wasn't going to return to FCI, although the chances that she would seemed to be vanishing since Rosa's account of what had happened on Saturday, when her family was still alive.

CHAPTER 24

Tessa could not get to sleep. She looked at the clock for the hundredth time and saw it was just after 2:00 A.M. She had wanted to get a good night's rest, so she would be sharp tomorrow when she saw Rachelle for the first time since being sent to prison. She would need to be at her mental best as she planned to rake the woman over the coals, and then some. Tessa would know if she was lying. She had spent most of her youth with liars, so she knew one when she saw one. Rachelle might act like a grieving mother, but Tessa knew that she of all people would be able to see through her lies.

She rolled over, punched the pillow into a comfortable shape, and closed her eyes. She tried to calm her mind, focus on nothing, so that she could fall asleep, but it was impossible. So she let her thoughts take her wherever they might, and after a while, she drifted into a deep sleep.

Tessa wasn't sure how long she had been asleep when she was startled awake. Glancing at the bedside clock, she saw that it was after four. She sat up in bed, waiting to hear if what startled her awake would become evident. A thousand thoughts went through her mind. She propped herself up in the bed, pulling the covers up to her chest. Thinking a reporter might have sneaked onto the property, she considered waking up Sam, but she knew that the newly installed alarm system would be blaring had anyone actually managed to get onto the property.

It was probably her imagination. She was so used to being awakened at night in her cell, it was most likely a continuation of her experiences over the years in prison. She had never been a heavy sleeper anyway and hadn't ever really required much sleep. She remembered that Mama Shirley used to tell her she didn't need much sleep because she was a true genius, just like the inventor Thomas Edison, who only slept a couple of hours here and there, according to historians. She didn't agree. If only Mama Shirley had known then why she rarely slept, she wouldn't have been so quick to compare her nocturnal habits with those of the great inventor.

Glenn. That sleazy slimeball who called himself a foster father had spent much of his nights prowling through the house, making pit stops in her bedroom. She knew she should have told Shirley at the time, but all she had wanted to do was live there long enough to finish high school. She knew that having an education was her only way out of the life she did not want to live, so she tolerated the nighttime visits. He would touch her breasts and tell her she would make a good model for Victoria's Secret one day. Thankfully, though, it never went further than touching. Little had he known that her aspirations were much grander than wagging her tits and ass in front of a camera for the world to see. But she had kept quiet, and Glenn continued to visit her room until her senior year of high school, when she finally confronted him. She was not long from graduating from high school and had already received a scholarship, so at least she knew she had a head start on bettering her life. The last time Glenn had paid her a nightly visit, she was ready for him.

While she mostly kept to herself in school, she knew a few girls who were not honor students such as herself. She had never judged them for their wild, crazy behavior because she didn't know what their life circumstances were. She had learned the hard way how hurtful it was to be looked down upon for things beyond her control, so she tried not to judge others when the so-called good girls would turn up their noses at them.

It was at lunch one day, and she remembered it as though it had happened yesterday. Norrine Sellers was sitting alone at a table in the back of the cafeteria. She had dyed, witch-black hair, black nail polish, and deep purple lipstick. Short skirts and too-tight tops garnered her a great deal of attention from the boys in their senior class. Tessa had thought she was quite the character and knew that she wasn't the slut that most of the school thought she was. They'd shared lunch more than once, and Tessa liked Norrine, and she knew that Norrine felt the same about her. It was during lunch once that Tessa had told her about Glenn and his nighttime visits to her room. Why she had spilled this to her, she wasn't sure, but she had needed to tell someone, and Norrine did not judge her. In fact, she had told her she had been through the same thing with three of her mother's boyfriends. She had asked Tessa to meet her after school that day, promising to help with her "problem." At first, Tessa was afraid she might tell someone, but true to her word, they met at the Starbucks three blocks from the high school. Norrine had slipped a can of pepper spray into Tessa's bookbag. "The prick comes into your room, spray him in the face. I promise you that he will never do it again. And with any luck, just the threat will give him a heart attack. Then they'll boot his perverted ass out of the system, and there goes his income."

Norrine had been right. When Glenn sneaked into her room the next night, she was sitting up in bed, and, instead of wearing her nightgown, she was still wearing the clothes she had worn to school. When he eased himself down on the edge of her bed, she whipped the can of pepper spray out from behind her back, then with her other hand, she had switched on the light. "See this, Glenn? If I spray you in the face, Mama Shirley is going to wonder why you're in my bedroom getting your eyes burned out of your pissy little head. And I plan to tell her. And the state."

He had never said a word to her, then or after. He left her room and never returned. The day she graduated from high school, she returned the can of pepper spray to Norrine and thanked her for her help.

She knew that what she had been through

with Glenn was not normal. However, she had lived a rough life with her mother and Lara, and as she got older, she knew there were men who preyed on young girls. All this came back to her that Wednesday morning when Piper and Poppy told them that their uncle had touched them in their most private places. They were only ten years old, for God's sakes! Tessa had tried to keep their lives as normal and wholesome as possible, and once they were old enough to learn about good touch, bad touch, she explained in very simple terms what they were. And always told them if anyone, it didn't matter who it was, ever tried to touch them, that they were to come to her immediately. Sadly, that had not happened. There were no tears this time as she remembered her daughters' tragic deaths. Maybe it was because she knew in a matter of hours she would confront Rachelle, and she would learn of Liam's whereabouts.

And then she would begin to plan. She would need Lara's help. Sam had her phone number. She would call her and tell her she had to come to the house. It was a matter of life and death. And she had to add that there would be money involved. That alone would bring Lara to her. If there was money involved, she could always count on Lara to show up.

Tessa tried to close her eyes again, hoping for at least another hour's rest, but sleep would not come, so she said to hell with it, went to the kitchen in her pajamas, and made herself a cup of coffee. As she waited for the Keurig to do its thing, she prayed that the DA would realize that the evidence that her family was still alive on Saturday made it impossible for her to have killed them. After all this time, it was painful for her to think that the jurors who convicted her actually believed a mother, *she,* could commit the crimes she was charged with. Had she looked that unsympathetic as she had sat at the defense table?

She didn't know the answer, as she was sure she had been in a complete state of shock. Her arrest, then the trial, which was only two weeks after her arrest, a fact she later learned was unusual, given the court's backlog, was the result of incredibly sloppy police work. How could she have killed people on Friday if they were still alive on Saturday? True, Rosa never came forward to tell her story, but how could a coroner mistake a Saturday time of death for a Friday time of death? Once they decided that she was the murderer, did they even bother to ascertain the time of death? Since she was on the mainland all day Saturday, she had to have committed the murders on Friday, to their way of thinking. Ergo, the victims were killed on Friday, and who needed to waste time on establishing scientifically when they were killed? They had to have been killed on Friday since she killed them.

Someone had wanted her out of the way, and she just knew that someone was Liam Jamison. And in only a few hours, she would finally have the opportunity to tell his mother how much she hated him and that it was her life's mission to find him. Tessa knew enough not to let on about her plans for Liam, but she would let Rachelle see what the years had done to her. She wasn't even fifty years old and knew that anyone looking at her would add ten years to her age, maybe even more.

"I take it you couldn't sleep either," Sam said as he entered the kitchen.

She had heard his footsteps on the stairs, so his appearance in the kitchen didn't surprise her.

"Not much," she said, taking her cup of coffee and sitting on the barstool.

He made himself a cup of coffee, and she couldn't help but admire him. She was a female. He must have showered — his dark hair was still wet — and she could detect a woodsy scent coming from him. He wore a pair of navy slacks with a white shirt, un-tucked, and buttoned only halfway. He was sexy and handsome, and why she had never really noticed this before, she had no clue. Handsome men hadn't been her priority.

"Darlene sent me a text message a while ago. Told me to tell you there was a dress and ankle boots in the closet, and the boots would cover your ankle monitor. Said they were in a box from Zappos."

"Zappos?"

"Darlene says it's the world's largest shoe store."

Tessa smiled. "I'd like to meet Darlene sometime, before . . . well, if I return to prison, I'd like to thank her for all that she's done for me."

"You are not going back to prison. You could not have killed people on Friday who were still alive on Saturday. You'll meet her today. She's going to meet us in Lee's of-fice. Darlene works part-time as a legal stenographer for Lee and a couple of other local attorneys. Gives her extra money for her grandsons, or at least that is what she tells me. Personally, I think Darlene is a workaholic, in a good way."

"I like her already."

"She's good people," Sam said. "Jamison Pharmaceuticals was lucky to hire her."

"No doubt," Tessa said, then went on. "Sam, what Rosa said about seeing Joel running from the house that day. Can we talk about this now? I was going to talk to Jill, given her profession, but I don't think this requires a professional opinion."

He brought his coffee to the bar and sat next to her. "Of course, Tess. You can tell me anything."

She nodded. "I'm just not sure where to start."

"The beginning always works for me."

"Of course." She wasn't sure what Sam would think of her after she told him her thoughts, but it didn't matter. This needed to be said, and she didn't want to wait until Jill's visit. "When Joel and I first married, we had what you would call a whirlwind romance. It felt right at the time, or at least I thought so. I still do, but there were times when Joel acted, I don't even know what word to use. Angry. And sometimes, he could be cruel. I remember when I was pregnant with the girls, I was just a few months along." She stopped, as this was still a bit embarrassing, but she was a big girl now. "Joel would laugh at me when I undressed, telling me I looked like a starving

298

Ethiopian. I told him how that offended me, and he said he hadn't meant to, but I think he did. Another time, right around this same time, he implied that I was way too fat for a woman to be in such early stages of pregnancy. Of course, I had no one to compare to. This really bothered me, and from that point on, I tried not to eat much in front of him, and I didn't undress unless he was out of the room or the lights were off." She took a sip of her now-cool coffee, got up, tossed it in the sink, then started brewing a second cup. "You want another?" she asked, and took the cup he held out to her. She finished brewing the coffee and returned to her seat.

"I have never been married, but I could see how this would hurt your feelings; you're bearing the man's children. I would think he would adore the changes."

Tessa blushed when he said this. "He didn't. It wasn't those things that bothered me so much. It was the twin thing. When I found out I was pregnant with identical twin girls, Joel was not happy. Not at all. He tried to act like he was, but I knew that he wasn't. When I confronted him, he told me he was just overwhelmed at the thought of becoming a father, and the prospect of twins, he said it was double the anxiety."

"Okay," Sam said. "I would imagine it

would come as a bit of a shock to anyone, but in a good way."

"I was thrilled. I wanted a family of my own so badly. I hadn't had anything like the best upbringing, as I'm sure you know. I wanted to be the best mother in the world, and I made myself a promise that I would never let anyone mistreat my children and that they would always be my first priority. Even before Joel."

"I think most mothers feel that way. Mine devoted her life to me; you know, I was an only child. My parents were older when they had me, but I was their world. When they died while I was in college, it totally brought me to my knees. They were the best. So I do understand the girls being top priority in your life."

"I didn't know, Sam. I am so sorry."

"There was no need for you to know."

She shrugged, not sure if that was the case. As the wife of the owner of Jamison Pharmaceuticals, she should have made it her business to at least get to know the company CEO and others who held high positions in the company.

"How well did you know Joel? In college, I mean? He said you were best friends, but I never really questioned his past."

Sam chewed on his bottom lip and took a

sip of coffee. "We were dorm mates, but I wouldn't say we were best friends. I was older by three years. When my parents died, I wasn't sure what to do with my life, so I stayed in school, lived in the dorm, even though my parents left their entire, quite substantial, estate to me. I didn't want to be alone. Joel was . . . quiet. Studied hard, wanted to go to work for his father. He was odd in some ways, and he had always had a bit of a temper."

"What do you mean by odd?"

"This is just my opinion, Tess. I roomed with him, and we were young. He would bring girls to the dorm, and he didn't have to, either. He was well funded, so he could have lived in an apartment. But he liked bringing girls to the dorm. I think a lot of them were much younger than he was. He would always try to impress them, and when they didn't appear impressed with his life, his cars, his bank account, all of his material possessions, he dumped them. And I do not mean that he just never asked them out again. No, he told them to get out. He threw them out. A few times I saw him smack a girl around."

Tessa didn't know what she had expected from Sam, but whatever it was, it certainly was not this.

"You're saying he was violent?"

"He could be when things didn't go his way," Sam said. "Was he ever violent with you or the girls?"

Tessa shook her head. "No, not physically. He was good at tossing crude comments here and there, but nothing that truly offended me other than the starving Ethiopian comment. After his father died, he said he had a lot of responsibilities. I thought he needed to vent, and being his wife, I was the recipient of his occasional ranting."

"Why do I feel like there is more? What are you not telling me, Tess?"

CHAPTER 25

"I keep thinking what Rosa said about seeing Joel running from the house. And that other man she said looked like him. I know it's not possible, but did he ever mention anything to you about . . . having a twin?" There. She had said it.

Sam seemed to give serious consideration to her question. "I think he would have told me if he had. That's a major detail to leave out when you're sharing a dorm room. Are you telling me that you believe there is some merit to what Rosa's been telling us?"

"I don't think so, but it certainly seems odd. When I found Joel, and the girls, I was hysterical, I know that now. But I remembered thinking that the body in the pool wasn't Joel's. To be sure, the face was unidentifiable, and I am trained in the pharmaceutical field and have some medical knowledge. The case against me said that I killed my family two days before, on

Friday. Decomposition, the water, I have taken all this into consideration. I have gone over that day a million times, and every time I come to the conclusion there was something odd about . . . the body. Something just did not seem right."

"In what way, other than the obvious?"

"Joel was tanned, a golden color, you know how he swam, always seemed to have the perfect tan people strive for?"

"Yes, he did like to swim and get in his daily dose of sun," Sam agreed.

"The body in the pool was pale, the skin looked like it hadn't seen the sun in . . . forever. Is it possible that . . . hell, I probably sound like a crazy woman myself. Look, forget this. I need to get a shower, get ready to meet Lee."

"We can discuss this later, Tess. We need to," Sam told her.

She nodded, rinsed out her coffee cup, then headed down the hall to the bathroom. She showered, then found a pretty floral dress with the matching beige ankle boots Darlene had mentioned. She slipped the boots on, and while the top part of her ankle monitor was exposed, the bulky part slid into the leather easily and was not too tight or uncomfortable. She returned to the bathroom, where she used some of the cosmetics Darlene had picked out.

Tessa looked at her image and did not like what she saw. Her skin was too pale, and there were too many wrinkles where they shouldn't be. Her hair was too long, and mostly silver instead of the honey blond of her past. She used the light foundation that matched her skin perfectly. Amazed at what a difference it made, she used the peach blush to add color to her face.

"Not bad for a convicted murderer just out of prison," she said out loud, knowing the words were for her ears alone. She used a taupe-colored eye shadow, then added a soft brown liner to her top lids. Deep black mascara on her top and bottom lashes caused her to gasp when she looked in the mirror. A tube of lipstick in the shade *sunny* completed her face makeup. Had she not known herself, she wouldn't have recognized the image staring back at her. Seeing what an improvement the makeup gave her, she twisted her long hair into a topknot and secured it with bobby pins. She almost could imagine the woman she used to be, of course, minus the wrinkles and silver hair. Smacking her lips together to set her lipstick, she returned to her room to get the small clutch purse that, of course, the ever-thoughtful Darlene had provided. Tessa couldn't wait to meet this kind, caring woman. She would see to it that she was financially taken care of in a very big way. Her grandsons would be provided with an Ivy League education; she would discuss the details with Sam later. At least she could use Joel's fortune, *her* fortune now, in a positive way.

She went to the kitchen, which was the most popular room in the house, and peered out the window while she brewed her third cup of coffee. There were two local news media vans parked behind the gates, but the big networks had obviously found another story to report on.

"Wow," Sam whispered when he entered the kitchen.

Tessa stepped away from the window, looked at Sam, and smiled. "Wow yourself." And she meant it. He wore a suit better than any man she had ever known, including Joel. Sam was broad-shouldered where Joel was lean and lanky. Sam was also taller than Joel.

"You look beautiful, Tess."

"It is an improvement. I saw that myself. Darlene thought of everything. I want to thank her. Sam, is there a way for me to set up an education fund for her grandsons? A lifetime income for her as well? I want to use all those millions for something good, at least while I can."

He laughed, and his entire face changed. The word *handsome* did not do him justice. "I think that can be arranged, though it's quite a big price tag for someone who just made sure you had all those girly things you needed."

"No, it's more than that. For the first time since the trial, I feel like a real person instead of a convicted murderer. It's not always the big things that matter, at least to me. I want to show my gratitude."

"Normally, I would ask Darlene to get the ball rolling, but I'll take care of this myself. Now, if you're ready, we can head over to Lee's office. I have already taken the liberty of contacting those who need to know that you're traveling to your attorney's office today."

She had almost forgotten about that. "I didn't even think about it. Thanks for covering my rear." Her face reddened, and Sam laughed.

"No worries, Tess. I've got you covered."

"How many times can I thank you? Now, I have another question: How are we going to get out of here with the media following us?"

"A member of your security is waiting in the garage now. He's been there for a while."

"Maybe that's the noise I heard this morning. I was sleeping soundly, then something woke me up."

"You didn't tell me that earlier."

"I'm used to noise at night. The prison was at its worst then. I probably thought I was back there and imagined I heard something," she insisted.

"Okay then, if you're ready, let's get out of here," Sam suggested. She went out the kitchen door that led to the garage, just as she had always done when she had lived here with her family, and saw a black Mercedes parked in the garage with a man in the driver's seat.

Five minutes later, they were speeding out of the gates, the members of the press apparently too interested in their early-morning coffee to pay them much notice.

"Dave, this is Tessa Jamison. Dave is a retired Secret Service agent."

"Good to meet you, ma'am," Dave said in a pleasant voice.

"Nice to meet you, too, and I appreciate you getting up so early to take us to Lee's office."

"My pleasure, ma'am."

She wanted to tell him he didn't have to refer to her as "ma'am," but given his former profession, she guessed it was a lifelong habit.

Once they had disembarked from the ferry and were on the mainland, it was a straight shot to the courthouse, the sheriff's department, the police department, and the federal courthouse.

"Where is Lee's office? I never even thought to ask," she said, as Dave weaved in and out of several side streets before parallel parking in front of a high-rise condo that overlooked the Caloosahatchee River. Prime real estate, she knew.

"In the penthouse," Sam said. "He owns the building."

She raised her brows. Lee was obviously a very good attorney; at least he'd achieved financial success. Inside, the foyer was plush, decorated in a Florida motif, pale greens and blues with light oak walls. Giant plants, all native to Florida, were placed strategically throughout the room, giving the area old Key West vibes.

She followed Sam to a private elevator. "Is this Lee's very own Trump Tower?" she asked, as they took the elevator up to the penthouse.

"I don't think he'd compare himself to Trump, but he does well for himself. And he has been very generous with his own money, having become very involved in funding cancer research. Just about devoted his life to it."

Tessa considered that quite a noble undertaking but kept her thoughts to herself as the elevator doors swished open, not giving her the chance to speak her mind even if she had wanted to.

Suddenly, she realized she was about to confront the mother of the man who'd wiped out her family. Her hands began to shake, and she felt sick to her stomach. She reached for Sam's arm. "Is there a ladies' room?"

"This way." He took her hand and led her down a short hallway. "In here."

She nodded, ran inside, and found an open stall. Entering the stall, she proceeded to empty herself of the morning's coffee. Before getting up to use the sink, she took several deep breaths, hoping to overcome the waves of nausea that had sent her into the bathroom in the first place. Using a piece of toilet tissue to blot her mouth, she waited until she felt stable enough before standing up and going to the sink. She should have stayed behind, she thought, and let Lee and Sam deal with Rachelle. But, no, she reminded herself, she had decided that she had to do this for Piper, Poppy, and Joel. At the sink, she took a paper towel and ran it under cold water, blotting her face and neck. She had read somewhere that placing a cool cloth on one's neck and wrists could stave off nausea.

She turned on the tap and let the cool water splash against her wrists. She rinsed her mouth out, wishing she had a mint or a piece of gum. She wasn't sure how long she had already been in the ladies' room, but she took a few extra seconds and reapplied her lipstick.

She was good at hiding things. No way did she want Rachelle to think she was frightened of her. When she stepped out of the ladies' room, she found the ever-faithful Sam still waiting. The man was really a gem.

"I was about to come in after you. Are you all right?"

She nodded. "Just a bout of nerves, I'm fine now."

"Lee's waiting with Rachelle. And Cal brought Rosa in, too, so we're all where we need to be. Are you sure you're all right?"

Tessa stopped and faced him. "Do I look all right? I mean, do I seem . . . nervous? I don't want that evil woman to think she's intimidating me."

"You look great, Tess, and I'd be nervous, too. You'll be fine. Remember, I'm here with you, and Lee is on your side." Sam held her close to him. Tessa thought she could stay in his arms forever, but she knew that was crazy. She had the sudden realization that she was *attracted* to Sam! Of all the times to have this . . . epiphany, now was not the time. In fact, it would never be the right time.

He eased her out of his arms. "Come on," he said softly. "They're waiting for us."

She nodded and let him guide her to Lee's office. He tapped on the door, a beautiful dark wood double door with elaborate carvings up and down its frame. When Tessa stepped into his office, it stunned her. A billiard table in the same dark wood as the door was in the center of the room. On the other side of the table was a wet bar, which was really a small kitchen. To her left was a giant desk, again, made of the same dark wood as the door and the billiard table. Surrounding the desk were half a dozen upholstered chairs constructed of the same wood, with cream-colored cloth that looked to be actual velvet. The wall behind Lee, who was seated at the desk, was floor-to-ceiling glass, giving one a spectacular view of the river.

Lee stood when they walked across the room toward him. He was dressed casually, in dark jeans and a light brown turtleneck beneath a tweed jacket. No pink, she thought.

"Tessa, you look wonderful this morning. I take it that both of you had a good night's rest?" Lee said, though Tessa noticed his voice was much more formal today.

"I slept well, thank you," Tessa replied, imitating the formal quality of his remark.

"Have a seat, please," Lee invited, gesturing to the plush chairs in a semicircle around his desk. "You want coffee? I have ordered pastries in case either of you are hungry."

Food was the last thing on her mind. She wanted to see Rachelle and get it over with. She had spent years fantasizing about such a meeting, and now that her fantasy was about to turn into reality, she didn't want to wait another minute.

"Where is Rachelle?" she asked. Tessa didn't care if she sounded rude. She did not want to wait for the meeting to begin any longer than necessary.

"Harry has her in another room. He's getting a DNA sample. Said he wanted to do it himself. Michael Chen is with him. A chain-of-evidence thing; a couple deputies, too. We don't want the slightest implication of impropriety. Remember the OJ Simpson case? I thought it best to get this over with beforehand."

Tessa breathed a sigh of relief. Lee really was top-notch. She was right to put her trust in him. "Yes, I suppose it's best to get things moving. Did Harry say how long before he has results?" Tessa was beyond anxious.

"At least twenty-four hours," Lee said. "That's working around the clock, which Harry will do. He's the best there is, and I wouldn't trust anyone else to undertake this . . . delicate operation."

"Where's that coffee?" Sam asked. "I need a jolt of caffeine."

"Minibar," Lee said.

Sam brought back two cups of coffee. She took a cup, and though it smelled divine, she didn't want to chance another stomach upset. She passed it on to Lee.

"How long before Harry finishes?" Sam asked Lee what Tessa wanted to ask.

"Anytime now, I would imagine," Lee responded. "They have been in there at least half an hour already."

Tessa felt like she was at trial all over again. The waiting. The nervousness that erupted into nausea, the fear of the un-known. However, this time around, she knew what she would be facing if somehow, some way, what they had already discovered, and whatever additional evidence they obtained was not sufficient to have the DA withdraw the charges against her or overcome the evidence that led to the first verdict if the case went to trial. Yes, in the worst-case scenario, she would have a new trial, according to Lee and Florida's Supreme Court, but a new trial was worth nothing if there was no new evidence to convince the jury that they should return a not guilty verdict the second time around. It all depended upon Rosa's story being accepted.

"How's Chen's attitude?" Sam asked. "He ready to blow a fuse or what?"

"Actually, quite the opposite. He's reviewed Poppy's artwork and agrees with Jill's assessment that she was most likely abused, molested." Lee looked at Tessa with sorrow in his eyes. "And he's wondering why the bones weren't found during the police investigation."

"Because there was no *investigation,*" Tessa told him. "They were after me and didn't listen to anything I told them. They tried and convicted me without a single piece of physical evidence. They went so far as not to bother to determine that my family had actually been killed on Saturday, when I could not have been the killer, rather than before I left the island on Friday."

Tessa found she could actually say the word *evidence* without cringing; though it bothered her and always would, it was necessary to say the word because that is what would clear her name. Or not.

Voices from behind her forced her to turn around.

"I got everything I need, Lee. I'm taking it to the lab now, with these kind deputies who have nothing better to do than follow me around. I'm rushing this. I'm going to do a test, I won't go into all the details, but it's quick and should give us answers by the end of the day," Harry informed everyone in the room. He carried with him three paper bags, which appeared to be sealed with evidence tape. Tessa saw writing on the bags but wasn't able to distinguish what the labels said.

"I appreciate this, Harry. You've got my cell-phone number. Call the second you know anything. Anything at all." Lee stepped out from behind his desk and followed Harry and the two deputies to the door.

When they were out of the room, another door opened, and Tessa was taken aback when she saw Rachelle. Where once Rachelle would have been considered gorgeous, with her slim build, but curvaceous in all the right places, long dark hair, and turquoise-colored eyes, she did not look at all like the woman Tessa remembered. Her hair was cut very short, striped with gray, her unique-colored eyes were bloodshot, and she had gained at least fifty pounds. No, Rachelle was not the stunner Tessa recalled from the past. If anything, she looked like an aging older woman who hadn't quite kept herself together.

"Tessa," she said in her heavy Southern accent. "I'm sorry, honey. I hate meeting like this, but . . . well, we both want answers."

Never in a million years had Tessa expected Rachelle to be so . . . kind. She had planned to launch a tirade the moment she laid eyes on her, but now, she was so taken aback, not only by her physical appearance but her kind words, and they were so sincere. Either that, or she was the best damned actress alive.

And it was this final thought that gave Tessa the courage she needed to speak. "I have been rotting in a prison cell waiting for answers. I have been plotting what I will do to your low-life, piece-of-garbage son if I was ever fortunate enough to have the opportunity. It looks like maybe the Florida Supreme Court has finally given me the opportunity."

Her heart was beating fast, and she felt a bit of the nausea she had experienced earlier, but she didn't care. She had fantasized about this moment, and no matter how Rachelle appeared, she was not going to let it pass without saying what she truly believed.

Rachelle just sat there, nodding, tears rolling down her face.

"Don't you have anything to say? An excuse? Your poor little son has been missing all these years. That is utter bullshit, and we both know it. Don't we?" Tessa said, her voice rising as the verbal blasts poured out of her.

"Lee, you need to have your client calm down," Michael Chen said, finally speaking.

Tessa hadn't paid him any attention once she had set her gaze on Rachelle. Now, however, she looked at him and saw that he was pretty much the same greaseball he had been more than ten years ago, during her trial. If he'd aged, it only showed in the graying hair, or at least what little hair he had. He was still fat, and she would swear that she smelled the same sour-onion miasma from all those years ago as he stood by her table at the trial.

"I think my client has the right to speak

her mind. This isn't a trial, Michael. Just us. Sit down, and let's allow Tessa and Rachelle to talk to one another before we get formal." Lee put extra emphasis on the word *talk*.

Before taking a seat, Michael Chen helped himself to a number of pastries from the platter on the table and a large mug of coffee. *No wonder he's so overweight,* Tessa thought. He'd piled enough pastries on his plate for at least five people. He disgusted her. She hadn't liked him at trial, and she didn't see that changing now, regardless of how agreeable he might be. Still, since whether or not she had to go through another trial might well depend upon his decision, she was in no position to come out and say anything that might antagonize him. She would try as best she could to be polite to this man, whom she despised and for whom she had no respect whatsoever.

"We're all civilized people, here, right, Mrs. Jamison? Mrs. Jamison?" Michael Chen looked at Rachelle, then Tessa.

Tessa felt dirty just being in the same room with the pig, but it's something she had to tolerate if she wanted justice for herself and the opportunity to get justice for her family. She wanted to tell him that she had lived with uncivilized women for almost a fifth of her life but knew it wouldn't win any brownie points, so she kept her thoughts to herself.

"Some of us are," Sam answered.

Tessa wanted to give him a huge smile, or a thumbs-up sign, anything to let Sam know she was grateful for those four little words.

"Well, well, Mr. McQuade, you are quite the aggressor this morning, aren't you? I thought we were here to . . . chat. To examine that new evidence you're all so excited about. Personally, I'm not one hundred percent sure it will matter, but I am the district attorney, and it is my duty to the citizens of Lee County to see that justice is served, no matter what my personal opinion is."

Michael Chen took a huge bite from one of his pastries, crumbs from which fell on his dingy white shirt, which looked as if it hadn't been washed since it came out of the package.

"Let's not start arguing. We're all here for a reason. Rachelle, if you wouldn't mind, as soon as Darlene sets up, I'm going to ask you a few questions, and Tessa as well, just for the record. Are you both okay with that?"

Tessa turned around and saw Darlene for the first time. The woman was petite, with pure white hair worn in a fashionable pageboy and dark eyes. She looked as professional as a woman could. She was wearing black slacks with a frilly red blouse and matching red flats and just enough makeup to enhance her features. *Classy* was the word that came to mind. She and Jill were on the same page, fashion-wise. Tessa smiled at her, and Darlene smiled back. "That dress looks lovely on you, Miss Tessa."

"Thank you, Darlene. I can't tell you how grateful I am for all that you have done for me."

"Ladies," Lee interrupted. "There will be time to get to know one another later. Sorry, Darlene."

"No need to apologize, Mr. Lee. I am here to work, but I do think that floral print looks quite lovely on Miss Tessa. Now that I have seen her wearing it, I just wanted to tell her how lovely she is. Right, Mr. Sam?" She winked at Tessa.

"Darlene, I know what you're doing, but let's get business out of the way first," Lee said, but he could not avoid grinning from ear to ear. They were all grinning, except for Michael Chen, who continued to smack his lips together and let crumbs dribble from his three chins to the small Mount Everest that passed as his stomach.

"Right, Darlene. You did a fantastic job.

You and Tess can talk later," Sam agreed.

"Of course," Darlene said. She had her stenographic machine set up by then and sat beside Lee, indicating she was ready to get started. During all this, Rachelle hadn't said a word.

"Rachelle, state your full name for the record," Lee began.

Rachelle did as instructed, with Tessa following suit. Once the basic identity questions were out of the way, Lee began in earnest.

"Rachelle, tell me the last time you saw your son, Liam Jamison," Lee asked.

"I saw Liam around the end of April of two thousand and eleven," she answered, but her voice quivered as if she were about to burst into tears.

Tessa wasn't sure she bought this sob story, but she listened, and she watched. She knew firsthand how a grieving mother behaved.

"Where did you see him in April?" Lee asked.

"He came to my house in Miami. We spent the day together." She stopped then. "Had I known that was the last time I'd see him . . . I would have told him how much I loved him, and that his father had loved him as much. But we had lunch and chitchatted, pretty much like we always did when he was in town."

"What do you mean by in town?"

"He lived in San Maribel. He wanted to be close to Joel. He idolized his older brother, wanted to be just like him. He used to tell me this when he was little, but frankly, I prayed he would never grow up to act like his older brother."

"You bitch," Tessa shouted.

"Tessa! Enough," Lee said in a stern voice she had never heard him employ before.

"Don't chastise her, Lee. The man was her husband, the father of her little girls. I understand how she must feel. But she didn't know Joel the way I did. The way Liam did. And she did not know Grant, the boy's father. He died before she ever met Joel."

Rachelle seemed . . . well, motherly, Tessa thought. She was an excellent actress; she would give her credit for that.

"Tessa, you need to refrain from commenting on Rachelle's testimony. This will most likely be on the record if we go to trial, so let's try to be as civil as we can," Lee said to her, his voice softening a bit.

"Sorry," was all she said. She had embarrassed herself, but she couldn't just sit here and let Rachelle bad-mouth Joel. She knew he wasn't perfect, but it was tough to hear about his faults from someone else.

"That last day you saw Liam, how did he seem to you? Worried? Anxious? Anything unusual about his behavior?" Lee resumed his questions.

Rachelle sighed. "He was troubled by something. I knew it, and asked him about it, but he said he was going to take care of it himself. I know that sounds horrible, given what happened, but it's what he said to me. I tried to get him to talk to me, thinking that whatever had been troubling him, I could help him with. He just said it would . . . I think he said, and this isn't exactly word for word, but he said something about 'changing the family dynamic.' "

The room was quiet; no one said anything.

Lee leaned on an elbow, cupping his chin in his hand. Michael Chen suddenly seemed more interested in Rachelle's words than the last pastry on his plate. "You never told this to me," he said to Rachelle.

"You didn't ask me about that visit, Mr. Chen," Rachelle reminded him. "Neither did the police. We mostly discussed Tessa and her past. Remember?"

Tessa was seething but kept her feelings and thoughts to herself.

"I don't recall us just discussing Mrs. Jamison's past. There were many other topics, and, of course, we have your testimony from the trial," Chen said.

"We're not going to get anything resolved if you're going to argue like kids on a playground. Rachelle, I have a few more questions, then Mr. Chen may ask whatever he needs to," Lee said to them.

"Back to that last day when Liam came to your house for lunch. When you said he seemed troubled, and that possibly whatever was troubling him might change the family dynamic, do you think he was referring to Joel and his family?" Lee asked.

Tessa observed Darlene's fingers as they moved at breakneck speed across the strange-looking stenographic machine.

"Yes," Rachelle said, her voice firm with conviction.

"Was he upset with Joel? The girls? Tessa?" Lee questioned.

"He didn't say. Just that he was troubled. He left later that evening, and I assume he went straight to his condo in San Maribel. That is the last time I saw my son. I am a mother. I would know if Liam committed this heinous act. Liam was a ladies' man, I know that, but I know for a fact that my son did not have a mean bone in his body. He loved his family, his nieces. He told me many times how cool he thought it was that Joel had twins. Once he asked me if I thought he would have twins when and if, he added, that I do recall, because we both laughed, if he ever married. I told him there was the possibility because twins ran in Grant's family. I believe his grandfather was a twin. Identical. Yes, I am sure Grant told me that at some point."

More silence.

"Tessa, did Joel ever mention that his . . . it would be his great-grandfather, was a twin?"

"No," she said. "When we found out I was expecting twins and that they were identical, I asked him, but he said there must be twins somewhere in his family because we were expecting them. I would remember if he said his great-grandfather was an identical twin." Tessa turned to Rachelle. "Did Joel know this?"

"I'm sure he did," Rachelle replied. "At one point, Joel became very involved in genealogy. He'd even mentioned to Grant that the company should gear some of their funds toward a genetics program."

"Tessa, you're sure Joel never told you this? Any of it, the genealogy, his interest in the subject?" Lee questioned.

"I would have remembered. I had identical twins, so it was a topic he and I discussed quite often, as you can imagine. He never even hinted that his great-grandfather was a twin, let alone an identical twin."

Tessa was beginning to wonder if she had really known her husband at all.

CHAPTER 26

Sam looked at Tessa, and she smiled even though she wanted to run out of the room and scream until she could no longer talk. To run as fast as she could and go as far away as humanly possible. Hundreds of images assaulted her, and she could not stop them from overwhelming her.

"Do you need a minute, Tess?" Sam asked. "You don't look too hot right now."

That comment brought her front and center to the present. "Thanks, I'm okay." She wasn't and she knew that Sam knew it, but she had to get through this because, she realized, she did not want to go back to prison. No matter how much she told herself that it didn't matter where she lived, now it did. Now she had a reason to go on. A reason that could bring her happiness if she allowed it, and right then and there, she knew that she would, and she would do whatever was necessary to stay out of prison. Legally. She could no more hunt Liam down and kill him than she could sit in this room now and slaughter Rachelle and Michael Chen. The thought was so far off that, for a second, she wondered if she had lost her mind, albeit, temporarily. Hunting down Liam Jamison like he was an animal would not bring back her daughters. Or Joel. And if Joel was alive, she would tell him that she thought he was a horrible husband and that he should have spent more time with Poppy and Piper. All these were just what-ifs, hypotheticals that would not amount to a hill of beans.

Though she needed much more than a minute, she kept that to herself. "No, I'm okay." Right.

"I can't believe Joel didn't tell you this," Rachelle said, her eyes filling up with tears.

She sounded truly surprised. Tessa was beginning to have a hard time believing that the woman was acting. She seemed to be genuinely sad. Grief-stricken, in fact.

"While I can't recall the exact time when Grant told me, I do know that he did. There wasn't much that Grant didn't talk about. He was a talker, and I enjoyed his stories. I encouraged him to write them down, but he never had time. He knew quite a bit about his family, and Lois's family, too, what there was of it anyway. Poor woman."

"Who is Lois?" Tessa asked, not caring that she was interrupting Rachelle's story.

All eyes turned to her. She began to feel like a pinned butterfly on a board. "What?" she asked. She hated this, wished she had never agreed to meet Rachelle here in this office, where there was no place to run and hide. She should've made them come to the house; at least there, she could run and hide.

"Darlene, we're finished here. You can stop. Michael, are you good with this?" Lee asked. "It seems pretty obvious that Tessa knows nothing, as you can see. I think Joel blindsided her."

"I do see where you're headed, and for once, we're on the same page. As soon as you have hard evidence, DNA, I'll go to Judge Crider," Chen said.

Darlene closed her machine and folded it into a small case. "Am I dismissed?" she asked sweetly.

"Shit, Darlene, you can do whatever you want," Lee said.

Tessa was surprised at his use of profanity in this setting. "Will someone tell me what I'm missing here because I am completely clueless," she asked the room in general. "What is going on?"

"Let me," Rachelle said. "Tessa, Lois was

Joel's mother."

Tessa nodded; she knew he had a mother. Of course he had a mother. Everyone has a mother. It's where we all come from. "He never told me her name. He would get upset when I asked about her, so I stopped asking."

"Of course he would be upset. When Lois died, Joel was at home with her. I think he was twelve. Grant said . . . never mind." Rachelle stopped.

"Please, Rachelle. We're way past keeping secrets from one another. What were you going to say?" Tessa pushed. "I need to hear whatever it is."

"No one was ever charged in her death, but Grant always suspected that Joel knew more about his mother's death than he told him."

"What?" Saying that she was stunned would not even begin to describe what she was feeling. "What are you trying to say, Rachelle?"

"I guess it doesn't really matter at this point since all of them are gone. I believe Liam is dead, too. He would never have run away, and if he had, he would find a way to contact me. He was my life. I know you all think he's still out there somewhere, but he isn't. Liam had many faults, but he was a good son and would never put me through this . . . hell that I have been through since he disappeared.

"Died. I suppose I should say it aloud. Makes it more real to me. I knew he'd never come back to me the day I found out about the girls. I hoped I was wrong, but a mother knows these things. Doesn't like to admit them, but it's been so very long ago. I just pray he's in heaven with his father and those precious girls."

It was obvious to Tessa that Rachelle hadn't mentioned Joel in the heavenly sense.

"Tess, Joel's mother fell down a staircase when he was twelve. There were suspicions back then, but they have never been confirmed." Sam stood behind her chair and placed his hands on her shoulders, squeezing them in a reassuring way.

"This is all so unbelievable. I don't know, I didn't know how his mother died. Joel told me that she had died in a tragic accident; I'm sure those were his words. I guess I just assumed she had died in a car accident or . . . I don't know what I thought. He never wanted to talk about her. Or about his father."

"Lee, call me when you have something concrete about this and after this Rosa woman takes and passes the polygraph test.

Obviously, if the girls and the adult male were still alive on Saturday, Mrs. Jamison, Tessa, could not have killed them on Friday. I feel like wringing the coroner's neck for this. Anyway, I'll keep my word and go to Crider. I'll let you all solve the family mystery. For now."

Michael Chen hefted his bulk from the chair, leaned across Lee's desk, shook his hand, then came up behind Tessa's chair where Sam stood, and shook his hand, too. Tessa smelled that rotten-onion odor emanating from his body. She wanted to throw up but took several deep breaths as soon as he stepped away.

"I'll hold you to that," Lee said before Chen left.

As soon as he was out of the room, Sam spoke. "Does that man ever take a shower?"

"I don't believe he even knows that they exist," Darlene said, with a giant grin on her face. "Miss Tessa, I look forward to seeing more of you in the future. Something tells me between Mr. Lee and Sam, you'll get a second chance. Now, I have just a bit more Christmas shopping to do for those grandsons of mine, so if you all need me, call me on the cell phone. I'll be at the mall." With that announcement, Darlene practically floated out of the room.

Tessa was unsure why they'd had the meeting with Chen. What, if anything, had the state gained by her and Rachelle's conversation? It wasn't as formal as Lee had expected it to be, that was more than obvious.

But then she realized that before she and Sam arrived, Lee must have told him about Rosa's story and the polygraph test she was going to take. That is the only way he could know that the people she supposedly murdered on Friday were still alive on Saturday, when she was on the mainland the entire day.

"I have a feeling the second Harry comes up with something 'concrete,' as Chen put it, he'll go to Crider and ask for a dismissal of all charges," Lee said with a grin.

"But beyond Rosa's story, we have nothing at this point," Tessa said, "except for Poppy's drawings, do we? While I think that's more than enough to show she was being abused, are you that confident he'll do what he says?"

"I am," Lee said. "He's a big show-off, but his legal career is his life. He would not allow new evidence to go unnoticed."

"I'm not so sure," Tessa said. "Remember where I have spent the past ten, almost eleven years? He convicted an innocent woman without even bothering to listen to my story. Why should I or any of you trust him now?"

"She's right, Lee. He's a swine," Sam said.

"In the true sense of the word for sure, but I have a feeling he knows he's screwed up on this case. Big-time. And in one sense, it might not even be his fault. Yes, the investigation was about as slipshod as one can find. But he is not the person who decided that the murders took place on Friday, when Tessa could have committed them, rather than Saturday, when she could not have. And he is not the one who identified the adult male as Joel.

"He'll do whatever it takes to make himself out to be a hero, regardless, so I trust he'll take the evidence provided by Rosa, assuming she passes that polygraph test, and whatever evidence Harry comes up with and, if it's in our favor, which it has to be, then he'll be the media's darling for a few days when word gets out that he's released an innocent woman and found the real killer. Forget that he is the person responsible for locking Tessa up. He is a manipulator for sure, but I feel good about this."

Tessa began to object to the assumption seemingly being made that the real killer was Joel but held her tongue. Instead, she asked, "Can we go?"

Then she said, "Rachelle . . ." Tessa never thought in a million years she would say what she was about to say, but she swallowed her past doubts about the woman, and asked, "Why don't you come back to the house with us? Sam can make us lunch. He makes omelets to die for."

"That's a great idea," Lee said. "I'll let you know how Rosa's polygraph turns out. Phil Dormands is the best polygrapher in the state. He should be here soon. I'm sure Cal is tired of babysitting Rosa in the lunchroom."

"You mean he's still with her?" Tessa asked in amazement.

"He is," Lee said.

"Rachelle, are you coming with us?" Sam asked. "We'll give you a ride."

Rachelle seemed to be considering the idea but shook her head. "I appreciate the invitation, but I'll stay at my hotel. It's just down the block. I don't want anyone to feel obligated to . . . manage me."

"I am sincere," Tessa said. "I don't believe you could be managed even if I wanted to, which I don't."

"Thank you, Tessa, but I want to go back and rest. Maybe another time?"

"All right, but do you mind if I ask you a

question before you go?"

"Not at all."

"Why aren't you staying at Liam's condo?"

"Honey, Liam's place burned to the ground, along with ten other units at Charter Ridge. It happened about a week after the girls and whoever the adult male was were killed."

"My God, was anyone . . . hurt?"

"One elderly gentleman died, I believe. He was wheelchair-bound upstairs. The elevators stopped working. It was on the news . . . Of course, you wouldn't have known about this as you were locked up at the time." Rachelle sighed. "I am so sorry."

Blinded with grief then and now, she wanted to add, but refrained. *What else did I not know? It seems that large parts of my life weren't exactly as I had imagined.*

"I didn't know," was the only response she could come up with.

"That's why I'm staying at a hotel. I'll be in town a few days longer. I want to find out if there's any DNA connection to me."

Honest, Tessa thought. She really didn't know this woman. All these years, she had built up such hatred for her. In another time and place, they could have been friends. She wasn't that much older, maybe early sixties now. She couldn't remember her age, and it was of no importance anyway.

"Of course," Tessa said, still shocked that Liam's condo had burned to the ground. "I'm sure Lee will stay in touch, let you know the results when they come in. The man is a true miracle worker."

"Good luck," Rachelle said, and Tessa was one hundred percent sure that she meant exactly what she said.

CHAPTER 27

The gentle people of the press were nowhere to be found when the Mercedes carrying Sam and Tessa turned onto Dolphin Drive.

"Thank God," Tessa said. "I feel like I'm being spied on."

"I'm sure someone else is about to feel that way, too," Sam said as Dave pulled the car into the garage.

"I hope it's not for the same reason," she replied, trying to remember how to use sarcasm. She had spent most of her life being dictated to in one way or another. Free for the moment to say what she pleased, she knew deep down inside that her sense of humor and spirit would return if she would just let go. And she would. Now that it seemed pretty certain that she was to remain free, she was going to try to be her best. Not as she had been when she and Joel were married, not the girl who'd been tossed in and out of foster homes, and not the little girl who'd been whisked out of class, only to learn her mother had died of a heroin overdose. No, Tessa would just be herself. Whatever that was, she would go with it.

"Dave, you're free to go. If I need a lift, I'll call," Sam said to Dave, who had remained in the driver's seat.

"Anytime, my friend." Dave gave Sam a two-fingered salute and backed out of the garage.

They went in through the door that led to the kitchen, the same way she had done in the past. She stopped dead in her tracks. "Sam!"

"What in the hell?" Sam said as he removed his cell phone from his shirt pocket. "Tess, stay where you are."

"Lee, it's me. Looks like there's been a break-in at Tessa's. I'm going to call the police unless you tell me not to."

Tessa waited outside the doorway.

"I'll call them now, then." He hung up and dialed 911.

The blue dishes that Darlene had picked out for the house were scattered all across the kitchen floor, in pieces. The Keurig coffee machine was completely smashed up. The garbage bin had been dumped out onto the bar area. Cans of soda had been opened and dumped all over the floor. The silver-ware was crammed into the garbage disposal, and from the looks of it, whoever did this had turned the disposal on. A low humming sound was coming from inside the sink. The disposal's motor was fried.

"I don't get this," Sam said. "I've got security watching the house, plus the alarm was on when we left. How could anyone get inside and stay long enough to do all this damage? You stay here while I go around to the back. I want to come in through the glass doors. See if this bastard destroyed anything else."

"Okay," Tessa said. She didn't like being left alone even if it was still early in the day, and Sam was just a shout away. This didn't feel right. She was brought back to the Sunday that she had returned from San Maribel. She had used this exact entrance, and though the kitchen had been remodeled, the layout was still the same. She had gone upstairs to search for the girls, for Joel. Of course, she had had the shock of her life, and now, she wasn't sure if the sheer fright of that day would ever leave her. But perhaps she could go back to that dark place where she had hidden the images of their slain bodies without having a full-blown panic attack. Prison took the fear out of you;

she knew that firsthand.

Sirens wailed in the distance, and by the time she opened the garage door, three squad cars, with sirens blaring, were parking in front of her house. She put her hands over her ears, wondering how one ever got used to the noise. They must have seen her because the sirens all went silent at the same time.

"Ma'am, you called nine-one-one?" a tall African-American officer asked her.

"Uh, yes . . . Sam called."

"Sam? Is he your husband?" the officer asked.

Sam chose that moment to appear from the side of the house. "I'm the one who called," he shouted before the four other officers pointed their drawn handguns at him.

"Guys, back off," the African-American officer said. Tessa looked at his bright gold name tag. Officer Ray Waterman.

"The place is trashed," Sam said to her and the other four police officers.

"Okay, sir. We'll need to secure the inside for the crime-scene techs. You two good with hanging out here for a while?"

Tessa spoke first. "I want to see the inside. You can follow me around. I won't touch a thing. I promise. I've been through something like this before," she added before starting to enter the house.

Officer Waterman clicked then. "You're the woman who allegedly killed her twins, right? We were talking about you a couple days ago. Saw where you're getting a new trial."

"You're not here to discuss Ms. Jamison's past, Officer Waterman. The place has been vandalized. You and your men do whatever you have to do, but do not discuss Ms. Jamison's past in my presence."

"Man, don't be so hard on us. No one, at least no one that I know, believes she killed her children or the husband."

"Really," Tessa interjected herself into the conversation.

"No, ma'am. No mother in her right mind could do that to her children. I've seen a few husbands get what they deserve in my line of work, but no child deserves to go out that way." He shook his head from side to side. "I'm sorry for your loss, Ms. Jamison."

"Thank you, Officer Waterman. That means more to me than you know." And it truly did matter to her. She was not just being polite. She had adapted to the belief that she would be branded a murderer for the rest of her life, so when she came in contact with anyone who believed in her innocence, she would tell them it meant something to her. If she was to remain a free woman, she vowed to always acknowledge those who'd believed in her. During the trial and afterward, during her more than ten years in prison, she had never cared, but now that she had the chance for a new start, she would not jinx herself with negativity just yet.

"Glad to, ma'am. Now, if you'll excuse us." Officer Waterman took charge of his men while Tessa waited for the go-ahead before entering her house.

Twenty minutes later, Lee arrived. Tessa was still waiting outside with Sam.

"Any idea who did this?" Succinct, that was Lee.

"No clue. The crime scene techs just got here. Said it will take them a few hours to process the scene," Sam explained. "Fingerprints, fibers, the usual laundry list of procedures they have to follow."

"They allow you inside?" he asked Tessa.

"Not yet."

"Tessa, I can arrange for you to stay someplace else. A hotel, a friend's house. It will be a while before they let you inside. What about Jill? Do you think she would let you stay with her for the night?"

Why didn't I think of that? And wasn't Jill

supposed to call me? "Yes, I can stay with her, but first I'd like to call and make sure she doesn't have other plans." Tessa knew that Jill had planned on staying at Tessa's house tonight. She was supposed to call after her scheduled client left. Obviously, she had either forgotten or called the house while they were still at Lee's office. And Tessa did not have a cell phone. "Sam, can I use your phone?"

"Sure thing." He handed her the phone, and she dialed Jill's office number because she knew that Jill left her cell-phone number on her answering-machine message for her clients, and Tessa had no clue what her cell-phone number was. She listened to the recorded message, then motioned to Sam for a pen. He removed a pen from the pocket of one of the police cars and handed it to her. Tessa scribbled the number on the palm of her hand and tossed the pen back to Sam, nodding toward the car. *Meaning put the damned pen back where you found it.*

After six rings, Jill's voice mail picked up, asking the caller to leave a short and sweet message. "Hey, Jill, it's me. I need to stay at your place tonight. Just giving you a heads-up." She ended the call and returned the phone to Sam.

"You didn't tell her your place had been trashed, did you?"

"No, it would only cause her to worry. I'll tell her later. She said she was going to call when she finished up with her client. It's possible she's still at her office. Let me try calling again." Sam tossed his cell phone back to her.

She repeated the call but instead of hanging up, she left a message. "Jill, it's me. If you can pick up the phone, do so; it's important." She waited for a clicking sound, something to indicate that Jill was picking up the phone, but she heard nothing.

"Okay, she isn't at her office or at home. I'll get a hotel. Where is Rachelle staying? Maybe she and I can have coffee or dinner, get to know one another." Given the intense hatred she had felt for the woman ever since finding the bodies in the pool, the words coming from her mouth sounded so strange. Her *past* intense hatred. Tessa felt sure, even though it opened up the door to so many other possibilities, that Rachelle absolutely believed that Liam was dead. And after learning that Liam's condo had been burned to the ground, she was beginning to think that Rachelle might be right and Liam really was dead. And, she suddenly realized, putting two and two together, that's what

Harry, Lee, Sam, and even Michael Chen thought. They thought that the bones that had been dug up were Liam's and that the DNA taken from Rachelle would prove it. And if Liam's body had been buried, then either Joel or the other man (his twin?) was the killer. *Oh my God!*

CHAPTER 28

The crime-scene unit gave Tessa and Sam the all-clear four hours after its arrival. Knowing what the kitchen looked like, Tessa went straight to her new bedroom. It, too, had been trashed, but there really weren't any personal items she cared about, so it was no loss to her, only to Darlene, who'd spent hours purchasing things for Tessa. Next, she entered the room across the hall that Sam had converted into a library.

When she stepped fully into the room, she gasped. All of her books had been knocked off the shelves, some with pages ripped out. "Who in the hell does this kind of thing?" she asked of no one in particular. She began putting the books back on the shelves, and those with torn pages off to the side. It sickened her that her college textbooks with the pages torn out of them were tossed around like garbage. Those were the only books with any type of sentimental value.

And that's when she remembered the boxes upstairs in the master bedroom.

She raced down the hall and up the stairs. She stopped outside the master bedroom before going inside. Now these things in here were personal, mostly things that belonged to Joel, but a thief could get a nice payout if they found Joel's expensive wristwatches and gold jewelry. She had a few pieces that were expensive, but she really didn't care about them one way or the other. Entering the room, she saw more of the same. Boxes torn open, the contents scattered all over the floor.

"Tess," Sam said. "Are you okay?"

"No, I'm not okay. Who in the world would do this? How did they get inside? Just look at this." She gestured to the floor.

"The police seem to think that whoever was here was searching for something."

"Isn't that obvious? The entire place has been destroyed."

"They didn't take your televisions, the laptop in the guest bedroom, things that burglars usually steal. Whoever was in here was not only looking for something, but they wanted to leave a message, and they want you to know it."

She shook her head. "Who?" Then it suddenly occurred to her. "Lara!"

"No, I know for a fact it wasn't her. That was my first thought, too. I called Lee right after he left. He says Lara has been in jail for the past forty-eight hours. Prostitution."

"What?"

"You heard it right. Prostitution. I can't believe she couldn't wait a few days. Damned girl needs to learn a lesson. I told Lee not to bail her out. I hope you're okay with that?"

Am I?

She knew what it was like to be locked away, to have your freedom taken. While there was no love lost between her and Lara, she was her only living relative. "I'm not okay with this, Sam. Call Lee and tell him to post her bond, but only on this condition: She has to stay with me. Or you, I suppose, if by some cruel trick of the lousy criminal justice system, I end up back in prison. Not *live with* you. I wouldn't put that burden on your shoulders." She stopped.

"I have burdened you with her for years. Why am I just now realizing this? I take back what I said. Let her stay there a few days, then I'll bail her out. Can she even be bailed out? I guess I should have asked that first. It's not like I don't have any experience in this area." Tessa rubbed her eyes, not caring that she had smeared her mascara. "My life is just one giant mess."

Sam looked at her, then stepped over the contents of the boxes on the floor. When he reached her, he took her in his arms and held her tightly. Then, before either of them realized it, his lips were on hers. He kissed her with such tenderness that tears filled her eyes. She tried to free herself from his embrace, and said, "I'm not your kind, Sam."

"Why don't you let me decide what my kind is? I think you're perfect, Tess. In every way that matters." He kissed her again, and this time she kissed him back and felt a tingling sensation in the pit of her stomach and parts lower. The familiar shiver of desire coursed through her, fogging her mind with images that told her that she wanted Sam in ways she had never wanted Joel.

Joel.

"Sam, I can't," she said, forcing herself out of the safe circle of his embrace.

"You can't or just don't want to," he whispered.

"Both. Neither. Not yet." She was so confused, she sounded like a schoolgirl with her first real crush.

He released her, and she felt empty.

"I know the timing isn't right, but it will

be. Someday. I promise."

She nodded because she didn't know what else to say or do. She and Sam together seemed wrong in some ways, but now wasn't the time to contemplate the why and why nots of a relationship.

"Sam, what is going to happen when Chen goes to Judge Crider? Is the case against me going to be dropped? And if it is, when will we find out? And if it isn't, when will we get a trial date?"

"Soon; we'll know very soon. Once the polygraph results are in Chen's hands, establishing that you could not have committed the murders on Friday since the victims were all alive on Saturday, they will have to drop the charges.

"As to establishing the actual facts of the murders, Harry's the key. He's good, and he's fast. I'm guessing we should know everything there is to know about the murders in a week at most. But by that time, the charges against you should have already been dropped since not knowing who the adult male was who was killed and who killed the girls is irrelevant to whether or not *you* were the killer."

"What if things don't work out? What if Rosa fails the polygraph test? What if the DNA results are useless?" She hated sounding wimpy and childish, but her veneer of toughness was breaking down moment by moment, especially when Sam was around.

"We will deal with it. Together. Tess. You and me." Sam smiled, and her heart melted. Despite all the negativity that surrounded her, he gave her hope, and if that's all she walked away with, she was okay with that because, until Sam, she had had no hope.

"Thank you, Sam." While her words were simple, their meaning was deep, and they came directly from her heart.

"We'll work this out, Tess. But later. First we need to find a place for you to stay. I would have you stay at my house, but I don't think we should. Yet." He grinned, and she smiled back.

Which reminded her. "Did Jill ever return my call? I can't believe I forgot all about her."

"She didn't call my cell, but obviously I can't tell you about the landline."

"I should call her again, let her know what's happened."

He handed her his cell phone. "Call her and see if she's okay."

Tessa scrolled through the recently called numbers, found Jill's cell number, and hit the CALL button. "I need one of these gizmos." Jill's voice mail picked up, and

Tessa left another message, telling her it was urgent that Jill return her call.

"No answer." Tessa gave him the phone back. "I do not think she would be at the office this late. She told me she had one appointment scheduled for early this morning, said it couldn't be rescheduled. This isn't like her. I'm starting to worry."

"It's just after three now. Are you sure she told you she would stay here tonight?"

"Yes, she was going to cancel her appointments for the rest of the week, so we could spend time together. The Jill that I know always does what she says."

"I can drive by her house, check to see if she's there. Her office, too."

"You're sure? It would ease my mind. I can start cleaning up this mess. I can stay here tonight; the beds aren't damaged. I know you're my guardian, and if you'd rather go to your place, I'm okay with that. As long as this" — she pointed to the ankle monitor — "is allowed to be wherever we go."

"I'm fine staying here. It's messy, but that's not a problem for me. There should be some Windex in the kitchen under the sink if you decide to clean the print powder. I have been told that it usually does a decent job."

"I'll keep that in mind," Tessa said.

"Are you sure you're okay being here alone?"

Honestly, she wasn't, but it was the middle of the afternoon, the place had already been searched and trashed, and surely that was enough for one day. Chances of anything happening for half an hour or so were slim.

"I'll be fine. Just check on Jill and make sure the alarm is on when you leave."

"Here, put this in your pocket just in case." He handed her his cell phone.

"What if I need to call you?"

"You're right, give it back, but use the landline. The phone in the kitchen wasn't smashed."

"Okay, I'll get started then," Tessa said, and began scooping up handfuls of her past, Joel's past, and her children's past. She wasn't crying. That was a good thing, she supposed.

Sam left without saying good-bye. Why was this thought running through her head when she was in the midst of cleaning up after someone who obviously thought she had something they wanted?

Taking her time, Tessa sifted through the contents as she picked through the mess. An old John Grisham novel; he'd been Joel's favorite author. Two sweaters, one red and one purple. She held them against her face, inhaling the scent, hoping for that familiar little-girl smell she loved so much. Sweet honey, fresh strawberries would always remind her of them.

But the sweaters smelled musty, and she placed them inside an empty box. She would pack up their clothes and take them to a place where they would benefit other little girls. She would keep some of their clothes, like the Harry Potter shirts, but she wasn't even sure how long she would have the freedom to pack up their belongings, so it was best to do as much as she could while she was still a free woman.

She bent over to grab a handful of Joel's dress shirts when an old photograph caught her attention. She dropped the shirts in a pile and reached for the small frame. She didn't remember this. It was a picture of Joel, maybe when he was in the seventh or eighth grade. A school picture. The background was the typical sky-blue color most school photographers used, but this photo looked different. Standing by the window to capture the light, she viewed the picture closely, then removed it from the frame. She traced the face, feeling the texture of the photo. It was sturdier than your typical, stock school photos. She looked at the back of the picture. On the bottom left of the picture in gold script it read: *Canterberry's, Savannah, Georgia.* "Joel never lived in Georgia," she said out loud.

She looked at the face in the picture. It was definitely Joel. But why hadn't he told her he had lived in Georgia? It was odd as he was a true Florida Cracker, born and bred, his words. There weren't many true Floridians, it being such a tourist state. Something they'd both shared, their birth state. The pharmaceutical company started by Grant was in Florida. Joel went to college at Florida State University in Tallahassee. That's where he met Sam, though Sam continued his education in Georgia. He'd said he went to Emory Law. Maybe there was a connection? It was perplexing, to say the least. She tucked the photo in her pocket and would ask Sam if he knew that Joel had gone to school in Georgia.

She started scooping up another handful of clothes when the thought struck her that there was something odd about the picture. She took it from her pocket and went back to stand by the window, where the lighting was better. The boy was Joel, but there was something different about him in the photo. She turned the photo left and right and viewed it from every angle possible before she realized what was slightly odd. It was the eyes in the picture. Joel's green eyes sparkled, it was one of his best features, she thought. But in this picture, his eyes were empty.

Lifeless. *Could this be a picture of Joel's twin? And could that be the other man who showed up at the house the day of the murders?*

She shoved the picture in her back pocket. Sure that Sam would know, or maybe Rachelle, she focused her attention on the massive amount of junk that had been tossed across the wood floor.

What had they hoped to find? Could it have been teenagers? Knowing the history of the house, maybe they thought trashing her house was a great way to spend their day? She knew that kids did this kind of thing for kicks, but it was a huge risk given the presence of the media vultures lurking outside like shadows. Had that been part of the challenge? The thrill of not getting caught? She could go on with a thousand different scenarios, and not a single one would help her in getting the house back in some kind of order.

She had boxed up most of the clothes when she realized that Sam had been gone longer than thirty minutes. She had assumed that Jill still lived in the same house in Whiskey Creek, south of here. It used to take her about fifteen minutes to drive there, ten extra if you were caught behind a school bus. Then it hit her. It was December. Prime tourist season for the Sunshine State. It would take at least half an hour to get to Jill's house. She felt better knowing the traffic was probably bumper-to-bumper. Plus, if he drove downtown to her office, he'd be at least another hour.

These were the issues of daily life that she hadn't had to deal with in prison. In prison, you did what you were told to do — nothing more and nothing less. She had lived by the rules of the prison, and maybe she would have to live out the rest of her life and die by those rules, but negotiating, planning, gauging driving times — these were things she would have to get used to, assuming that Sam was right and she would avoid being returned to prison, that she could live the rest of her life as a free woman.

This was only the third day she was away from prison, yet it was beginning to feel like her life in prison belonged to someone else. Still, adjusting to the day-to-day activities of normal life was going to take some time.

She hated the word *adjusting*. That's what

they called acclimating to your situation in prison. In reverse. Prisoners *adjusted* to their new seven-foot-by-ten-foot living quarters. They *adjusted* to every-other-day showers. They *adjusted* to lights out at the same time every evening. She prayed she wouldn't have to return to that hellhole. She had made no friends in prison; though a few of the convicts had tried to befriend her, she wasn't stupid. She knew what went on when the lights were turned out. And she swore to herself that she would never allow herself to be victimized for however long she was there, and in ten years, she hadn't succumbed to participating in the nighttime passion that most inmates engaged in.

Her thoughts were careening all over the place when she thought she heard a noise downstairs. She stopped what she was doing and went to stand by the door of the master bedroom. Nothing. Probably her imagination. She turned around and was ready to go back into the room to do more cleaning when she heard the noise again.

She paused just outside the master bedroom door, waiting.

Footsteps. That was what she had heard. Someone was making crunching sounds as they walked over the broken dishes in the kitchen. The phone was in the kitchen. Damn. She inched her way past the bedroom's entrance but kept close to the wall. She waited, careful not to bump into anything. Again, she heard footsteps walking over broken glass. Whoever it was, they were trying to be quiet.

They knew she was alone in the house.

Tessa dared to ease away from the wall where, if she could lean far enough, she could see past the wall into the kitchen. Stretching as far as she could without falling, she saw a pair of feet clad in black boots. Obviously, it was a man.

Wishing she had kept Sam's cell phone, she tried to remember if there was a phone jack in Poppy's or Piper's room. Not that it would matter since the portable phone she had had was crushed in a pile downstairs, most likely by her intruder.

She watched the black-boots-clad feet move around in the kitchen. Back and forth, back and forth; then the man stopped walking and stood still. Tessa could tell by the position of the boots that the man was now facing in her direction. She practically mashed herself into the wall.

The man just stood there. Had she made a noise? No, she was being very careful. She listened, then stretched out a second time for another look.

She could not see him anywhere in the kitchen. The booted man was gone.

Or he was in another room.

Her heart rate quadrupled. Sweat trickled down the back of her neck.

Think. Think. Think. I have to get out of this house!

This place was evil; she could feel it in her bones.

There. A noise. She heard it again.

Afraid to chance a look, she tried to place where the sounds were coming from.

The hallway.

Her bedroom.

Had the son of a bitch forgotten something? Had he returned to steal her clothes?

Suddenly, it occurred to her she had only one chance, to race down the stairs to the kitchen, where the phone was.

If only he stayed in the bedroom long enough.

Or should I stay put? Wait for Sam?

No! Sam could die! Whoever it was could kill him when he came into the house.

She wouldn't let another person she cared for die.

Never.

She strained to hear.

Yes!

He is still in my room.
For now.

Carefully, she removed her ankle boots. One, then the other.

If she kept them on, they would make noise.

If she took them off, she would only risk cutting her feet.

She would take her chances on her feet. They would heal.

It was now or never.

Without a second thought, she flew down the stairs, as quietly and quickly as possible.

She stopped when she reached the bottom of the steps.

Holding her breath, she inched her way around the wall.

Only half of the living room was visible from where she stood.

Lowering herself onto her belly, she eased her way across the main living area, behind the leather chairs facing the pool.

One inch at a time. Move. Stop. Listen.

Move. Stop. Listen.

She was almost there.

Move. Stop. Listen.

She didn't hear him.

She eased her way across the threshold into the kitchen.

Her hands met slivers of glass.

Blood trickled from her palm to her wrist.

The phone was on the countertop.

Only a few feet away.

What was that?

She heard him.

Closer.

She smelled him.

Oh. My. God!

"You thought I was dead, didn't you, Tessa?"

Was she dreaming?

Yes.

"Didn't you?" He shoved her face into the glass.

He pushed harder. She felt the glass slice into her skin.

But you didn't feel pain in dreams.

Or did you?

This was not a dream.

"Answer me, Tessa."

This was real.

The voice. The smell. The positioning of those black boots.

"Joel?"

Wrapping his fist around her hair, he jerked her head back so far, she thought surely her neck would break.

Cold, hard steel touched her neck.

"Please, don't do this."

"You bitch! You ruined my life! Get up!"

Tessa pushed herself into an upright position as soon as he released her. She leaned against the bottom cabinets, using them to steady herself as she tried to stand. Her legs felt like Jell-O. She tried to think. *Think. Think!*

Joel is alive. Here in the kitchen. Their *kitchen.*

The telephone rang.

"Answer it, and you're dead."

She nodded.

The phone continued to ring. Was the answering machine on? Did she even have an answering machine?

The ringing stopped.

She must reason with him. "Joel . . ." Her voice didn't sound like her own. Fear stole her breath, her voice. Fear took her daughters' lives.

Shaking as if the temperature were more like the Northeast at Christmastime and not Florida, she tried to speak in as normal a voice as she could muster. "Joel, listen to me. Please. I don't understand anything. Please. Tell me what you want." *There. Now I sound more like myself.*

"You were planning on leaving me. Just like Jack did. He didn't want to be around me. All he wanted to do was play with Mommy. All the time. He was mine. She

365

said she was going to send me away. You're just like her, you know that?"

Tessa focused on the man she had once loved. He had aged badly — his hair was thinning, and his green eyes glinted with pure evil. His skin looked like old leather. The sun. Wherever he'd been, he had lived in the sun.

"Like who? Who am I just like? And who is Jack? What are you talking about?" she dared to ask, almost sure that she already knew the answer. Understanding, finally, why the body in the pool had seemed strange. Understanding why Joel was so upset when he found out that they were going to have twins. Understanding why he never spoke of his mother and had never told her his mother's name.

"Mommy. Jack's very best friend. Lois. The whore."

Dear Lord, he was totally mad!

I have to keep him talking. Surely, Sam will be here soon.

"I never met your mother, remember?" she said, hoping he would focus on what he was telling her and not on what she was doing. The drawer where Sam put the knives was just within reach.

"You're just like her. Stupid whore."

She moved her hand slowly so as not to

draw attention to her movements. An inch at a time, she traced the edges of the drawers, feeling for the knob.

"You think you're home free now, don't you?"

She shuddered at his words. "I don't understand."

"I watch the news, Tessa, or did you forget that little detail?

Back and forth, his personality veered between childlike petulance one minute and insane, evil Joel the next.

"Yes, I remember now."

"When I learned you might have a chance at freedom, well, I couldn't allow you to one-up me, could I?"

He really is batshit crazy! Completely off his rocker.

"Just kill me then. Get it over with." Her voice was stronger, louder. Maybe she should scream for help. It would be a good time for one of those nosy reporters to do their job. Spy. Sneak. Search.

He laughed.

"Tessa, I have a question for you. If you give me the correct answer, you will add five minutes to your life. Yes, let's play a game. I always enjoyed playing games. This game is the game of life. You always liked to play games. You played games with *them.*

You always stopped when I came home. Remember? You didn't let me play."

For God's sake, the extent of his insanity was off the charts. She couldn't even begin to understand the deranged psychopathic man he had become. No, cancel that thought. The sick son of a bitch he had always been. *How,* she asked herself, *could I have lived with him for eleven-plus years and not known how sick and evil he was?*

"The game. Let's play. I'm going to ask you a question, and if you answer correctly, you win. And your prize — there has to be a prize for the winner — is that five minutes will be added to your life." Once again, his voice was the singsong voice of a child.

"Ask me the question, Joel. Let's play your game of life."

"Number one. I like to play this way. It's like school. Okay, here is the first part of the first question: What is sodium hydroxide?"

His voice no longer sounded the same as before. The singsong quality was gone, though it was still the voice of a child. It was as if a different child had taken the place of the other one.

Multiple personality disorder?

"Tick tock, tick tock. Better hurry, Tessa, time to answer is running out."

"I forgot the question."

"Stupid bitch. You get one more chance." Evil Joel voice.

"I'm sorry."

"What is sodium hydroxide?" He'd reverted to the singsong voice again.

Now he was sitting on one of the barstools, and she could see the hunting knife where he had placed it on the countertop.

"Lye," she said.

"Part two of question number one: What do sodium hydroxide and the human body have in common?"

She tried to think, and when the answer finally came to her, she lost her breath. Gasping, she tried to push the words out of her mouth. "Why?"

Manic laughter, and his eyes lit up like Satan's might upon consigning another soul to the depths of hell. But all he said was, "All those science classes you took in college. I was right. You are a stupid whore. Tick tock. Tick tock. Ding, ding, ding! Time is up!"

"You sick son of a bitch! What do you want from me?" She screamed the words as loud as she could. If he was going to kill her, he'd better get started.

He jumped off the barstool and reached for the hunting knife. "You're gonna die this time! No more minutes added to your miserable life, you fucking whore!" He came toward her then, the knife raised high above his head. Tessa cowered in the corner but didn't dare to run. In one swift motion, her neck would be severed.

The reality of what he'd done hit her full force.

"You insane son of a bitch! You killed my daughters! And before that, you molested them!" Her breath came in short gasps. "You don't deserve to live!"

"Wait, wait, wait! You're not the leader, Tessa. I am. You're just like Mommy, always wanting to be first." The singsong childlike voice again.

Before she changed her mind, she tucked her head into her chest, rolled onto the floor, and grabbed his ankles, knocking him to the floor with her. The black boots were heavy, but she didn't care. She was going to kill him or die. There was no other choice.

Twisting his ankle into an unnatural position, she turned her body with the movement to avoid getting entangled herself. Bits of glass cut into her arms, but in the adrenaline rush, she couldn't feel any pain. Her strength seemed as if it were ten times more than normal. She had almost succeeded in twisting the foot she was holding completely around when his other foot smashed into her face.

Tessa felt a sharp snap, then felt warm blood oozing from her nose. She continued to hold his ankle as blood dripped onto her hands and his boot, causing her to lose her grip. His boot came down a second time, only this time it caught her on the edge of her left shoulder. Another snap, and a hot jolt of pain ran down the length of her arm. She tried to move her left arm, and a hot, icy pain traveled up her arm, to her shoulder.

She rolled onto her back; with her right hand, she used her shirt to wipe the blood from her eyes. "If you're going to kill me, you sick, perverted piece of shit, then you better have the guts to look me in the eye when you do it!"

"You are stupid, Tessa. Aren't you?" He kicked the back of her head.

She winced. She would not give the bastard the pleasure of hearing her beg for her life. If he was going to kill her, she wanted every single moment etched in his sick mind forever.

"Wait!" She needed to know; she didn't care what he did to her after, but first she had to know. "Joel. Why did you kill them? Why? They were just little girls! Why?"

Tessa was sobbing now, and she didn't care. Hot, salty tears burned the cuts on her face, yet all she could think of is what her precious daughters had gone through. Here. In this house. Right under her nose. The entire time?

"Answer me, goddammit! You at least owe me that much!" Struggling to keep from passing out, she forced herself to stare up at him, her gaze unwavering.

"They were just like you. And Jack. And Mommy. Never wanted to play games with me." The plaintive, singsong voice of the child was back again. "I was trying to teach them how to play the game, just like Mommy taught me."

Oh dear God!

Then it hit her. Liam! What had he done to Liam?

"Did you kill Liam?" she asked, her voice muffled from pain and the blood from her broken nose.

"That little bastard! Of course I killed him. What do you think I used the sodium hydroxide for? And I killed Jack, too! He actually came to the house. I was a bit surprised."

The evil Joel voice again. "But it was the perfect ending for my new beginning. I already had a new identity set up, with more than enough money to lead a carefree life, just in case something went wrong. And when you decided to go to San Maribel, I knew that you were going to leave me and take the girls. I couldn't allow that to happen.

"Then Liam showed up, and he had to be killed. And so did the girls. Jack's appearance was just bad luck for him and incredibly good luck for me. And when you were convicted of killing me and the girls, I knew it was the perfect ending to that game of life. But then they let you go, so I had to come back and put an end to the game once and for all."

Tessa rolled away from Joel seconds before he lifted the hunting knife, aiming it at her throat.

"Freeze!"

Joel's bright green eyes sparked with fire. When he saw Officer Waterman's gun aimed at him, he tightened his grip on the knife, and this time, he used both hands as he raised them high above his head, garnering all the force he could to stab her in the forehead.

Tessa's world went black.

EPILOGUE

Eighteen months later

Sam reached for Tessa's hand as the newly elected governor prepared to speak.

"Good evening, ladies, gentlemen. First, I would like to thank each and every one of you for your vote. It was a close race, but it only takes one more vote than the other candidate to win." Applause.

"Tonight, as your newly elected governor, you all know why you're here." He paused. "Almost thirteen years ago, one of the city's most horrendous tragedies took place. The lives of Piper and Poppy Jamison, along with those of their uncles, Liam Jamison and Jack Jamison, were taken by a vicious, callous man, who was the father and the brother of the victims." Michael Chen looked at Tessa. "I would like to formally apologize to Ms. Tessa Jamison. I was the lead prosecutor in the case, and I made a very bad mistake. I did not listen to her. So bent on getting a conviction, I and my staff focused all of our attention on her, a woman, a wife and mother who'd just lost her entire family. I can't begin to think that my words will have any healing effect on the survivors, but I hope in some small way, they will. Rachelle Jamison lost a son."

Sam leaned over and whispered in her ear. "Now?" she mouthed back.

He nodded.

Tessa took Rachelle's hand, then whispered in her ear. "Already?" Rachelle asked in a low voice.

Tessa nodded.

"I'm coming with you."

Quickly, and hopefully, they quietly eased out of the auditorium without distracting too many people who had come to listen to Governor Chen discuss a new bill the Florida Senate had recently passed.

The Jamison Bill. The bill protected women who had been released from prison and were being stalked, harassed, or had an attempt made on their life by their significant other. Tessa had worked tirelessly with Lee and Darlene to take the bill to the Florida Senate. Surprised and proud when it was passed, Tessa's loss might prevent another woman in similar circumstances from losing her life or that of a family member. It was a simple thing, nothing too complex. When a woman was released from confinement in a jail, prison, or halfway house, if she was harassed by a significant other who had been instrumental in her having been convicted and served time, the harasser would automatically be jailed for ninety days, then would receive a full mental evaluation before being released. It wasn't huge, but it was something dear to her and to Rachelle, who had become a surrogate mother to her. Rachelle had sold her house in Miami and moved to Naples, where Tessa now lived in a ritzy condo overlooking the Gulf of Mexico.

As soon as they stepped outside, the June heat hit them full force. "Can you believe it's this hot at night?" Rachelle asked. "Or am I having another hot flash?" she added, laughing.

Inside the car, Tessa's bright red Porsche, Sam cranked over the engine and clicked the air-conditioning on. "Do you think Lara can handle this?" Tess asked the others as Sam backed out of the parking garage.

"I do, Tess," Sam said. "She's not the same girl she was. She has finally grown into a woman, at least in my opinion."

"She has," Tessa agreed. "I think her finding out about Joel, Liam, and Jack, the poor twin who'd spent most of his life in Savannah, and the girls changed her. Made her realize that life was too short to waste it on dope and dresses. What do you think of Logan?"

"He seems like a decent guy. He married your little sister, so he better take care of her, or else," Sam teased.

"Did you call Lee and Jill?" Rachelle asked from the backseat.

"No, Logan did. They should be there by the time we arrive."

"I hope we're in time. I would hate to miss this life-changing event, plus I can't wait to see Lara's face when she sees her baby for the first time."

"As it should be, a surprise. I don't think I'd want to know the gender of my child if I were lucky enough to have one," Sam said.

Tessa remained quiet. While she and Sam were in love, and planned on getting married in the fall, in Vermont, she wasn't so sure about children. She was almost forty-nine, and he was fifty-three. But never say never.

Look at Jill. She was ready to burst with a baby boy. Lee was so excited, he'd replaced all his pink ties and shirts with pale blue ones. They were older, too, but Tessa knew that Jill would make an excellent mother, and Lee was already the stereotypical doting father.

Sam pulled into the parking lot at Gulf Coast Hospital.

Inside, they took the elevator to the second floor, where the birthing suites were located. Inside room number 216 were Lara, Logan, and the baby.

"You've had the baby already?" Tessa said as she hurried across the room.

"Yep. Here. You want to hold . . . her?"

Tessa eyes filled with tears. "A baby girl."

She took Elizabeth Marie Rivera and cradled her in her arms. Tears dripped down her face.

Life hadn't always been good to her, but right now, she was happy. Lara was happy, and baby Elizabeth would be the most spoiled niece in the whole world.

Sam stood behind her. With a finger, he traced the baby's cheek. "Soft as down," he said, smiling.

Tessa cradled the baby in her arms, then inhaled.

Strawberries and honey.

She looked at Lara and smiled.

She remembered.

Jill and Lee arrived, her belly entering the room a few seconds before she did. When

Jill saw the baby, she sat down and cried.

"She is absolutely beautiful, Lara. She has Logan's eyes."

They all looked at her. "What?"

"She hasn't opened them," Tessa said, laughing.

"But when she does, she'll have those gorgeous blue eyes," she insisted.

"Of course. Lara and Logan both have blue eyes."

They all laughed and took turns holding the new addition to the family. Rachelle was now designated as Nanny to baby Elizabeth. In the short time since Joel's death, they had all become a mishmash family.

Tessa had had the house torn down and the property totally excavated. After she had received permission, the entire property had been converted into a grassy retreat amidst all the beautiful and expensive houses in the gated community. And on it were two memorials, one to the Jamison girls and one to their uncles.

The memorial to Jack and Liam consisted of a large, Calder-like mobile of two manatees swimming around and around a small whale that spouted water into the air every minute. The memorial to Piper and Poppy, she had placed at the base of the lighthouse at the edge of the island. It was a very large sculpture of a kitten's paw and a jingle seashell. The lighthouse was ringed by a newly planted semicircle of different kinds of red flowers that bloomed all year round and a semicircle of purple flowers that was also perpetually in bloom.

Harry's work proved what Joel had told her the day he tried to murder her. He had indeed killed both Jack and Liam. After dousing Liam's body with sodium hydroxide, he had buried his remains in the yard, which was confirmed by the DNA analysis of the bones that had been dug up.

Jack's body had ended up in the swimming pool, and everyone had assumed it was the body of his twin brother, Joel. Jack, it turned out, had spent his life after his mother's death at the Canterberry Institute, in Savannah, Georgia, an institution for the mentally challenged. He had been released only two days before his death. From his doctor, they had learned that Jack had witnessed Joel push their mother down the steps. Jack had always been slow, and after Lois's death, Grant had had him placed at Canterberry for his own protection.

She didn't want to know any more than that.

Right now, for the first time, her life was hers, on her own terms.

ABOUT THE AUTHOR

Fern Michaels is the *USA Today* and *New York Times* bestselling author of over 150 novels and novellas, including *Holly and Ivy, High Stakes, Crash and Burn, Fast and Loose, No Safe Secret, Double Down, In Plain Sight, Perfect Match, Eyes Only,* and *Kiss and Tell.* There are over 160 million copies of her books in print.

Fern Michaels has built and funded several large daycare centers in her hometown, and is a passionate animal lover who has outfitted police dogs across the country with special bulletproof vests. She shares her home in South Carolina with her five dogs and a resident ghost named Mary Margaret. Visit her website at www.fernmichaels.com.

The employees of Thorndike Press hope you have enjoyed this Large Print book. All our Thorndike, Wheeler, and Kennebec Large Print titles are designed for easy reading, and all our books are made to last. Other Thorndike Press Large Print books are available at your library, through selected bookstores, or directly from us.

For information about titles, please call:
    (800) 223-1244

or visit our website at:
    gale.com/thorndike

To share your comments, please write:
    Publisher
    Thorndike Press
    10 Water St., Suite 310
    Waterville, ME 04901